THE MAN IN ROOM 423

CATHERINE CURZON & ELEANOR HARKSTEAD

The Man in Room 423
ISBN # 978-1-83943-893-6
©Copyright Catherine Curzon & Eleanor Harkstead 2020
Cover Art by Erin Dameron-Hill ©Copyright May 2020
Interior text design by Claire Siemaszkiewicz
Totally Bound Publishing

THE MAN IN ROOM 423

Dedication

CC – Say no to polyester!
EH – To Jen.

Chapter One

Lizzie saw him in the light of his uncurtained hotel window. He leant one hand casually against the pane, looking back at her across the dark December street.

She watched him over the rim of her glass. Office Christmas parties were loud in the bar around her, but she was barely aware of them. All she could see was the man at the window, immaculate in a dark-coloured suit, the white of his shirt as crisp as frost.

"Earth to Lizzie. Come in, Lizzie!" Long, coral pink acrylic nails snapped in front of her eyes and Donna set down two glasses of a bright red cocktail, a cherry bobbing on the surface like a drowning man. "You need a crowbar to get served in here tonight!"

She wasn't going to tell Donna about the man in the window. She wanted him for herself, so that she could pass through what remained of this evening with her sister in the knowledge that she and she alone had seen him.

And that he had seen her.

The interested glance of a stranger.

"What on earth sort of cocktail is that?" Lizzie attempted a grin. She put it to her mouth to taste it and exaggerated her recoil. "Gosh, that's strong!"

She allowed herself a quick look. He was still there. He was still watching.

He might even be smiling.

"Aaaand still nothing from Matt." Donna's frosted pink lips turned down into a frown as she stared at the phone she held. She sighed and threw it down on the table, sending it skidding into a puddle of someone else's spilled beer. "He finished training *hours* ago, where is he?"

"Maybe he's busy? You did insist on marrying a footballer."

"*You did insist,*" Donna mimicked her sister, a petulant child once more. "And he's not playing tonight, he's not training tonight, he's not *here* tonight. So where is my Matt? There're some strange people out there, Lizzie, and he doesn't look out for himself sometimes!"

"I'm sure he's okay. Maybe he's drinking with the squad. Lads' night out. Or maybe he's at his mum's, eating beans on toast!"

"I hope so." Donna shook her head and swirled the cocktail glass by its stem. "We've had to get the police involved, you know. He's had some horrible messages sent to the club, really nasty stuff. They've said not to worry, but... Well, I love him. I don't like to think of someone being out to get him."

Lizzie reached across the table and gave her sister's hand a reassuring squeeze.

"That's terrible, Donna! But you've done the right thing, going to the police. It'll be okay."

Would it be? But her sister had chosen this existence, had sought it out, pursued it and embraced it.

"That's celebrity life, Don. I've heard similar from some of my clients. And you know what they say to me? *I knew I'd made it when I got my first stalker.*"

That seemed to please Donna, just a little reminder that she had won her premiership striker, that she was the closest Manchester came to royalty. Donna beamed a bright smile and patted her poker-straight blonde hair into place, though it was immaculate already. "I always said I'd be a WAG, didn't I? When you were stitching dresses for your dolls, I was dreaming about my footballers! A girl's got to have ambition, after all."

"Mine was to run my own business and be my own boss." Lizzie smiled. "And I am."

She took a sip of her cocktail, punctuating her comment, then pushed the glass away. It tasted like medicine.

Her sister just laughed in response and glanced around, her attention caught by a group of loud, tanned, gym-honed young men by the bar. As if by habit, her eyelids fluttered and she dropped her gaze, forming her lips into a perfect selfie-pout. Donna de Luca was confident in her glamour in a way that Lizzie had never quite been.

Lizzie propped her elbow on the table and peered outside again. He was still there. Had he watched her, even as she'd looked away at her sister?

Never breaking his glance, he slowly unbuttoned his jacket and flung it in one smooth movement onto a chair. His hands were at his throat, and seconds later, a tie went after the jacket. And now he was attending to the cuffs of his shirt. Although a street and several floors divided them, Lizzie was sure that he must have been wearing cufflinks. They went into his pocket.

She swallowed, her free hand toying with the beads of her wooden necklace.

He was unbuttoning his shirt, from the neck down. Then it was off. But on the floor this time, at his feet.

He pressed both palms to the glass, his toned, bare torso on show for her.

For someone. Had a complete stranger really just stripped for Lizzie Aspinall? Partially, that is.

His hands drifted to his belt. Then he turned his body away, his glance lingering for just a second longer before he strolled across the room and vanished from her sight.

"Matty!" Donna snatched up her mobile as a text buzzed across the screen. She swiped her thumb from left to right on the glass and immediately started to tap out a reply, her finger moving with confidence from key to key. "Oh my God, Lizkins. He was *tanning*!"

"A special coat of creosote for Christmas?" Lizzie laughed. "Is he going to come to our parents'? It would've been our turn at Neil's parents, but seeing as we've split up… I was thinking of going to our parents', but I'm tempted to lurk about the flat by myself. Just enjoy being on my own, in my PJs, even if — Donna, are you listening?"

"Just a mo, sweets." Donna didn't even look up from the screen, her finger moving swiftly from letter to letter. "I can't listen to you and text. I've had too many drinkies for that!"

Not for the first time, Lizzie wondered why she had agreed to come out. Because Donna had insisted, *'because you've got to go out and meet people'*. But Lizzie would've been content to stay at home. Even though home was makeshift, it was hers.

She looked again at the hotel room. It was empty.

Minutes passed, then from the corner of Lizzie's eye, there was movement. The man was back in the window.

Donna was still intent on her phone. Lizzie placed a hand to the side of her face, as if she were merely relaxing, but instead, she was staring.

The man was wearing nothing but a towel.

Neat and white, it was tucked in at his waist and hung to just below his knees. He ran a hand through his dark hair and slowly shook his head from side to side. Even from where she was, Lizzie could see the water droplets fly away. He resumed his pose, leaning with one hand on the glass. Leaning and looking across the street at Lizzie.

Who does he see when he looks at me?

Then he lifted his hand. The palm was still facing outward as though he was about to wave but instead, he folded his thumb down, to hold up four fingers. After a few seconds had passed, he folded down two of his fingers as though giving a victory salute then, finally, held up his ring finger alongside the others.

Lizzie held her breath. Had he just signalled to her? But what?

423.

She gestured with her hand, below the level of the tabletop so that Donna wouldn't see, but the man in the hotel room could. Her hand flicked back on her wrist.

What does that mean?

But even as he signalled again, Lizzie counted up the floors to his window. He was on the fourth floor.

He was in room 423.

And he wanted her.

A warm flush spread over her skin. A prickle of desire, of recklessness. *Why not. Why bloody not?*

"I'm— I'm off now, Don."

Donna still had her head in her phone. Lizzie knew she wouldn't be missed.

She took her coat from the back of the chair, tied on her scarf, shoved on her woollen beret, pulled on her gloves.

"I've literally *just* bought you a drink!" Donna looked up from her phone, her face set in a dark pout, but then she shrugged, glancing at the screen once more. "Matt wants to grab sushi, so I'll just tell him to head over here. He can have your cocktail since you're too boring to hang around and drink it!"

"Well, yes, I *am* an extremely boring person, as you have so often told me. Bye, sis."

"Hugs!" Donna pressed a kiss to her fingers and threw it to her sister. "And behave!"

"Yes, I shall behave in my slippers, with my cocoa… Night…"

Lizzie walked out of the bar, but once she was in the corridor outside, she ran. She jabbed her finger on the lift button, her reflection showing her the boring person her sister saw. The boring woman who was running to the bedroom of a stranger.

The lift was taking an age. Lizzie had to move, had to answer the thudding of her pulse. She pulled open the doors of the staircase and ran down, two steps at a time, jumping off each bottom step, propelling herself around each landing to the next flight, down…down…

Wrapped in her winter clothes, she barely felt the intense cold when she arrived in the street. She stopped and looked up at the window again. He was still there. And he saw her. She raised her hand slightly. A small wave. Just to be sure. Just to be certain that it was her, definitely her, that he had invited.

He turned from the window, almost disappearing, and for an awful, embarrassing moment, she thought there had been a mistake. He had been signalling to someone else, someone who even now was on their way over here too. But then he was at the window again and had in each hand a glass of what looked like champagne.

Waiting for her, for Lizzie Aspinall, with a glass of chilled champagne.

She hurried across the road, over the metal tramlines, and round the corner to the hotel's grand entrance. She couldn't run here. They'd find her out. She glided up the steps, nodding to the doorman who opened the door for her.

She tried not to stare at the opulence of the reception, of its leather armchairs and palms in brass pots. Up a flight of marble stairs and to the lifts. She pressed the button.

But nothing happened.

"Not got your room card, love?"

Lizzie shrugged at the other guest, a businessman in a pinstripe suit, his hair turned grey.

He waved his card over a brass panel and the lift doors opened at once. "What floor?"

"Fourth, please."

The doors closed. The businessman got out at the second floor, nodding an acknowledgment. The lift doors closed once more, the gears and cables clanking as Lizzie ascended through the building.

A robotic voice announced the floor and the doors smoothly opened. Lizzie paused.

Am I really going to do this? Sensible, boring Lizzie?

Yes. Yes, I am.

Out onto the plush carpet. A sign straight ahead. 423 indicated to her right. She tried to steady her breathing as she got nearer, counting down the numbers on each door she passed.

427, 425, 423.

She cleared her throat and knocked.

Seconds passed. Silent seconds, the moments ticking by as the world slowed to a crawl. Then the door opened and there he was, the man in the window, the man who had summoned her. His wet hair was slicked down, droplets of water glistening on his shoulders, smoothing down the light scatter of dark hair on his torso. The depths of his dark eyes sparkled. He stepped back into the room without saying a word, holding the door open for her.

Should she say hello? Tell him her name, comment on the coldness of the weather?

No.

Lizzie followed him into the room and shut the door behind them. She pressed her back against it, recovering her breath, gazing at him. His dark eyes… there was passion there, but something tentative too. Almost unsure. Did he think she would change her mind and run away?

She was aware of his clean, masculine scent, of the presence of him. Waiting. His soft, full lips fell slightly open. Did he still want her, now that they were face-to-face?

She reached one hand towards him, her palm up. Offering him her permission.

His palm met hers, their fingers entwining. She could feel the warmth of his skin through her glove, felt the strength in his hand and the fizz of electricity in the air between them. She drew him towards her and he came to her willingly.

She brushed her free hand against the side of his neck. He leant into her caress, lowering his eyelids, and she brought her mouth to his, not quite touching, but breathing the same air. His grip on her hand tightened, his eyes opened again, and Lizzie placed her lips on his.

Something tore itself free from the sensible inside of Lizzie Aspinall. Whatever had propelled her here demanded satiation, and with a hunger she hadn't even realised that she had, she was holding the nameless man against her, kissing him with an urgency she had never felt before.

His put his free hand on the door beside her face, the same door that she now felt against her back. And the kiss went on and on, their tongues exploring, tasting, the scent of his botanical aftershave as suddenly exotic and forbidden as this encounter on a winter night.

He could be anybody—she knew that, was thrilled by it. He could be whoever she wanted him to be, and she? She was free. For one night at least, she could live.

She moaned into the kiss, the first sound she had made in his presence. There was so much power in the body that was against her own, and she shifted herself so that his hardness pressed between her legs. He deepened the kiss. He understood what she wanted.

She untangled her hand from his, still kissing him as she pulled off her gloves. She ran her bare fingers through his hair, so thick, still wet. She brushed one hand down his back, feeling the muscles under her fingertips. Her hat had already fallen off, and she tried to remove her scarf with one hand, but it seemed only to knot all the more.

His hands joined hers on the scarf, deftly unknotting it and tossing it aside, then his fingers were on the buttons of Lizzie's coat, nimbly unfastening each one. When the coat was finally open, he pressed his hips to her again, the layers between their bodies growing fewer, the evidence of his desire sending a shiver through her. He brushed his lips against her cheek, across the place where her dimples showed when she laughed, then he was kissing his way to her earlobe, moving his full lips with gentle certainty.

She trembled, moaning again as he kissed his way across her face, each breath she took punctuated with a sigh of deep, overwhelming need.

He caught her earlobe with his teeth, teasing and nibbling around the wooden bead of her earring, soothing the same spot with his tongue a moment later. His lips were against her ear then, and he finally spoke, the words a low purr.

"Let me fuck you."

"Of course I'll let you, whoever you are," Lizzie whispered. "I need you, oh, God, I need you…"

He pressed his hand to the fabric of her blouse, cupping her breast. Then he slid his tongue over her earlobe again and he whispered, "Tell me how hard you like it."

Lizzie couldn't muster a reply at once. No one had ever asked her before. Panting, she gripped his hair and circled her hips against his.

"Hard. Very hard. So hard." It was an answer, but not what she'd wanted to say. She ran her tongue over her lips. Breathless, she told him, "I want you inside me."

And his mouth was on hers again, fierce and rough, claiming her. Lizzie clutched his hair tighter, squeezing out more water from the dark, thick locks that were entwined between her fingers. He groaned his approval, heard her own answering moan, felt his hand caressing her breast and, all the time, the length of his erection was pressed to her thigh, promising what was to come.

She arched her back. "Undress me…"

He eased her coat down her shoulders as their lips met again, and it fell at her feet, taking with it the last suggestion that she might still leave, might change her mind. She wouldn't, though, because this was one chance to say, *I lived.*

With a nameless man in the low light of a plush hotel room as the air grew icy outside, I lived.

Then the door was at her back again, tracing the outline of her breast once more and his lips a whisper on her throat.

She took his other hand, guiding it to the buttons on her blouse. As he unfastened the first, his mouth warmed her newly revealed skin. She trembled against his caress, cradling his head as he undid the next button. He gazed at her deeply, wolfishly. The unfastened button revealed the chaste, pale pink bow of her white bra, resting in the valley between her breasts.

He pressed his lips to hers again, his palm over her breast as he traced the outline of her nipple with his thumb, teasing the stiffened peak. All the time his free hand was unfastening the remaining buttons on her blouse, fingertips lightly brushing her skin as they moved down to part the fabric. She heard a catch in his breath then his hand slid round behind her, teasing down her back to rest on her bottom. A moment later he pulled her body to his, the muscles of his torso hard against the softness of her skin.

Soon, she would feel that powerful torso eliciting lust, bringing her intense joy. Even with their kiss, she could feel her pleasure building, a hint at the now-unimaginable heights that he could take her to.

And she him. She would match this stranger's passion, kiss for kiss, touch for touch. She wanted him not to forget this one snatched night. She wanted him not to forget her.

Her blouse and cardigan had slipped off her shoulders. He nuzzled her neck, his mouth travelling to nudge the straps of her bra away with his kisses. Her breasts almost freed from the plain white bra, he slipped his fingers into one of the loosened cups, caressing her.

He strengthened his grip on her bottom, caressing through her corduroy skirt. He began to hitch it up, slipping his hand underneath to reach up her thigh, fingertips just brushing, through her thick winter tights, the sensitive spot where her thigh met her buttock.

At this lightest of touches, Lizzie shuddered with a need that she could not control. Her hands slipped from his hair, down his back, exploring, enjoying the muscular planes of his body as he kissed the exposed skin of her breasts.

The man whose name she didn't want to know scooped Lizzie into his arms, seemingly without effort, sweeping her feet clear of the floor. As though she was a bride on her wedding night, he carried her to the bed, his lips hungry against hers, even as he laid her down atop the snow-white duvet.

It was then that she noticed, as her hand swept down his back, onto a bare bottom, that he was naked. The towel must have fallen halfway between the bed and the door as he had carried her. He must have realised that she had noticed. He broke from the kiss and his lips quirked into a smile, his dark eyes glittering. He didn't move. Once again, he was inviting her gaze. Enjoying it.

She curled her arm behind her head and stroked his face as he kissed her hand. His nudity was more impressive than she had dared hope.

"Shame..." Her voice was a whisper, her cheeks dimpling. "I'd have liked to strip you."

"Damn," was his murmured reply. Then he slipped the blouse and cardigan from her arms, tossing them onto the floor beside the bed. For now, he left her bra fastened and began to move down, dotting kisses over her collarbone, the swell of her breasts and down to her stomach, coming to rest at the waistband of her skirt. Her hips rose slightly off the bed, their gazes meeting.

She wanted to remember, forever, how he looked at her at that moment. As if she was the most desirable woman on the face of this earth. And the trail of his kisses made her feel, for the first time in her life, as if she were.

He slipped his leg between hers and moved farther down the bed until his hands were on her boots and he could remove first one then the other. He stroked over her foot, even through the thick tights, a breath escaping her when he slipped his hand along the length of her leg to the hem of the skirt. Then he hitched her skirt higher until it rested at the midpoint of her thigh, a delicious forbidden *something* in even that.

Yet there was something even more forbidden about the feeling of his fingers curling over the sensible, thick waistband of her winter tights. He shifted to kneel beside Lizzie, his eyes fixed on hers as he peeled the tights down with an agonising slowness, easing them lower with each passing second. There was something utterly wanton in the ease with which he knelt there, naked, hard, no trace of shame or embarrassment on his handsome face.

With a half-grin, he flung her tights over his shoulder. His hand was on the waistband of her skirt, and she guided it to the zip at the side. He bent and took it between his teeth, his mouth brushing her naked hip as he tugged the fastening down. She lifted her hips and he pulled the skirt away in one swift movement. She closed her eyes. A nervous giggle escaped her, and she wondered what on earth he would make of her knickers, which were white with a small bow to match her sensible bra. They were not the knickers to wear for a passionate assignation with a handsome stranger. But he didn't seem to care.

Lizzie gave a gasp as he pressed his body to hers once more. Their legs entwined again, the hint of his erection against her leg sending a flare of heat through her veins. His lips met hers, his tongue teasing in a long, languorous kiss, and behind her back, his graceful fingers glided over the fasteners of her bra until they came apart. In response, Lizzie thrust her fingers into his thick hair, holding him to the kiss, lifting her hips until she felt his cock pressed to her, the slight, involuntary jerk of his body promising so much.

Her hands were still in his hair when he shifted lower, drawing a trail of kisses from her mouth to her neck. In one smooth movement he pulled her unfastened bra down her arms and away. Then, with a moan of desire, his lips were on Lizzie's bared breasts.

He responded to her every sigh and every shudder, as if he were learning the desires of her body as he kissed and sucked and nibbled without a word, without instruction, as if there were no point to this unless he gave her pleasure. He was utterly unselfish, even for a man who seemed to be so aware of his own attractions. He could have lain back and had anyone, effortlessly. Instead, he had chosen *her*, and he was drawing out her bliss, tantalising with lips and tongue and teeth.

His powerful arms were around Lizzie's waist and he lifted her body just a little, his hands smoothing over the arch of her back with a practised elegance. She tipped her head back on the pillow, her lips parting and the fingers of one hand once again in his hair, the other clutching his toned shoulder. She could feel the power in it beneath her palm, the strength in the muscle when it flexed to lift her body to his lips.

He circled her nipples with the very tip of his tongue before he drew it down, barely brushing her skin until he reached the unfussy cotton knickers. Yet even then he didn't stop, and he dipped his tongue beneath the elastic at her waist, tasting the warmth that lay beneath. Lizzie gave an involuntary jerk of her hips and he rested the flat of his hand on her thigh, stilling her movements so he could tease her, exploring the skin that had yet to be revealed.

The more she tried not to move, the more her muscles tensed, the more her pleasure intensified. Her moans were growing more breathless as the stranger made his exploration of her body. He gradually pulled her knickers down farther, the curve of her stomach appearing to him. He ran his kisses over it and, once her navel was revealed, he dipped the tip of his tongue into it.

So intimate was this that a deep shudder rolled through Lizzie, a prelude to orgasm, but at an intensity that she had never experienced before. He met her eyes then, the man who wanted to *fuck* her. Did he notice her rising tears of joy and relief? Would he wonder why? A sliver of tenderness entered his glance, but it was soon overwhelmed by a look of devilish passion, and he continued to slowly undress her.

He slipped the last of her clothing down and cast it aside. She was naked now, shamelessly so, carried away on the tide of passion. Still, his kisses traced heat over her skin and Lizzie shut her eyes, her breath coming in gasps. The man's hands were soft when they drifted over her hips and urged her body nearer. Then, with a delicate touch, he pressed his tongue to her.

Lizzie groaned, pressing her head back into the pillow as he swirled his warm, wet tongue around the most tender part of her body. He teased with the tip of his tongue, then laved her with a powerful lick. Lizzie trembled in response to him, her breaths urgent.

"Make me come, oh, please…"

He lifted his head for just long enough to purr mischievously, "All night long."

Then he flicked his tongue over her in one sinuous movement, darting it inside her. His fingers dug against her hips with each languorous movement and he held her there, alternating between those strokes at her core and short, teasing flicks of his tongue over her clit.

Lizzie's toes pressed into the bed. Her necklace, which had been entirely forgotten, had heated with her body, the beads clicking with her every movement. Their sound reminded her that, after all, she was not entirely naked, but the man between her legs was, and the thought and the sight of it made her arousal keener. She lifted her legs, crossing them at the ankle behind his back. Feeling the strength of his body as he pleasured her, his unselfish attentions became all the more intense to her.

That shudder, that prelude, repeated through her body, followed almost at once by another, more intense. Every muscle in her body strained towards one place, that spot where the nameless man whose presence she had been in for less than an hour was pleasuring her. The shudders came faster, deeper, but the man wouldn't break away, and she was carried up into an intense space of bliss, a long cry falling from her mouth. As that ebbed, he took her higher still, and she shouted in her ecstasy, wordless, formless sounds of utter joy.

Only when Lizzie sank back on the duvet, her eyes closed and her lips parted as she gasped down sated breaths, did he finally withdraw his tongue. Just as he had drawn those heated kisses down the length of her body, now he retraced his path until his lips had passed over her stomach and breasts, her throat and jaw, and was kissing her again.

I want you to remember me.

His erection was pressed against her thigh, and Lizzie, still trembling, reached to caress it. He deepened his kisses in response, and she closed her hand around him, learning how he felt. He murmured something in her ear. A gasp of pleasure, or a word, she didn't know.

She whispered, "You have a splendid cock."

His reply was to close his hand over hers and whisper, "You taste like pure excitement."

Lizzie giggled, her breasts wobbling a little with her laughter, but she made no attempt to conceal them or be embarrassed that they had behaved in a less than perfect way.

She felt so completely unhindered in the presence of this man. He could be anyone, but she felt at ease with him. Aroused, but at ease. Wanton. Lustful. All manner of things that she had not felt for so long. If she ever had at all.

"Look... I wasn't planning to be ravished by a handsome stranger this evening. I haven't got any..."

She tightened her hand around his cock and he moaned in time with her rhythm.

"You do know what I mean, don't you, mystery man?"

"Champagne?" It was a teasing, breathless murmur.

"That's not what I meant!" She grinned at him. "But…since you're offering…"

Her *mystery man* lifted his head and looked across the room to where the two filled glasses waited on the table beside the window. The curtains were closed now, but this was the place that he had stood, his hand on the glass, and his clothes were still neatly placed where he had left them, his shirt in a crumpled heap on the floor. The ice bucket with its bottle of champagne reflected the bed back at them, beads of condensation making it a surreal scene.

His gaze drifted from that suddenly far-distant table down to where their linked hands were still moving on his erection and asked, "Right now?"

Lizzie rested her cheek against his, enjoying the scent of him, the warmth of him, the tangle of their bodies.

"Oh, I'm a patient girl. I wouldn't want to rush you." She pressed her mouth to his ear, her polite tone changing to one of desire. "How hard do you want it?"

"So hard that you still feel me there tomorrow." He dipped his tongue against her ear. "And every time you look up at this window."

Lizzie swallowed, and his mouth brushed her neck.

"I…I want that too."

His free hand skimmed down over her hip, resting there for a moment until it travelled lower, teasing her. Then his fingers were moving again, and she gasped as she felt him deep inside her core.

She took his wrist in the circle of her hand, guiding him to slide slowly, deeply, in and out of her. Each time she had him as far inside her as his elegant touch would reach, she held him there, and tightened her muscles around him as his fingers moved. His thumb circled at her clit, and still their linked hands stroked his cock.

They didn't look at each other as they murmured their pleasure.

Nor did they speak, the only sounds those of their breathing and soft, pleasured sighs. It was as though he instinctively knew just how to draw out her deep waves of pleasure and shivers of delight. From the way his hips pressed to her hand, the brush of his lightly stubbled jaw rasping her cheek, the heat in his skin, she knew that she shared that instinct, that her caresses were just as electric.

Lizzie Aspinall, able to elicit abandoned moans and gasps of anticipation from a man like this, a man who, less than an hour earlier, she had never laid eyes on before. Yet now here they were, their bodies already attuned to each other.

Should she wonder who he was? A besuited businessman in town for one day, one night only for them to be together. And she would return tomorrow evening and look up at his window. By then, another guest would be there, and all trace of this evening would have disappeared. Except for what remained in the memory of her skin.

Still his fingers maintained that steady pace that seemed to reach a place she so rarely explored. He caught her ear between his teeth, nipping and tasting, rolling his tongue around the smooth shape of her earring.

His mouth moved to her throat, taking a bead of her necklace between his teeth, then he kissed the skin that had hidden behind it.

Lizzie felt another shudder building in the core of her being. It rippled through her, her hand stilling on his cock but not letting go. Her nameless lover didn't even seem to notice and instead kept his fingers moving, apparently devoted only to her pleasure, driving her on to reach the heights. And all the time his lips were on her neck, her collarbone, teasing under her necklace, tasting her pulse.

She lifted her leg over his waist, bringing him deeper into her. Then she was caught there, the intensity of his touch increasing with each of his movements within and outside her as her climax engulfed her.

How had he brought her to such pleasure again so soon? All she wanted to do was hold him, feel his strong body against hers as the remains of her orgasm trembled away.

He took his own hand from hers and rested it instead on her bottom, holding her leg around his waist, then shifted slightly until he could flip them so he was the one on his back, Lizzie's body atop him. He still caressed her, and she let her head rest on his shoulder, feeling his lips soft on her hair.

Even in this moment of tenderness, she did not want to tell him her name. She did not want to break the spell.

"Thank you…whoever you are."

As the moments passed, his caresses were sweet, his kisses gentle. But Lizzie was more than aware that he was still erect, entirely unflagging.

She placed her lips by his ear, her whisper heavy with anticipation and desire.

"I want your cock inside me."

His breath caught before he stretched out his arm to the bedside table. From the corner of her eye, Lizzie saw that he had reached for a smart wallet of black leather. That wallet, so small, so inconsequential, would tell his story and break the enchantment. It would bring mundanity and disappointment and the truth of the man in the hotel room who was hers for tonight. Lizzie closed her eyes and kissed him again, determined not to see *anything* that the wallet might contain, only to keep her stranger in her arms.

She could hear that he was preparing himself. The crinkle of a foil wrapper, then his mouth broke away from hers. She opened her eyes then, in time to see him tear the small packet with his teeth, then his hands moved out of sight as she gazed into the depths of his dark eyes, and she couldn't look away.

He guided her hand down to his cock, letting her feel that it was now sheathed.

"So." There was a playfulness beneath the heat in his voice, a hint of southern England suggesting he would be far away by this time tomorrow. "How do you want me?"

"Just as you are now. Lie still."

Lizzie raised her head from his shoulder and sat up on the bed. She was aware of the way his eyes travelled across her, settling on her breasts, moving to her stomach, a smile as his gaze roamed lower. But then he returned his gaze to hers.

Lizzie straddled him and guided his erection to her body. She watched him, saw his teeth catch at his lip for a second, saw the darkest brown eyes she had ever seen, flecks of emerald catching the light deep in each iris. His hips lifted just a little, betraying his hunger for her.

Lizzie gazed at him from under eyelids heavy with desire.

"Let me fuck you, mystery man."

She was so aroused, so wet, that despite her best intention to take him inside her as slowly as she could, in moments she had sunk her hips onto him and he filled her completely. The sensation robbed her of her breath.

She guided his hand to her waist and tensed her thighs, rising slowly up, holding him tight with her muscles then sinking down again. Delicious moans that she matched with her own came from his full lips as she rose and fell. She took in the sight of him as his stomach tautened with each of her thrusts. His thick, dark hair on the white pillow was a slash of night-time through the snow.

His hand tightened on her waist and his hips rose to meet her. He reached out with the other hand to circle her nipple with just the tip of his finger, exploring as though she were the most exotic thing he had ever laid eyes on. Then, never breaking the gaze or the rhythm as his hips lifted to meet her, the man dragged his finger over her hot skin, skimming her stomach and lower still until he was pressing his fingertip against her, circling and teasing.

She placed her hand over his on her waist, their fingers tangling as he rose again between her thighs. She reached for his nipple, combing her fingertips through the hair on his torso, teasing and tweaking.

"Please—" He gasped and it was like someone had flared fire through her blood. That breathless plea had been elicited by *her* fingers, fingers that even *she* hadn't felt in so long, and the thought that she could have his back arching like this, his eyelids falling and his gentle lips pouting, was utterly intoxicating.

Answering his need as his fingertip still worked at her clit, she took his nipple more firmly, twisting between finger and thumb. Nothing mattered, nothing at all, other than giving pleasure to this unknown man who was giving such pleasure to her.

Her necklace bounced and a light patina of sweat gleamed on her skin. The heat of her body reawakened the rose perfume she had innocently put on earlier.

Deep shudders began again at her core. He moaned, his hips bucking harder as he held her waist tighter, keeping her body latched to his, not allowing her to go.

And he spoke. Amid the groans, the sighs, he asked huskily, "Do you want me deeper?"

Lizzie's hair had tumbled into her face, but she made no attempt to push the tangle away. She gazed at the man and his glittering dark eyes through the loosened strands.

"Yes, yes, I do!"

His fingers gripped Lizzie's hips and, in one agile movement, he flipped them. Lizzie was on her back now, her lover's body over her, deep inside her. He reached up to curl the fingers of one hand around the headboard and began thrusting harder, each movement drawing a loud moan of pleasure and exertion from his lips.

Lizzie bent her legs, and with his free arm he caught her under the knee and forced her leg back farther, allowing him to enter her even more deeply.

Just as she had promised, Lizzie grasped his buttocks. There was a desperation in her hips to buck, but he seemed to sense it and pressed her down with his body, transforming her urgency into the beginnings of another orgasm.

They breathed in rhythm with his movements, Lizzie's sighs becoming louder and higher as a deep tremble ran through her. He was bringing her to bliss again.

His mouth fell to her throat, teeth grazing her skin, his tongue tracing the line of his kisses to her ear. She could hear every moan, every gasp, every breath, could feel every inch of his body both within and without her, could sense the intense need in them both. Their bodies moved in perfect harmony in the low light.

Lizzie shuddered, shaking in his arms. Words tumbled from her lips as her orgasm began to claim her.

"Don't—don't tell me your name! Please don't tell me! Don't...don't...!"

"Don't forget me—" Her lover's voice was lost in a gasp of release as every muscle in his body seemed to tense as one. His hand darted up to grip her shoulder, as though she might somehow be swept away from him.

He let go of the headboard and held Lizzie's hand, squeezing it as his orgasm faded out in smaller and smaller thrusts.

"I won't— I won't forget you, *ever*, Four-two-three."

"Another life..." He kissed her shoulder. "Another room... Who knows?"

Was there a nostalgic tone in his voice, like the sigh of the wind in autumn?

Lizzie felt him withdraw from her, then he snuggled down onto the bed. He drew her into his embrace, one arm around her waist, and murmured, "I promised you champagne..."

"You gave me something infinitely better than champagne."

He grinned tiredly at her and his eyes closed, his long, dark lashes twitching for a moment before they were still. But his arm was still tight around her, and she propped herself up, gazing down at him as he slept.

Whoever he is, whatever he dreams of.

But she had to go. She didn't want to, but she couldn't rush into another man's life. She couldn't let another man hurt her, even *this* man, who had awoken everything in her that had been shut down and locked away for so long. And what if she hurt him? It was too soon. She would have to let him slip away.

And if they knew each other's names, they would be too close.

Yet still she stayed, drinking in the sight of the man in room 423, the man she would never see again and whose touch she would remember to her dying day. She committed him to her memory, the toned body with just the hint of a suntan that had almost faded to nothing, the disordered, still damp black hair with its odd thread of silver, the tender expression on his sleeping face. How old was he, she wondered, this man with just the barest hint of gentle lines on his face, the slight sprinkling of silver in his hair? Then, painfully slowly, Lizzie lifted her lover's arm and slipped from the bed. For just a moment her eyes were drawn to his wallet, sure that its contents would give up all his secrets. She looked away.

Barely making a sound, she gathered up her clothes. She paused by the desk, her eye falling on paper and pen. She had to say something. And he might not even see it before it was tidied away by a chambermaid. She would never know.

423 – remember me.

A floorboard creaked underfoot as she went into the bathroom. She closed the door and ran water into the sink, splashing her flushed, perspiring skin. Her eye wandered across her anonymous lover's things. So prosaic. His toothbrush, his razor, his...

Lizzie inhaled a shivering breath.

The walls felt as if they were moving in on her.

On the glass shelf above the sink was a plain gold wedding band.

Chapter Two

Ben Finneran opened his eyes as soon as his hand found the empty bed beside him, already missing the warmth of his unnamed lover. She was standing at the desk, pale lamplight warming the contours of her naked body. He forced himself not to speak, not to ask her to fall back into his embrace. Instead he watched her now as he had watched her from the window, committed the waves of her dark auburn hair to memory, safely locked away the exact cornflower shade of her blue eyes so that he could recall them, recall *her*, when she was gone. He could still feel the soft warmth of her skin beneath his hand and now he studied every inch of her, every curve of a woman he would never forget, no matter how long he lived.

In her arms she held her clothes as though the bundle were the most precious thing in the world. Her head was bowed, and it was only now that he realised she was writing something on the notepad.

Don't forget me, he pleaded silently. *Don't forget us.*

As she laid the pen down beside the pad, Ben closed his eyes and listened to her light tread across the deep carpet, the bathroom door closing a second later. There was the sound of running water followed by silence. He pictured her dressing, hiding the curves of her body once more beneath the layers, tucking the wooden necklace under her thick scarf and, finally, fastening her coat.

Then she would leave, and he would be alone again.

When the bathroom door opened Ben closed his eyes. He heard her footsteps, clad in boots now, the dip of a floorboard and her gentle breath. She was looking at him one last time, he knew.

Don't forget me.

The door opened and closed, the electronic lock clicking into place.

Ben Finneran was alone.

He was on his feet a second after she left, praying that maybe she had left a number on the pad, but she hadn't, of course.

423 – remember me.

"Always," he told the empty room, breathing in the rose scent of her perfume.

With one deft movement Ben tore the sheet off and folded it. He put it into his wallet, a treasured memory for a man who had known precious few of those lately. Then he padded into the bathroom and took his vintage paisley bathrobe from the back of the door. As he pulled it over his arms, his eyes settled on his wedding ring and he felt a sudden, painful pang of shame. What would Holly say if she'd seen him there in the window, if she'd heard the noises of wanton pleasure, witnessed the utterly abandoned liaison that had ended as suddenly as it had begun?

What the hell would she think?

Yet that didn't stop Ben from returning to the window to part the curtains and look out, to see his mystery woman one last time. And there she was, her gloved hand on the door handle of a white minicab. She wouldn't look back, even though he was willing her to with every passing moment as the door opened, the dark interior of the car about to swallow her forever.

And at the last, the woman glanced over shoulder and up at the room. They couldn't see each other's eyes, yet he felt their gazes meet one last time, recalled her body in his arms, as fleeting as a dream. Then she slipped into the cab and closed the door. Ben let his forehead rest on the window as the car pulled away, carrying her out of his life forever.

Chapter Three

"This fabric is so soft. Hold the nap to your cheek, Jordan. Feel it?"

"Like a bub's arse, boss." Jordan winked as he held it to his pale cheek, then grimaced. "That sounds awful, doesn't it? I don't go round rubbing my face on baby bottoms, whatever you may have heard!"

Lizzie giggled. "Oh, Jordan! Let's clear our minds of that image. I was thinking more...the kiss of a...a lover."

She saw the man again—in her mind, at least. The tenderness in his eyes, and the fire.

She had to stop thinking about him.

"But...we are upholstering a country hotel, and I'm not sure if deep, dusky pink damask says 'rural retreat' or...or 'courtesan's boudoir'."

He had lain on the bed beneath her, his pleasure building, and she had been above him, wild and wanton and free.

"Country hotels are always fawn, aren't they?" He screwed up his face. "Maybe they need an injection of boudoir!"

Jordan leant one elbow on the table and cupped his chin in his palm, musing.

"If you were enjoying *the kiss of a lover* in your country retreat, wouldn't you rather be kissed amid gorgeous pinks than boring old brown and cream?"

Lizzie touched the back of her hand to her cheek. She turned away from Jordan, knowing that he would spot her blush at once.

"I rather think you're right. Will you go through the rest of these, Jordan? Now…where did Claire go with those swatches?"

She left him to it with the bales of fabric in reception.

Elizabeth Aspinall Interior Designs occupied the entire top floor of a sandstone edifice on Deansgate, a business she had built up from her parents' dining table. A business which kept her sane and drove her mad in equal proportions. But she was doing well. She had two staff, an enviable roster of clients and, perhaps most importantly of all, she had respect. Even if her single-minded focus made people like her sister think she was boring.

She gazed out across the rooftops of the city from the long window outside her office.

Night was falling. He must have left the city by now, gone back to his life in the south. Back to his wife and a world that Lizzie had no part in. Lights glittered across the darkening streets, like jewels on a haphazard necklace, the city girdled by the dark moors beyond. One of those buildings, some collection of glass and steel and concrete, had contained for a few hours the stranger who had taken her to his bed and pleasured her.

But she really had to stop thinking about him.

She opened her office door.

"Lizzie!" Donna was sitting in Lizzie's chair, her feet crossed at the ankle and resting atop her sister's desk.

"Donna? What are you doing in my office?"

Donna waved her mobile phone in greeting and asked excitedly, "Have you seen my photo spread? My first *proper* go at the *Mail!*"

"No, I haven't, I—"

She was already rifling through her enormous handbag for her iPad. She dropped it carelessly onto the surface of Lizzie's desk, then her fingers were moving like lightning over the screen.

"There you go!"

Donna working out. No, not working out. Donna stretching on a park bench, stretching against a wall, stretching at a white painted fence. Donna in a full face of makeup, her blonde hair in a casually tousled topknot, her figure perfectly on display in form-fitting yoga pants and a bright pink crop top. Donna, the premiership wife, in full, glamorous flight, ready for the next photoshoot.

"Some people have made horrible comments." She pouted, then shrugged. "Jealous, fat Jeremy Kyle viewers wearing Kappa. Haters gonna hate, Lizkins!"

Lizzie squinted at the images. People really were stupid if they thought this was an adult human being actually exercising. Whenever Lizzie went to the gym, she did her level best to avoid all mirrors, not wanting to be reminded of the way her hair frizzed at the ends or how red-faced and sweaty she ended up.

But then she had looked like that quite recently, without stepping through the doors of a gym.

She really had to stop thinking about 423.

"Do you never break into a sweat, Donna?"

"Not when there's a camera pointed at me!" Donna scrolled down to the comments. "Look at this one. *'That's what I call a real woman. Gorgeous!'*"

"That's almost sweet! Erm…what's that one say, just underneath?"

"*'I'd smash her back doors in'.'*" Donna frowned. "That's sort of a compliment, I guess."

"They sound unhinged! You have to be careful, Donna. What if it's the stalker? Have you shown that to the police?"

"They said that they're going to look at all our coverage but— I mean, if you look on any of these sorts of stories, there's always one or two loonies. You only have to look at the girl who got spiked last week and dropped dead, you never know who's around!" Yet Donna frowned and glanced at the screen of the iPad, the light reflecting onto her face. In that moment she looked like a little girl again, far from the gorgeous young woman of a thousand perfectly executed paparazzi shots. "I'll let the club lawyers know. They're handling it for us."

Lizzie leant against the filing cabinet, her arms folded.

"They might be able to trace them by IP address. It's amazing what they can do, I've seen it on the telly."

"It's all gone a bit Scandi-noir in here." Donna laughed, still admiring her own photos. "I don't want to think about what people can be like. Some of these comments are gross. *'I'd smash her back doors in.'* Horrible stuff!"

"What does Matt say about all this? I still remember that time he split open that poor bloke's nose because he winked at you in a bar. You don't think he'd go after someone who posts those things online, do you?"

"Even Matt's shaken up by it." Donna shuddered. "He says it's just a United fan with a sick sense of humour, but we feel like we're being watched all the time. You look around at people and think *is it you?* They've threatened to kill him!"

"Why would anyone want to kill Matt? Well…apart from the bloke who he punched in the nose. But he's a local boy done good, a Manchester hero. *Moss Side's finest* and all that. Unless… You don't think he was involved in anything dodgy, do you, and some hard-man's after him?"

"He's *famous*, Liz. A lot of people get very upset when someone does well for themselves." She shook her head and closed the neon pink cover over the screen of her iPad. "We're talking about loonies."

Donna swung her long legs down and stood, towering above the desk thanks to her skyscraper heels. She trotted round to embrace Lizzie and announced, "Anyway, you can't live your life for random nutters, can you? Matt's treating us to dinner at Australasia because I've been so hopped-up on all this stress."

"Lucky old you! Have a great time, won't you?"

Lizzie meant it. At least one of the Aspinall sisters should be happy. And it wasn't Lizzie, who had thrilled to the caresses of a stranger and would never see him again. If only she had given him her number — at least there would have been a chance for something. But her need to protect her heart had decided for her. She had seen his ring and left him sleeping, with only the memory of their encounter. She hadn't even said goodbye.

Remember me.

Two glasses of champagne, waiting on a table, poured but never drunk. It bothered Lizzie like a fly in an empty room.

Chapter Four

An hour later, Lizzie was on her way home. She'd bundled her coat tightly around her, the cold wind buffeting. Her scarf had partly unravelled and drifted on the wind in her wake.

The streets were busy with the prelude to Christmas. Bright windows were lit up with gifts in luxurious displays, showing themselves to the street to tempt and tantalise. Lights festooned the buildings, bastions against the encroaching winter evening.

She turned down the road that ran alongside the hotel. It was on her route home, a building she had walked past hundreds of times and had never been inside.

Until last night.

The façade of Victorian grandeur rose up before her and Lizzie studied the mellowed red brick and yellow stone, the filigree metalwork at the lower half of each window, the swagged velvet curtains in each room.

Some of the rooms were occupied, the curtains open and lights on to reveal guests unpacking suitcases, taking off their shoes, peering out at the city night then pulling the curtain closed.

A tram went by, packed with commuters. By the time it had passed, Lizzie realised she was level with the room she had visited the previous night. She would dare herself to look up. She needed to see that the room was empty or that another guest was at the window, another guest who would not even notice her in the winter darkness.

She steeled herself and tipped back her head.

He was there again, by the window.

She blinked, just to be sure that it wasn't her brain playing tricks, transforming another man into *her* man, her stranger, but it wasn't. The man in the towel was the man in the suit once more, a sharply cut jacket of dark blue like a shadow on his white shirt. He was gazing into the bar where their eyes had first met and the look on his face in that fleeting instant was one of such ruefulness that she couldn't help but feel a jolt of *something*, though she didn't want to consider what that something might be. Then the tide of pedestrians carried her on and the man in 423 was lost to her.

She could go straight home, forget him, tell herself that last night had been a one-off. Enjoyable, maybe one day even regrettable. But a one-off, not to be repeated, because she had thought she would never see him again.

But she just had. He was still in the room, within those four walls where Lizzie Aspinall had cavorted with a stranger, where their bodies had connected in the most immediate way she had ever experienced.

Going back into the hotel was barely a conscious decision. Something led her there, an invisible thread.

The same doorman nodded to her as she went up the steps. Did he recognise her? Did he know?

But she had to see the man in room 423.

She strode over the plush carpet towards the receptionist. She was on the phone and held up one immaculately manicured finger to Lizzie. As Lizzie waited, her heart thudding hard in her chest, it occurred to her that she had no idea what to say. He didn't know her name, and she wasn't about to say, "Tell the man in 423 that the woman he tumbled into bed with yesterday has arrived."

And she couldn't even be sure that he'd seen her from the window. He had been staring at the bar, not down at the pavement. He would have no idea that she was here. If she went up to the room, if she knocked, if she asked through the panels, *Do you remember me?* he would have a choice. He could open the door, or sit in silence until she went away.

She headed to the lifts. With any luck, a helpful person would arrive with a room card and she could go up. With any luck, this would be before someone noticed that she shouldn't be there.

She stepped back as a lift door opened in front of her.

And Lizzie smiled.

There, in the brightly lit, mirrored interior, deliciously respectable in his blue suit and understated silk tie, was her lover. He beamed so brightly that he was as far from a brooding mystery man as it was possible to get and asked her, "Champagne?"

"Yes, please!"

He reached out his hand, inviting her to take it, and she placed her own atop his warm palm, their fingers twining. Then he caught the attention of the receptionist and called, "423. Best champagne you can get?"

With the phone still pressed to her ear, the receptionist acknowledged with a smile and wave of her hand, then the man was drawing Lizzie into the lift with him, already pressing the button for the fourth floor.

After staring at each other in amused amazement for a few seconds, their mouths met once again. There was no trepidation. Their kiss was fire and passion at once. They held each other tightly, and in moments, Lizzie was pressed to the wall of the lift, pulling the man to her.

The pressure of his body held her there and his fingers caught in her hair, combing through the strands. There was nothing soft about the kiss, though, a wild, fierce embrace that didn't stop as the lift began its slow ascent.

The scent of him, the closeness of him, dragged Lizzie back to their few stolen hours of the night before. She clasped his buttocks, to remind him of yesterday, and held him close to her, his hardness pressed to her hip a promise of pleasure she had not thought to feel again.

They were still locked in each other's arms when the doors of the lift finally glided open at the fourth floor where, less than twenty-four hours earlier, she had made her uncertain way towards the man in the towel. Now she wasn't alone, far from it, and he kept his lips pressed to hers as he stepped back a little, clearly reluctant to end the embrace, even now.

"I kept thinking about that champagne." There was a note of mischief in his voice, though it was heavy with desire. "And hoping you'd come back for it."

Lizzie's dimples were reflected into infinity in the lift's mirrored walls. "I did too! And I *have* come back." She tugged his silk tie out from his suit, bringing his mouth near to hers again. "But...not just for the champagne."

"Good to know," he murmured, catching her lips for another kiss, coaxing them to part. She felt the heat in him as he claimed her, then in one sure movement, he scooped her clear of the floor and into his arms again. This time there was no convenient towel to lose, and with Lizzie cradled safe in his embrace, the man in room 423 strode from the lift.

They didn't kiss now, but gazed at each other, taking in the reality that the Fates had ordained them to meet again.

"I thought you would've left the hotel by now and gone home. I wasn't expecting to see you again."

"I'm in no rush to leave."

Lizzie nodded. She was afraid of what she might say if she allowed herself to speak.

He managed to open the door to his room without dropping Lizzie, and as soon as it was shut behind them again, he lowered her to her feet. He pressed her to the door, just as he had yesterday, and their heated kisses went on. Lizzie traced her fingers down his side, to his waist, and slipped her hand between them, stroking at his erection through his clothes.

As his hips pressed closer to Lizzie's touch, she felt his teeth catch at her ear, his tongue teasing and tasting. His breath on her skin was warm, yet she felt goosebumps of anticipation where his lips caressed, and once again, those nimble fingers were skipping over the buttons of her winter coat.

They threw it aside together. He had to negotiate another set of buttons on her velvet jacket before he could get to the blouse underneath. Lizzie was desperate for their contact again and, sensing that he would encourage such wantonness, unbuckled the belt on his trousers and tugged down the zip. No sooner had she done so than he took her hand in his and pressed it to his erection, held now by just the thin fabric of his boxers. His fingers were busy on Lizzie's blouse and his mouth followed the buttons down, kisses dotting her collarbone. He drew the tip of his tongue down between her breasts and she arched her back, gasping her pleasure.

"All day—I kept—thinking about—you!" From beneath her half-closed eyelids, she saw him smile. She squeezed his hand. "I need you inside me. I felt you all day, as if we had never stopped."

"You wear roses in your perfume." The gentle observation, more innocent than she might have anticipated, momentarily stilled Lizzie. He met her gaze for just a moment before he pressed his lips to hers again, his hand coming to rest against her hip.

In the heat of their renewed kiss, she slipped her hand under the waistband of his trousers and edged them down, along with his boxers, to the tops of his thighs. She caressed his revealed erection in response to the deepening of his kiss. Those hands, elegant, graceful, that had brought her such pleasure last night, now slid to the button of her own trousers, and with agonising slowness, he unfastened it, then drew down the zip at the same speed. He nipped her ear again and asked, "Right here?"

"Yes…"

As soon as the man released the zip of her trousers, they slipped down to pool at her feet and his hand was brushing over the smooth skin of Lizzie's thighs. His lips remained at her ear, the tip of his tongue circling her earring, his gasps of pleasure pushing her on.

Had she planned to come back at some subconscious level when she'd dressed this morning? It was a thought she dismissed, but for the first time in so long, she had felt desirable, beautiful even, and leaving that sensible cotton underwear in the drawer and wearing lacy ones instead had been a tiny, private secret to celebrate what they had done last night.

Her eyes were closed but Lizzie heard his wallet opening then the thud of it being cast aside onto the floor. His hands left her skin for just as long as it took to shrug off his suit jacket and then her lover's body was pressed to hers again, their tongues moving together in a deep kiss. Lizzie heard the condom wrapper tearing, a few seconds lost as he sheathed his cock, but his hands were on her again soon enough, more insistent than ever. She gave a murmur of assent when his fingertips played over her hip, teasing her knickers down just a little.

Lizzie tangled her hand in his hair, revelling in the way he tantalised. She took his wrist and guided his fingers into her underwear, gasping as he touched her delicate flesh.

"Am I ready?" She pressed her mouth to his ear. "Am I wet enough for you?"

He withdrew his hand and brought it up to her lips, drawing one finger along Lizzie's pouting mouth. The very tip of his tongue followed the path his finger had traced, ending in a long, slow kiss.

"You're ready."

"I better get these off, then, hadn't I?"

There was no elegant way of removing her knickers. He let her out of his arms while she nudged them lower and kicked them away, along with her shoes. Naked from the waist down, she returned to his arms.

A tremble of anticipation hurried through her. "Are you ready?"

Her lover nodded, his gaze locked on hers. "Since you stepped into that lift."

She kissed him again, gasping her approval as his strong arms encircled her waist and lifted her clear of the floor. He teased the tip of his cock against her body, easing into Lizzie bit by bit, pushing her back against the door. She held him about his shoulders and lifted first one leg, then the other, crossing them behind his waist.

Once he was all the way inside her, Lizzie shivering at the sensation of him filling her, he paused. He kissed the tip of her nose, such a sweet gesture for such a voluptuous moment, then, as if he couldn't hold back a moment longer, began to thrust. His movements were hard and fast, his kisses fierce on her throat and lips, full of heat.

The door rattled with each buck of his hips, but anyone passing by wouldn't have heard it over the sound of the woman pressed against the other side of it, sighing out her pleasure with total abandon. His own gasps of exertion blended with hers in the silent early evening, each stroke bringing them closer to the moments of blissful release.

Ripples of pleasure started up from Lizzie's toes, trembling through her legs as she crossed them more tightly around him. All sensation drew into the core of her body and she shuddered and shuddered as her orgasm went on. Her lover held her firmly, tenderly, even as his thrusts went on, even as his own peak claimed him in a deep shiver. He sighed formless words against her ear.

Now his kisses were more gentle, his movements growing slower, less deep, as the wave of his orgasm subsided. His head dropped to her shoulder and she clung to him, running her fingers through his hair.

"When I saw you tonight—" He laughed then, leaving the sentence unfinished. Instead he lowered her feet back to the floor, kissing her all the time.

"When *did* you see me? I tried not to look up, and then when I did, you were staring at that bar across the road."

"You weren't looking up, but I *knew*— It sounds ridiculous—but I recognised your hair."

"My hair?" Lizzie giggled. "It wasn't in a big messy tangle. How could you possibly have realised I was the same woman as the one you had in your bed last night?"

"You tidied it before you left." *So he had been awake,* Lizzie realised. She wasn't sure then whether to be relieved that she hadn't known or not. "And didn't put your hat back on until you were outside."

Of course, he had watched. Because that was what he did.

"I'd better... If we're going to have that champagne...I should make myself a little less—naked. If you don't mind?"

"Do you mind if I—" He pointed to the bathroom.

"Not at all..."

With a last kiss, he stepped over his discarded jacket and into the bathroom, closing the door behind him.

Lizzie, still woozy from her orgasm, pulled her trousers on again and buttoned up her blouse and her jacket. She did what she could with her disordered hair and smudged makeup, which was reflected back at her from the large mirror, but there wasn't a great deal she could do about her blushing face or her enormous smile.

She picked his jacket up off the floor. Such a beautiful piece of clothing, hand-stitched in places, with a silk lining of purple paisley. She hung it carefully over the back of a chair. His wallet was on the floor. Trying to be tidy, she picked it up, but it burned in her hand with the knowledge that she had only to flip it open and she would know who he was, what name to murmur as he pleasured her. Without looking at it, she put the wallet on the table.

And—*because why on earth not*—she stuffed her knickers into his jacket pocket. A gift for later, once she had gone. She tucked the chair in, blushing even more at her recklessness.

The bump of the chair against the table awoke the screen on his phone.

She glanced at it, only because it had caught her eye, and she hoped that he wouldn't think she had been snooping. But there, on the screen, was a sunny photo taken in an American theme park. A fairy-tale castle filled the back of the photo, and in front, an adult in costume as Tigger from Winnie the Pooh, waving. On one side was the man, in sunglasses, his bright, white teeth smiling into the camera. He looked effortlessly smart, even in a loose, short-sleeved shirt and shorts that stopped just above his knees, revealing his tanned legs. And on the other side…

Good lord, she was young! But she shouldn't be surprised. A trophy wife for a businessman. Slender, in a sleeveless summer dress, long legs like a colt. Hand slightly obscuring her face to catch a strand of her brunette hair. The same happy smile for the camera.

But your husband just fucked me against a door.

Lizzie wasn't proud of that stab of triumph. But he was a nameless man in a hotel room, a stranger who was just passing through. It wasn't permanent, it didn't matter, she didn't need to know about his life outside of this room. And he didn't need to know about hers.

But she had spotted it, his discarded wedding ring, on the table by the window, where a huge television was balanced. Lizzie bit her lip. She wouldn't think about the man's wife, even if it made her the other woman. She couldn't ignore the pull between them, their mutual, inescapable desire.

An efficient rap at the door and a brisk call of "Room service!" alerted Lizzie to the arrival of the champagne.

She hurried to the door, peered through the spyhole and opened it. A member of hotel staff in neat uniform, a brass name badge on their shirt, presented the champagne on a large tray. There was a bottle in a metal cooler and two glasses next to a bowl of halved strawberries.

"Your champagne, madam. Shall I bring it in for you?"

"No, no, that's fine. I'll take it."

"Will there be anything else, madam?"

Lizzie heard the bathroom door unlock. She grabbed the tray. She didn't want anyone to intrude on her moments between her and her mystery man. Not even the room service person with their champagne.

"No, no, that's everything, thank you."

She nudged the door shut with her foot.

The bathroom door opened and the man emerged, somewhat more presentable than when she had last seen him. His shirt was once again neatly tucked into his trousers, but he had shed his tie and was now barefoot. She couldn't help but notice that his hair was no less disordered though, and he paused and ruffled his hand through it, meeting her gaze with a smile.

"You stayed."

Lizzie took his hand.

"You…you thought I was going to leave while you were in the bathroom?"

"I hoped not." He lifted her hand to his lips and kissed it. "I wanted us to enjoy our champagne. And strawberries too, which was unexpected!"

His laugh was just a little bashful and he released Lizzie's hand and lifted the bottle from the bucket. She watched his sure movements as he stripped off the foil from the neck and took the cork in his fist.

"You might want to take cover," he warned merrily.

Lizzie ducked behind him, giggling, her arm about his waist.

"I don't like the bang. It scares me!"

"Consider me your hero," was his deadpan response. He squared his shoulders, as though he were about to face a raging bull. Then he gave one flamboyant tug of his hand and the cork left the bottle with a resounding *pop*. "How're you doing, my damsel. Still in distress?"

"The champagne will calm me down, I'm sure."

"I don't know if I want you calm. I like you as you are." He poured two glasses and held one out to Lizzie. "To the woman with no name, dancing eyes and the sort of smile you can see from four floors up."

"To hot, nameless men with hair as dark as midnight, who strip at windows and pose in a towel."

"Hot, you say?" He pouted. "Show me where. I'll knock him out!"

Lizzie dimpled up at him, drinking the champagne, her arm still around his waist.

"Oh, he's very, very hot indeed. In fact, he's the most handsome man I've ever seen. He's gorgeous. And he's amazing in bed."

"The bastard," he growled darkly. "I can see I'll have to up my game."

Lizzie leant up to kiss him.

"He's even amazing *out* of bed, as well!"

"How does he perform in a hot shower?" He kissed her. "Or a very bubbly bath?"

"I'm sure that would be amazing too! I'm... I'm glad we've got to drink our champagne, at last. I hated thinking of those glasses just sat there. Like a missed opportunity, something sparkling just...left behind."

Lizzie realised she'd revealed more of herself in those words than she had intended to and looked away from him, but only found herself staring at his discarded ring.

"How long can you stay?" His hand moved up to cup her face, long fingers brushing her hair back. "Long enough to finish the bottle?"

"Yes... Give me two hours. I have work tomorrow... I have to get home and I have to sleep. I have to — " Was this really the moment, but when else could she say so? "I have to do normal things. And then...and then remember that I was up here with you. And be so bloody happy that I was."

Her companion met that with such a bright, disarming smile that she couldn't help but return it. He took a sip from his glass and told her with a sigh, "It's nice to close the door on real life though, isn't it?"

"It absolutely is."

His hand left Lizzie's face and he brushed his fingertips down her arm until that strong arm was around her waist once more, his dark eyes blazing into hers. "Let's enjoy our two hours."

Lizzie rested her head on his shoulder. Another tram clattered by outside, but it didn't break the peace of that moment. Two nameless people, who had somehow found a deep, timeless connection, embracing in a plush hotel room in the cold heart of the winter city.

"Seeing as you're dressed, mystery man, unlike yesterday...perhaps it's only fair that you give me the chance to strip you?"

"I am entirely at your disposal, Ms. Mystery." He took another sip from his glass. "And ready to please."

Lizzie put her glass down on the desk. Too late, she remembered that this was where he had left his phone, but this time the screen didn't turn on. She kissed him as she slowly unbuttoned his shirt, tenderly exploring and tasting. The quality of the cotton was very fine under her fingertips, soft, immaculate. Still kissing him, she brushed his newly bared skin, eliciting a tiny shiver in his body. He carried that botanical scent with him again. He must've preened in the bathroom while she had accidentally snooped. He stood motionless, the champagne still in his hand. When she broke away from the kiss for a moment, he quirked up his lips and took a sip.

"I like a man who wears cufflinks." She twisted them out of his shirt and put them aside. "I also like a man who's just had them taken off."

She slowly swept the shirt off his shoulders and stepped back to admire him. She knew he would like it, and he gripped the back of the chair behind him, the muscles tensing. He sipped the champagne, his dark eyes glittering at her with desire.

"Now, lie down on the bed."

"I like the way this is going." He tensed his muscles one last time before he let go of the chair, caught the natural confidence in his walk as he crossed to the room to obey her command. He took his time, setting the glass down on the table before he finally settled on the bed, his arms pillowed behind his head and one leg crooked at the knee, just casual enough to not be casual at all.

Lizzie knelt on the bed. Her breath hitched as she looked at him. She crawled up the bed until she was at his side. She unbuckled his belt, then unfastened the top button on his trousers. His hips strained just a little off the bed, but Lizzie laid her palm flat on his stomach and stilled him.

She reached for the glass of champagne beside the bed and took a sip. Then, at his side again, she leant down to his torso and tipped a tiny rivulet of the cold drink onto his flat stomach. His breath escaped in a gasp of delighted surprise and the fingers of one of those pillowed hands clenched momentarily, catching his own hair.

She dipped her head to lick the champagne and swirled it across his body, across his stomach, up to his chest. He lifted his head, as if wondering if she would kiss him. She gave him a quick peck, sipped from the glass, then bent to take his nipple in her mouth, the bubbles on her tongue tickling.

The sound that escaped his lips was neither a moan nor a shout but something in between, perhaps an expression of abandoned pleasure. His back arched from the bed and one of his arms darted out from behind his head, his fingers gripping Lizzie's shoulder. She felt his breathing quicken, saw it in the rise and fall of his chest, heard the gasps of pleasure, even as her head filled with the taste of champagne and the scent of botanicals. The scent of *him*.

This man who had patiently brought her bliss the night before, a stranger he had seen across the street. And she would bring him bliss too.

She licked and kissed her way down to his waistband, his body stirring beneath her. Keeping her gaze on his, she teased down his zip. He gulped, and it seemed he was trying to still his hips but failed in spectacular fashion as they bucked up from the bed, a grunt of pleasure escaping him. They smiled at each other, Lizzie suppressing a giggle in her throat. Then the zip was unfastened.

His hips rose off the bed again and Lizzie tugged his trousers down. She pressed her hand onto his raised knee and he obediently lowered it as she straddled him. His boxers had gone and that splendid erection rose up before her.

She balanced the champagne glass on his flat stomach.

"Don't move."

She reached for the champagne, topped up the glass on his stomach and put the bottle on the bedside table.

Then she held his hips steady and kissed the tip of her lover's cock.

"That champagne won't spill," he told her optimistically. "Not with my *legendary* self-control."

She swirled her tongue around the tip. Then, taking her mouth away, she placed her tongue at the base of his cock and swept up slowly to the tip.

The glass wobbled a little, the lines of bubbles rising in the champagne only slightly uncertain.

On she went, tasting the saltiness of him, as he groaned at her touch. A determined rhythm entered his breath, so she stopped, sat across his thighs and drank the champagne as casually as she could manage while the aroused man below her gripped the bedsheets, his hips stirring.

She clasped her free hand around his erection, enjoying the shape and the width and the warmth of it. He put a hand over hers, guiding her. Their eyes met again.

"Do you want to come?" she whispered.

He nodded, his lips parting in a sigh of, "When you're ready."

She relinquished her hold on him and got off the bed. She leant down to kiss him. His eyelids drooped, the long lashes brushing her cheek.

"I'm ready because you are."

She pressed her mouth to his and pulled away, the man straining after her lips. She lifted his chin, to make sure he was watching, and tipped the glass up to her mouth. It was empty now, but she hadn't swallowed. She put down the glass and returned to the bed, still holding her mouth full of champagne. Careful not to spill a drop, she took her lover's erection between her lips and let the bubbles tickle and burst against his skin.

His whole body seemed to jerk up from the bed towards her, one hand clutching tight at the pillow whilst the other grabbed the bedsheet in a tight fist. This nameless, naked man with the pretty young trophy wife had entirely surrendered to Lizzie Aspinall, to the promised crescendo that she controlled.

Now, now she would thank him for all the pleasure of yesterday, when he had unselfishly carried her to ecstasy. She took him into her mouth as far as she could, champagne dribbling a little onto his skin from her lips as she rose and fell. She followed the bucks and jerks of his body, finding his rhythm with ease and staying there with him. He roared unrepentant groans as finally his hips sprang up and his moment of bliss arrived.

It took a little while, of continued shivers and moans, until he was still. He managed to give her a darkly seductive smile, and Lizzie, in answer, flung off her jacket. She unbuttoned her blouse and lay down beside him, taking his hand and placing the palm on the bare skin just below her bra.

They kissed slowly, sensuously, the man languorous in the penumbra of his *petit mort*.

"I do hope that was all right."

"I do hope that was a joke." He wetted his lips and smiled, running his hand down over her stomach. "I don't think I've ever met a woman like you."

Lizzie blushed at his compliment, unable to meet his glance.

"I'm quite boring really. You bring the devil out in me..."

"I guarantee that I win in the boring stakes." He brushed a kiss to her shoulder and laid his hand on his stomach, atop the very place that Lizzie had balanced the champagne glass. "And our devils seem well-matched."

She laid her hand over his where it lay on his stomach.

"You're all sticky now!"

"What do you propose we do about that, mystery girl?"

She gave him a pert grin.

"You have a very nice shower in there. Perhaps I could help you scrub off?"

"Those dimples…" he murmured fondly. "Will you soap me down slowly?"

"If you're good."

"I promise to be very" — he leant forward, punctuating each word with a kiss — "very. Good."

Lizzie nearly let herself fall into a kiss, but with effort, she got off the bed. She pulled her unfastened blouse across her chest.

"I want to strip for you, like you did for me at the window."

Her companion pushed himself up to sit against the pillow, resting his hand behind his head again. At her words his eyebrows quirked in anticipation and he breathed, "Please do."

Lizzie held the man's gaze, smiling through her pout, swaying her hips just a little, as if someone were playing music somewhere and only a hint of its beat could be heard.

She popped the collar forward on her blouse, peering at him over her shoulder as she turned her back on him. She rolled her shoulders and brought the blouse down to her waist in three sharp tugs. She paused, enjoying his eyes roaming her bared skin, then she pulled one arm free of the blouse. Hand on her hip, she slowly circled the arm that was still in the blouse, turning it like a windmill at her side.

And she flung the blouse across the room.

With surprising force, it hit the television, and she started to giggle, but she recovered herself.

She stepped back to face the man, her arms across her chest, buoying up her bosom as she winked at him. He gave her such a saucy glance that Lizzie thought he was about to wink back. She reached behind, watching him over her shoulder, and unclasped her bra. That too went the way of the blouse.

On the bed, her lover sat forward, his eyes narrowed just slightly and focused entirely on Lizzie. The arm that had been so casually tucked behind his head was now withdrawn and he chewed on his thumbnail in abject concentration. Only when he sensed her gaze on him did he blink and murmur, "Go on…"

She swept her toe across the carpet in an arc as she swayed back to face him. She cupped her bare breasts in her hands and wriggled her bottom as she leant towards him. With a wink, she dropped her hands away.

His eyes widened in an involuntary gesture when she revealed her breasts, his hand falling away from his mouth and into a very stirring round of applause. His face wore an expression of mischief mingled with desire and Lizzie realised that she couldn't recall a time when any man had looked at her with such undisguised appreciation. His gaze lingered, even as he reached for the bottle and brought it to his lips, taking a deep swig.

Lizzie gripped him by his hair and took the bottle from his hand. She tipped back her head and poured the champagne into her mouth. It spilled down her neck, over her wooden necklace, over her breasts. She passed the bottle back to him and sank one knee onto the bed, almost brushing him.

She undid the top button on her trousers, and still with that beat that was somewhere in her hips, she drew the zip down. For the last time, she turned her back on him and brought the back of her trousers down from her waist, revealing her bottom. She dragged them down farther and finally kicked them away.

Not quite able to sustain her prancing persona for much longer, Lizzie, naked now, sat down on the edge of the bed. She nudged her face into the man's neck.

"In case you're wondering… I learnt that on a hen weekend."

"In case *you're* wondering" — he set the bottle back on the side — "I'm having the night of my life."

"Me too." Lizzie kissed his warm skin, her arm around his naked waist. A shiver of anticipation went through her. "And now *I'm* all sticky with champagne… Still want that shower?"

"After that, more than ever." He let his cheek rest against her hair. "I'd make it a cold one, but since I'll be sharing with such a hot girl…"

Lizzie took his hand and rose from the bed. Her voice was soft and adoring.

"Come along, then…hot man."

"You forgot something." He slipped from the bed and Lizzie felt his fingertips brushing at the nape of her neck, unfastening the clasp of her necklace. A few strands of her hair had tangled in it and he freed them before he lifted the wooden beads from where they rested on her skin and put them down beside the bottle. "There."

The last vestige of the world outside had sloughed away.

"Will you think I'm a proper saucy chancer if I stop by my wallet on the way?" His face took on an expression of utterly comical disgust then, and he said quickly, "Not for cash, I hasten to add!"

Lizzie, lightly sarcastic, said, "Two naked people in a shower... What could possibly happen? I just don't know! But...thank you for asking. You're a gent."

"I want you." He released her hand and scooped up his wallet, opening it with a well-practised flick of the wrist. "But I'm still a gentleman."

Lizzie pressed her lips to his ear.

"A very handsome gentleman."

"With a very beautiful woman." He reached to take her hand again and together they went through into the gleaming white bathroom. The light seemed bright after the soft illumination of the bedroom and she cast her eye over the bottles on the glass shelf. Yesterday there had been so few things here, and Lizzie realised now that she had been right to guess that he was a new arrival in the city, because he had *definitely* unpacked, and an array of toiletries were now clustered on the shelf above the sink.

He dropped the wrapped condom onto the chrome soap dish and turned a dial. As a light rain began to fall from the jets, he took Lizzie's hand and escorted her into the shower. She clasped her hand against her shoulder, shivering slightly as the water splashed over her.

"And I feel like I should tell you that I don't make a habit of stripping in hotel windows." A slight smirk reached her lover's lips as he spoke. "At least, not since I gave up the job in Amsterdam."

Lizzie giggled at him. But his light-hearted comment begged a question.

"Why *did* you, then? Why for me? If you don't mind me asking."

He closed his eyes and turned his face to the water, and for a long moment she thought that he might not answer at all. His hands slicked his hair back and he blinked away drops of water before meeting her gaze again.

"It felt as though there was a thread between us, tied on at either end." His palm skimmed her cheek, eyes full of tenderness. "And I couldn't ignore it."

"Of course there is a thread. Because I followed it to find you."

Blushing at her sincerity, Lizzie couldn't say anything more. She let water pool in her hand and poured it over the man's stomach, where not long before she had licked off champagne. In reply he caressed his fingertips down her face then put his lips to hers for a kiss that felt lighter than a whisper.

Wet skin against wet skin, so sensitive and sensuous. Lizzie sighed as she ran her hand down his back, dancing her fingertips over his firm buttocks. He wanted her, to give her pleasure, without expecting anything in return besides her touch.

Would she return tomorrow or the night after that, and when the weekend was upon them, would they see out his dying hours in the city together? She couldn't allow herself to think of it when they had this *now*, each other and the water cascading down their entwined bodies in this room where the whole of her existence seemed to be contained.

She brought his hand to her breast, and as he closed his fingers over it, that look of desire kindled in his eyes again. Water glistened on their skin as he caressed her, and they kissed deeply. There was nothing frantic in their movements, only tenderness.

"I don't know what I was going to say when I got into that lift." It was a soft admission against her lips. "But I couldn't let you just walk past."

"I was going to try to get up to your floor and knock on your door, and hope you remembered me."

"I've been remembering you all day. It's been hard to concentrate on anything else."

"You kept distracting me by appearing in front of my eyes when I least expected it."

"I kept your note," he admitted.

Lizzie held him more tightly and sighed.

"I'd hoped you'd find it. I'm glad you did." She kissed him along the collarbone before bringing her mouth up to his. "I want you. I know it's greedy, but I do. I can't help it."

His reply was a kiss and then another, his hands sliding confidently over her back, skimming through the water as it fell over them. Then the kisses came faster and deeper and she felt the almost imperceptible tightening of his arm around her waist, holding her to him.

"Possess me," she whispered.

"I might not want to let you go." The response was a low murmur and he kissed her again before she could respond, his tongue exploring tenderly, his hands still roaming over her skin.

At that moment, so intimate and sweet, she wanted him to hold her forever, even though she knew that he couldn't. That, loathe as she was to admit it, there was a workaday world outside, where for Lizzie couldn't walk arm in arm with her handsome stranger. A dull world that had none of the burnish of this room, a grey land that had no place for whatever it was that two nameless people might feel for each other.

There was none of the fevered rush of their earlier encounter this time but instead long, languorous kisses, their hands exploring, their lips moving together. His embrace was almost protective and Lizzie sank gladly into it, his body hard against her softness, faintly tanned against her paleness. Her stranger, her man with no past. No yesterday, no tomorrow, just tonight.

He tenderly circled his thumb over her sensitive flesh and Lizzie moaned, yearning for their bodies to combine again. She gripped his erection, her hand moving swiftly over his wet skin. His breath quickened and caught, his fingers moving in reply, teasing what was to come.

"Don't be shy, mystery man..." Lizzie took his earlobe in her teeth, tugging playfully. "*Have* me. I'm yours for this evening."

"I'm never shy." His voice was lower, thick with desire, and he closed his hand over hers, encouraging her to stroke harder. Then he slid his fingers into her and whispered, "And neither are you."

She gasped and circled her hips with his fingers moving and turning inside her. As she continued to caress his erection, she was aware of a slight jolt in his hip. With her free hand, she reached for the condom.

"Leave it." His hand snapped up to seize her wrist. "I'll tell you when."

Lizzie's surprise turned into a giggle, and she pressed her kisses to his shoulder as his fingers still moved in her core.

"Oh dear, have I been naughty?"

"I hope so." With his fingers thrusting harder, he released Lizzie's wrist and slipped his hand round to land a playful smack to her bottom. "I'm still waiting for you to soap me down."

She blushed and ran her finger down the side of his face, telling him, she hoped, that she absolutely hadn't minded that smack at all.

She put the condom back on the soap dish with a grin. There were all manner of bottles to choose from, so she took the one that most resembled shower gel and squeezed. The gel lathered up quickly and she washed it slowly across his chest while gazing at the droplets of water that had caught in his long eyelashes. As her hips rocked, she took both of his nipples and, echoing his movements inside her, she caressed them.

"Is this the soaping down you were after?"

"I could probably stand a little harder, if you're woman enough?"

"If you're sure…"

She tweaked and twisted them, and he shut his eyes. His knees almost gave way but he caught himself at the last minute, his hand shooting out to grab the shower fixture as he gasped, "Christ!"

Instinctively, Lizzie let go of his nipples and caught him around the waist.

"I wasn't expecting *that* to happen!"

"You've got a talent for it." He withdrew his hand and, slipping through her embrace, dropped to his knees. Lizzie looked down through the water, following his lead as he encouraged her to lift one leg over his shoulder so he could bring his lips to her. This time there was no gentle exploration, just the sense of his tongue and fingers working together to taste her and push her onwards.

She clutched her hands in his hair and everything fell away until she was pure sensation. The warm water caressed her and made each sensation keener. And this man, this mystery... Somehow he knew what she wanted. Even before she knew herself.

Tremors started up in her toes and she shivered, her grip tightening on his hair, her orgasm drawing near. He slid his hand up over her thigh, round to grip her bottom and lifted it, bringing it down with a gentle but still firm smack.

That smack was just enough to send Lizzie spiralling into intense bliss. She trembled, her nerves thrilling at her pleasure. With admirable speed, he was back on his feet and reached for the condom, tearing open the packet as if there wasn't a second to spare—and perhaps, Lizzie thought as she took the condom from him, there wasn't.

If someone had told her twenty-four hours earlier that she would be rolling a condom onto the erection of a man she didn't even know, she would've been as amused as she was appalled. Yet here she was, her hands moving with confidence, his kisses more fevered and her own heart slamming so loudly it could probably be heard next door.

As soon as he was ready, Lizzie lifted her leg around her lover's waist and he caught it in a strong hand, holding her steady so he could enter her.

"Tell me your name?" It was a whisper, almost a plea, against her ear.

She couldn't.

That name didn't belong here, not in this room, not with her stranger, who was inside her, bringing their bodies closer and closer. *Lizzie.* It was a name from another time.

But she began to speak.

"It's...it's L—" She swallowed. "It's Louisa."

"James," he replied, and she wondered if that were true. She would never know.

"*James...*" She grinned at him, even as she felt something in the region of her heart wither. Why the hell had she lied to him? But she couldn't tell him the truth now. The moment was lost. For them both. "It suits you."

"I would never have guessed Louisa...not in a million years." Then he kissed her, and she told herself that it didn't matter, so why did it feel as if it *did*?

"What...what did you..." Should she really ask him this? But what was the sensible response? "What did you think it was?"

"Doesn't matter." James gasped. "Louisa."

Would this be their last time together, or would she return? But she would enjoy what she had now, this man, this—James, so passionate and tender. She would file away his every touch, his every moan, his every dark, glittering glance.

"James..." She said his name in a drawn-out sigh. Some day soon, someone else would be sleeping in room 423, and she would never allow herself to look up at the window again.

She tipped back her head, the water splashing over her face, her makeup long washed away. James' lips were on her neck, trailing up and down as he gasped her fake name again. She could feel the strength in his body as he pressed himself to her, the heat in his gaze, and the warmth of his skin. Their two hours were dwindling, moving too fast and sweeping them both along on the tide of passing time.

Lizzie felt the change in his body as he slowed his hips to a gentler rhythm, drawing out their encounter for her. She took his face in her hands and kissed him tenderly. All that existed in that moment was their two bodies meeting in bliss.

She trembled again, all her nerves alive to pleasure. And she knew that he was there with her, beside her, filling her, and that one day, he would be somewhere else entirely.

They sagged against each other, satiated, happy, at least for now. At least for this moment.

"I wish I didn't have to leave you." She meant it. Because if she hadn't needed to leave him, then she wouldn't have lied to him about her name. She had to leave. She couldn't curl up with him and sleep. She couldn't be the other woman. Even though she knew that she already was.

"So do I," James whispered. "It's a lot quieter without you, Lou."

They kissed once more, then Lizzie reluctantly slipped out of his embrace.

"I suppose we better get dried off?"

He nodded and turned his face up to the water, slicking both hands back over his wet hair. With effort, Lizzie dragged her eyes away from him. She stepped out of the cubicle and stood on the bathmat, wondering how to dry herself off without losing her air of mystery. She took a large, thick towel from a shelf and wrapped it around her so that it draped over one shoulder, aiming for a look akin to a Roman goddess.

"Throw me a towel?"

Lizzie was in danger of her carefully constructed toga collapsing. She reached for another towel with one hand, her other clasping her toga. As she passed it to him, she tried not to make it too obvious that she was admiring his nudity.

When she looked away, she caught her reflection in the bathroom mirror. Her hair was a soggy, tangled mess. That was not how she wanted him to remember her.

"At the risk of sounding boring, I don't suppose this room comes complete with its own hairdryer, does it?"

"It does." He turned off the water then took the towel and wrapped it around his waist, just as he had on the first night. "But I can do better than that."

Lizzie took her glance from his torso and raised an eyebrow at him.

"You're full of surprises, James."

At the door, he paused to take his dressing gown from the hook and hold it out to her.

She took it from him and put it on. It carried his unique scent.

His hand patted her bottom opportunely and he padded away, leaving her to prepare. She heard the chink of bottle on glass, the muffle of someone in the hallway.

Lizzie leant on the doorframe, watching him. Two glasses of champagne were waiting. James had pulled out a chair in front of the mirror.

"Your throne awaits, madam." He gestured to the seat and pulled open a drawer to retrieve a hairdryer. She caught a glimpse of the hotel's standard-issue dryer before the drawer closed again and she realised that this was his own, and a far better model at that. *So that casually relaxed hair doesn't become casual on its own.*

James looked up and caught her eye. He pouted and held the dryer to the side of his face, as though he were posing with a gun. "I'm the dandy highwayman— Are you too young to get that?"

Lizzie chuckled and held up her hands. "Stand and deliver, your money or your life!"

"Can I choose a kiss instead?"

She brushed her mouth lightly over his, just a hint of her tongue's tip emerging to tantalise him. Then, leaving him wanting more, she sat down.

She had brought a comb through from the bathroom and tried to get the tangles out of her hair as best she could. When she switched on the hairdryer, hot air escaped it at such force that she nearly dropped it.

"That was…somewhat alarming."

She was relieved of the hairdryer a moment later when James took it. He put a glass of fizzing champagne on the table in front of her. Then, still holding the dryer, he opened the drawer again and took out a bottle, which he held up for her to examine. "Nothing sinister, don't worry."

"Heat protection spray?"

Her dimples were reflected back at her, and James crinkled his eyes, amused. Then his gaze fell to her hair and his expression became one of concentration as, bit by bit, with painstaking and gentle care, he began to tease out the tangles. She watched him through the glass, enjoying the two sides of one man, the toned but not overworked body and the towel recapturing the frisson of the previous evening. Then, alongside that, the gentleness of his hand running over her hair, the careful dividing of each section before he combed it out straight.

Lizzie sipped her champagne and still he worked, the hum of the hairdryer settling into a rhythm that was almost soothing, coupled with his gentle ministrations. Eventually he turned the dryer off and leant over her shoulder to put it on the desk. Then he stood back a little and looked at Lizzie through the mirror before he stepped back to the chair and, without a word, returned his attention to her hair once more.

And still she watched him, wondering who he *really* was, what he did when he wasn't here with her or in Disneyland with someone else.

She didn't want to let go of this, whatever it was, this deep connection, this tenderness, the thread that pulled them together. But he'd be gone soon. And perhaps that was the point. They would only ever have a few evenings together and would never move on to arguments about DIY or hanging baskets. It would always be a shimmering moment that had no time to fade.

He turned off the hairdryer and stepped away for a moment, just enough to bring the bowl of halved strawberries to Lizzie. Before he went back to her hair, he picked one of the berries up and held it to her lips.

She bit into it, her eyes never leaving his.

Outside the window, the relentless Christmasification continued, the unstoppable march to the big day, all twinkling lights and forced smiles. Would James be on a tropical beach somewhere, or perhaps even a ski slope? Would he wake early or late and place a languorous kiss on his young wife's lips before presenting her with an effortlessly stylish, ridiculously expensive gift?

What would life be like if I woke up next to James every day?

Surely he wouldn't have seen what she was thinking? If only she could allow herself to stay, just this one night. Sleep through the hours of darkness with her head pillowed on his chest. But that wasn't wanton abandon. It was the prelude to... *No, don't think it, don't allow your thoughts to wander there.* This was enough. Because it was all they could have.

"You're very good at this. You've made my hair all shiny."

"A hidden talent," James told her, and she realised that he had moved on already. Her hair, sleek and combed, was being transformed into a neat, even plait. He was looking down again, intent on his work, his brow furrowed in concentration.

I don't care who you are outside of this room, Lizzie reminded herself. *It doesn't matter.*

Eventually his hand returned to the drawer to retrieve a sewing kit and he finished off the plait in a tight loop of thread that matched the shade of her hair perfectly. His fingers brushed over her hair one last time then continued to her shoulder, resting atop the silk dressing gown that she wore.

Lizzie placed her hand over his, then followed his bare arm, up to his shoulder, caressing all the way. In the mirror, his reflection half-closed his eyes.

"Thank you, James."

His fingers tightened on her shoulder before he released her and untucked the corner of the towel that was wrapped around his waist. He let it fall before running his hand down his reinvigorated erection, all the time matching her gaze in the mirror.

"Stand up." The low request was neither a question nor a command, his tone as heated as his eyes had become. All the time his hand was moving, leisurely working his cock.

Lizzie rose from the chair. She looked at him in the mirror, her face flushing with the urgency of her desire at the wanton sight of her lover. She untied the belt of the dressing gown, and it fell open, revealing a glimpse of her naked body.

He pressed his lips to her shoulder, teasing the tip of his tongue along to the curve of her neck. His arm slipped around her waist and there in the reflection she watched his hand slide over her stomach and lower until his fingers were teasing between her thighs, moving over her skin in a gossamer dance.

"James…"

Lizzie rested her head back against his shoulder, sighing the name that might not be his name. She could feel his hardness through the dressing gown. Ripples of pleasure were beginning in her body again, at the promise in his body of the bliss he would give her.

The pressure of James' fingers increased as they slid against her. All the time his mouth was insistent at her neck, nuzzling and tasting, her gaze locked on her own reflected eyes.

"I want you so much…" *And I can't and I shouldn't but it's impossible to fight.* "Have me, oh, James, for God's sake, *have* me."

She brushed the dressing gown from her shoulders and it dropped away, susurrating against her skin as it fell. James stepped back from her a little, just enough that the dressing gown could fall to the floor. Then he pressed his body to her now-naked back, his fingers working faster.

"I want to feel you come," James whispered, the heat of his breath rasping on her throat. His cock pressed to her and she watched the reflection of his free hand as it traced the contours of her body. He was tanned against her pale skin, fingers moving with a graceful confidence over her breast to tease her nipple.

Lizzie was so aroused that she struggled to turn her desires into words.

"I—I need you—inside me."

"You want me to fuck you again?" His teeth caught her earlobe, tugging it gently.

"Yes…yes…" She swallowed, her hand unsteadily reaching behind to his hip. "I want you to fuck me. As hard as you can."

"Wallet." His fingers tweaked her nipple more firmly. "Now."

It had been there, at the corner of her eye, all along. And now she reached for it, her arm straining for it, so that she wouldn't have to break from his contact.

"Here."

And both James' hands left her body as one, denying her the pleasure that had been building so rapidly. The reflection of his body was hidden by her own, yet she knew from the sound of the tearing wrapper, the movement of his shoulders, what he was doing. Then his lips were at her ear again and he whispered, "I've wanted you all day."

"I dreamt of you last night," Lizzie murmured. "I hardly remember what, but you were there, holding me…"

"Skin against skin…" James gasped and she felt his erection pressing against her, needing her.

"And I'll dream of you again tonight, I'm certain of it." *And every night ever after once we are lost to each other.*

He kissed her jaw, one arm around Lizzie's waist, urging her forward just a little until her hands rested on the table and she bent forward. She could feel the strength in him, his body pressed tightly to her as his hardness teased her and she parted her legs a little farther until he could truly possess her.

He kept one hand on her waist, returning the other to stroke her tender flesh. Lizzie sighed at his touch, and it was all it seemed to take to show him that she was ready. She was so aroused, so wet, that he entered her easily and she moaned. Once he was fully inside her, their eyes met in the mirror. So much desire, so much longing burned in his gaze that Lizzie had only to look at him in that moment to feel her pleasure begin to build again.

He filled her, his body claiming hers with every long, deep movement. She moved with him, her body matching that steady rhythm, their gasps and moans mingling in the night.

She didn't utter his name. She wasn't sure it was truly his. He kept her on the precipice of pleasure, drawing out the moment so much that they passed somewhere beyond words into a place of only intense sensation. She thrilled to the sensation of his fingers on her body, of his hand gripping her waist, of his breath on her naked back, of each deep thrust.

James ran his hand tenderly over her waist and travelled higher, those elegant fingertips drawing shivers that seemed to grow from her very core. She felt the tickle of her plaited hair brushing her skin, then his fingers caught hold of the plait and held it, gentle but still strong enough to draw her head back. She turned to meet his lips for a kiss, her eyes still on their reflection.

Her limbs strained, then, taking her by surprise, her body tightened all at once and her orgasm came to her. Lizzie shuddered, and her lover went on, his rhythm not breaking. She cried out, somewhere in a region of light and joy. She was aware, only a little, of a thud as she knocked something off the table, a shatter as she flung out her arm and caught the bowl of strawberries, smashing it as it fell.

And that name, which she didn't know was lie or truth, was wrenched from her throat as the dying trembles of her bliss took her.

"James!"

James' arm grew stronger around her waist and then he gasped the name that wasn't hers, his hips rocking hard as pleasure surged through him. Still her plait was tight in his hand, his mouth hungry at her throat, and she closed her eyes, arching against him. Together they shared the final moments of ecstasy, two halves of one.

"Will you hold me, James? Just for a moment?"

He turned her in his arms and placed a tender kiss on her parted lips, murmuring, "Louisa…"

My name's Lizzie.

But even now, something stopped her from telling him. She would be Louisa here, a woman who could not be hurt, whose heart was safe from ill-aimed barbs, who would not fall asleep in the arms of a nameless man even if he gave her extraordinary pleasures.

"Give me two minutes?" James asked gently. "You've got time to relax before you have to run off?"

"Yes, for a little while. But I can't stay the night."

He nodded his understanding and withdrew his arms with one last kiss before he disappeared into the bathroom and closed the door.

She picked up his dressing gown and laid it across the foot of his bed. She surveyed the damage she had caused and stepped around the remains of the glass bowl. His phone and wallet had landed on the floor. She didn't dare tidy up, either. She rounded up her clothes, to make her exit smoother when it came. Then she sat on the edge of the bed, her plait over one shoulder, admiring the loop of thread he had so deftly tied.

It was only a minute or two before the door opened and James emerged. He paused on the threshold and watched her for a moment. She saw his mouth quirk into a smile before he padded across the room to sit on the bed beside her, his hand coming to rest over hers.

"I'm sorry about the mess I made. Do watch out for the broken glass."

His tenderness made her awkward, as if she were only now naked.

"I'll deal with it later." James reached up to draw the duvet back, revealing the bright white sheet beneath. He studied her gaze and brought his lips to hers for a kiss as gentle as their evening had been wild.

She hung her arms loosely about his shoulders, and as they kissed with one accord, they slipped under the duvet. They embraced for a while. After the passion of the last couple of hours, there was something so innocent about their cuddle in the cool, white bed.

But I can't stay the night.

"Tomorrow," James whispered against her hair, "let me buy you dinner?"

Lizzie hoped that he didn't notice her surprise that he could suggest they leave the sanctuary of this room. *Dinner?* But Louisa would go to dinner, Louisa would not be hurt.

She squeezed his hand.

"I'd really like that."

"Seven o'clock in the lobby?" She caught a stifled yawn in his voice, felt it in the movement of his chest where it was pressed to her. "Dinner and wherever the night takes us?"

"Yes, yes, that sounds perfect. Seven o'clock, downstairs, then."

She could see that he was smiling, but his eyelids were growing heavier, as if they were struggling to stay open under the weight of his eyelashes.

She placed a kiss on his forehead.

"I better leave you in peace... You're worn out!"

"Will you leave your glass slipper?" His voice was playful and he nuzzled a kiss to her shoulder. She felt it become a sigh, the inevitability of their parting impossible to stave off. "I'll look forward to tomorrow evening."

"I am already. And...I *have* left you something. You'll just have to find it!"

One more kiss...then another... But she couldn't stay. And he was sleepier by the moment.

"I'll get dressed in the bathroom."

Lizzie slid out of his arms and collected her neat pile of clothes. Once in the bathroom, she stared at herself in the harshness of the light. What he would do when she left? Would he ring his wife and tell her he had spent the evening in front of the TV, perhaps claim to have been going over papers for whatever his business up here was? Or would he just stay beneath the crumpled duvet and go to sleep, tired and sated from their encounter?

Or maybe, just maybe, he would think about her a little longer.

When Lizzie emerged from the bathroom, the bedroom was oddly peaceful. Her lover was a shape under the duvet, his soft, regular breathing suggesting sleep. Lizzie crept across to the bed and crouched beside it.

"Goodbye, James. I'll see you tomorrow. You won't be out of my thoughts for a minute until we're together again."

She placed a light kiss on his cheek.

"Will you be safe getting home?" James pushed himself up against the pillows, his eyes dreamy with sleep. "Can I get you a cab?"

Lizzie smiled and ruffled his hair.

"There's a taxi rank on the square. I'll be fine. I haven't got far to — It's okay. Don't worry about me."

"Tonight was wonderful." He blinked and caught her hand, bringing it to his lips. "Let's make tomorrow even better?"

"Yes, yes, let's. But sleep now, James." She kissed his mouth, then stood again. "Goodnight. Will you dream of me? Because I'll dream of you."

Lizzie went into the corridor and closed the bedroom door behind her. As she waited for the lift, she hugged herself, pretending her arms were his.

Chapter Five

Light snow had been forecast. As Lizzie made her way to the hotel again, tiny flakes whirled in the freezing air. They caught in her fake fur hat, in her eyelashes and her plaited hair. She hurried up the steps to the hotel's front door, her knee-high boots tapping over the cold stone.

There was a different doorman tonight, but he nodded in welcome. Lizzie smiled back at him.

Her reflection in the polished glass doors showed her a woman wrapped up elegantly against the winter night, a red-haired version of Lara from *Doctor Zhivago*. She went through into the crowded hotel lobby. The weekend was beginning, the lobby thronged with crowds of people.

It was five minutes to seven. She would be with him again soon, the man from room 423. *James, if that really is his name.* Whatever he was called, he had been in her thoughts all day. Sometimes it had even felt as if his body were still against hers.

Buffeted by one group of people after another — a melange of hen parties, a phalanx of American tourists with a lot of matching luggage, a troop of businesspeople — it was difficult to spot James. And it really shouldn't have been. She would be able to see those beautiful dark eyes from a mile away, and besides, he was tall enough that she would see him over the crowds.

But she couldn't.

She circled the armchairs near the lifts, peering behind the tinsel-festooned palms in their brass pots.

He wasn't there.

Seven o'clock came and went. A door opened at the far end of the lobby, the sound of loud conversations coming from the hotel bar. Maybe that was where he was.

She didn't like going into bars on her own, especially ones full of large groups of happy friends. But she was emboldened by the thought of seeing James, so she went in. She trod over the thick carpet, examining every face she saw in case it was his. Inevitably, there were men who thought they might be able to cheer her up, reaching for her with over-friendly hands.

"You all right, pet?"

Lizzie nodded politely and continued on her way. The bar was so full of people that she could barely squeeze her way through. What if he was here and she couldn't see him in the crush? She toured the room twice…then a third time. Still searching, still hopeful.

But she couldn't find him. She stood in the middle of the bar, jostled by laughing people, and she wanted to cry.

This can't be the end. Not tonight. Not now. Not like this.

She ran her tongue slowly over her bottom lip. Maybe his young, beautiful trophy wife had called him back early for the weekend. Maybe even now he was on his way home to her. Maybe he had forgotten about Louisa and room 423 already.

It had been wonderful while it had lasted, but it was gone, like the last reflections of a sunset against the cloud, fading with the night. She had been a fool to think he'd wanted her. She had been convenient, and she had let herself be used by a bored businessman on a boring business trip.

But she couldn't accept that. The way he had looked at her, touched her, the way their bodies had combined. They were joined by a thread, and it couldn't be severed.

After two nights? What's wrong with you, Lizzie? Go home, and never look at another man again. Don't let yourself be hurt.

She wandered slowly past the bank of lifts and into the lobby. She paused and reached into her pocket for a tissue. She wasn't going to cry. No, she wouldn't. They weren't tears. It was only from the cold.

It was horrible, a sense of abandonment that Lizzie hadn't really expected to feel, because she really hadn't expected him to do it. Even though he had a life and a wife and probably kids and a house in Southern France and Christ knew what else, she had really believed that James wouldn't let her down. Yet he had, because karma had to bite back, didn't it?

And it had bitten down hard.

"Lizbob?" It was Donna's voice, questioning and disbelieving as it sailed over the noise of the lobby and she saw her little sister, immaculate, glamorous, effortless as she stepped from a lift straight in front of

Lizzie. There in her skin-tight jeans and a long, floating blouse of baby-pink silk, Donna stood on towering heels and pouted a frown. Her gaze swept over her sister then she took Lizzie in her arms and whispered, "Are you okay, sis?"

Lizzie shook her head. "No. No, I'm not. I've been played for a fool."

Donna's blonde hair brushed Lizzie's face as her sister's head snapped from side to side in search of the unseen villain. She steered them both out of the centre of the busy lobby, her heels clicking a percussion on the polished floor.

"Come back to ours, sis? We'll hit the vino and you can tell me all about it?"

Lizzie wiped her hand across her eyes, smiling despite the anguish and despair that gnawed at her. "I'd love that. Thanks, Don."

Donna had a car outside, of course, the sort of car that might ferry a bride to her wedding or a WAG home from a fashion shoot in a plush hotel. A square-jawed man in a smart uniform was at the wheel, a peaked cap atop his flawless hair. He greeted them with a well-drilled tip of the hat then they were off, smoothly cruising through the Christmas lights and out of the city. Lizzie peered from the darkened glass of the window at the crowds, the drinkers and the colleagues and the lovers, and wondered where he was now, who he was meeting with those twinkling dark eyes, that gently desiring smile.

"So," Donna crossed her long legs and pursed her lips, "who is he and what's he doing fucking with my sister?"

Where on earth did Lizzie start? And what on earth would her sister think of her? Her recklessness had caused this, running off to a liaison with a stranger. She was an utter idiot. She had imperilled herself. She was lucky that it was only her spirit that had been hurt. It could easily have been so much worse.

"Promise not to judge me. I…I made a terrible mistake." Lizzie turned her attention from the festive streets and the happy people to look at her sister. "You see, I can't tell you who he is, because…*I don't know.*"

Donna's eyes grew into saucers and she gasped. "You're joking? Spill it! Did you swipe right?"

She reached out and clutched Lizzie's hand, her acrylic nails just catching the skin. "Was it the first date? Did the bastard stand you up?"

Lizzie pressed her eyes tightly together. Oh, why hadn't she told him her real name, why hadn't they swapped numbers? What she had done to stop herself from being hurt had only resulted in hurt.

"We'd already… Please don't tell *anyone*. That night we were at the Mezz, he beckoned to me from his hotel room. And I went to him, and we… It was amazing. And then I went back again last night. I can't describe…" Lizzie was conscious of the driver behind his glass screen. Could he hear her? "I told him my name was Louisa, and he told me a name which I don't think is his. Not really. And it was incredible, all of it, but… He was supposed to meet me. Tonight. *And he wasn't there.*"

Lizzie couldn't hold her tears back any longer. Shame and anger, disappointment and rage rushed through her. She sobbed and, as far as the seatbelt would allow, Lizzie cried onto her sister's shoulder.

"Look, let's go back." Donna patted her arm comfortingly. "Let's go and leave a note? Ask what he's playing at. Have you rung him?"

"I don't have his number. He doesn't have mine. Maybe it's for the best if I walk away." Something inside Lizzie had shattered. She should never have gone back on the second night, but she had. She deserved every twinge of pain she now suffered. "I've been such an idiot, Don. He's...he's married."

"Wow! That was... Well, it's not typically Lizzie, is it?" Donna let out a long exhalation, a sigh that said, *my sensible big sister?* "So we either leave a message at the desk or you say, *I was a bit silly, probably lucky I didn't get found floating in the ship canal*, and you and me get pissed as two farts?"

And wasn't that the problem? Sensible Lizzie, who ran her own business. How could she have been so stupid? And how could she have continued with him when she'd seen that photo of his pretty young wife? But a message? She couldn't leave him a message. She couldn't trust herself, in her state of humiliation and defeat, to write anything that wouldn't be thoroughly undignified.

"I can't go back there. If I did, I'd only tell him to shove it. And he's already done that to me." Lizzie tried to smile. "I'll rise above it, Donna. Let's get smashed."

"It's just... With Matt having this stalker, it's taught me that you don't know who's out there, Liz. I mean, your mystery date could be Matt's loony. You just don't know!"

"Please don't say that." Lizzie's blood had turned to ice. Could those glittering dark eyes have hidden *that*? No, she couldn't believe it. "He couldn't be."

"He *beckoned* to you and you went? Oh God, Liz, what if he had AIDS or something?"

"We were careful!" But then wasn't it strange, a married man who carried condoms about in his wallet?

He must make a habit of bedding random women. "People do it all the time. All over this city, right now, there's drunk people falling into taxis with someone they've snogged in a bar, and they'll go and have sex, and they won't remember each other's names the next day, if they even heard them over the music in the first place."

"But what if you'd gone into that room and he'd raped you, or fucking stabbed you, Liz? He wasn't someone in a bar, someone who'd at least *spoken* to you first! You could be dead in a ditch by now. You've had a bloody lucky escape if you ask me!" Donna shuddered visibly. "You always needed me to look out for you, Lizzie. It's a good job I was doing that shoot tonight. You shouldn't be on your own."

"Please, Donna. Stop it! I've learnt my lesson. I know it was dangerous, and silly, I know. But he was so gentle. Considerate. And yet so—" No, she couldn't allow herself to think of that. His heat and his passion, tempered by tenderness. Because then she would want him, would go back to the hotel and wait for him, curled up outside his door like a faithful dog. And she wasn't that person.

She had to think of something else.

"A shoot?" Lizzie smiled with false breeziness. "Was it for a magazine?"

"If you fly BA first class to Dubai, you'll see me featured! I'm talking about life as a prem wife, and the challenges of living with a superstar."

Lizzie stifled her laughter. An evening with her vacuous sister was the tonic she needed. "Yes, it must be very difficult for you. All that shopping must be exhausting!"

"And I'm *shopping* for an interior designer as we speak. Happen to know any good ones?"

"Well, there's always your good ol' sis. And that new house of yours is could do with a makeover. It's so..." *Sterile.* But Lizzie wasn't about to say that. Insulting potential clients was never a good way to get a commission.

"It's horrible, Liz." Donna laughed, then opened her eyes wide with excitement. "But we get our a-mazing new gates fitted tomorrow, to keep our nasty loon out. Wait until you see them. They're like...Buckingham Palace!"

In Alderley Edge. Lizzie raised an eyebrow.

"Consider yourself hired, but we'll talk about it when you're less stressed and I'm less full of champers. But the job is *yours*, Ms Aspinall." Donna reached out and patted Lizzie's knee. "And your shit of a booty call can jog on!"

Lizzie gave a sharp, determined nod. But inside her, the world was ending.

'Let's make tomorrow even better.'

But you didn't. You destroyed it.

Chapter Six

Jordan took Lizzie out for a spin in his new Smart car, a vehicle of which he was excessively proud. They were off to Alderley Edge, to the *des res* of Donna and Matt de Luca, premiership footballer, occasional thug and his WAG amongst WAGs.

Jordan thumped his palm on the steering wheel, laughing.

"You mean, that's his brief? City colours? He doesn't have any other ideas in his head at all?" His eyes left the road for too long to look at Lizzie. "Look at my sky-blue house with its sky-blue walls and sky-blue loo. What happens if he leaves and goes to United? What a nutter!"

Lizzie giggled for the first time that day. She had got her head down and worked, the only way to ward off the inevitable avalanche of sadness when she thought again of what she had lost, what hadn't been hers to start with. Each evening, on leaving her office, she had told herself, *I'll take the long way round. I won't go past the hotel*. And each time, she had found herself on that route anyway. The window of room 423 had always been uncurtained, but the light had been off and James — or whatever he was called — hadn't been there. She had, once, started up the steps to the hotel, half-determined to leave him a message. But she'd faltered. He'd gone back to his wife. That was it. He regretted their liaisons. Lizzie could leave him one hundred messages, and he'd never see them. He wouldn't care.

But she didn't need the distraction of men. Not Neil, not James. She had her business to run, and her only thoughts should be on the challenge ahead of tarting up Casa de Luca.

"Oh, Jordan! Please don't say anything while we're in his presence. I'll split my sides laughing if you do!"

The satnav on the dashboard demanded a left turn.

"I suppose that must be it…"

Stood in the middle of a field up ahead, a new-build palace in grey bricks awaited them. The only trees were saplings, tied to wooden stakes.

"I can't believe my sister comes out here to this place. It makes me shudder."

"Oh, look!" As they drove between a pair of enormous open gates that stood in the middle of an eight-foot brick wall, Jordan slowed and pointed out the initials DL, *de Luca*, picked out in wrought-iron thorns in the centre of the gates, the initials broken in half, thanks to their being open. Atop each letter bobbed half the galleon of Matt's team and Jordan howled with laughter, his finger pointed straight at three blue cars that were parked at perfectly opposing angles outside the house. To the left, a two-seater convertible, in the middle a four-wheel drive and to the right, another sports car, this time with an *actual* roof.

"That's more cars than my mum and dad have had in all my days." Jordan laughed. "And all sky blue, I note!"

"Are we being terrible snobs, Jordan? I mean, are we really?" Lizzie held her hand over her mouth, trying to control her laughter. "But this *is* the naffest thing you've ever seen, isn't it?"

"He earns more in a week than I do in a year." Jordan pouted. "Can I have a pay rise?"

"Can *you* kick a ball?"

They climbed out of Jordan's city runaround and Lizzie pressed the doorbell. They were reduced to silent laughter when it chimed out a recording of the chant that echoed around the Etihad whenever Matt was on the pitch.

He's Matt DL, he's Matt DL, he gives 'em hell, he's Matt DL!

"Stop it. Stop it *now*, Jordan."

"Oh my *God*!" Jordan bit his lip. "I might get a doorbell like that. *He drives a Smart, he drives a Smart, he's no old fart—*"

He stopped abruptly when the door opened and there stood the hero to a million children, a God to a million men and the man who, Donna claimed, every woman in the world wanted to get into bed with. Matthew de Luca was the jewel in the team's crown, the most expensive transfer in a decade and Lizzie's newest client. He leant one shoulder on the doorframe and let his gaze roam over her, barely offering Jordan a second glance. Finally he said, "All right, sis?"

Lizzie waved brightly. Her smile was excellent cover for her insatiable need to laugh. Very loudly indeed.

"Hello, Matt. How's Donna?"

"Yeah, she said she'd be down when you got here but she's still chilling on the sunbed, topping up her tan." He stepped back and gestured into the enormous foyer. "Step in, yeah? Relax."

"Well...here we are, then. This is my colleague, Jordan..." Lizzie nudged Jordan forwards.

"Mr. de Luca!" Jordan beamed, clearly appreciating Matt's skinny jeans and very, very tight grey T-shirt. "Don't mind me. I'm on camera duty!"

Lizzie took one look at Matt's figure-hugging outfit and thought of a man in a dark blue suit, framed by a window. She dismissed the image as soon as it arose in her mind.

Matt, however, kept his eyes on Lizzie and told her, "Let's grab a coffee, yeah?"

"Tea for me, please, Matt. Erm...Jordan?"

"Yeah, no tea here," Matt told her. "Coconut water?"

"That'll do me!" Jordan informed him.

"Could I just have water-water, please?" *A house, without any tea in it? How on earth is that even allowed?*

They were already drifting into the inner sanctum. The house's interior had been painted entirely in magnolia, presumably exactly as the builders had left it. Yet there was something there that shouldn't be, that hadn't been when she'd been there just a few evenings earlier. It was a gleaming mountain bike propped against the wall of the foyer — sky blue of course — a bike that she knew because she used to have to live with it. She'd tolerated the mud on the carpets, the chunks the handlebars had dug out of the walls, because she had loved its owner. Once.

Neil was here. Neil Mellor, City physio, friend to his squad and the man who had broken Lizzie's heart.

"Oh, Neil's over for FIFA, yeah?" Matt shrugged by way of an apology. "But before Don went up to tan, she told him to do one. He's just draining the snake."

Brilliant. And now, in her mind, she could see Neil's penis.

Just as that thought occurred to her, the owner of that penis appeared. He was clad head-to-toe in Lycra, of course, more muscle-bound than she had ever seen him, a hulk of a man, even beside Matt de Luca. His hair, always fair, was now definitely blond, and he greeted Matt with a matey handshake, their palms clasped as though they were about to arm-wrestle.

"Hey, Lizzie!" Neil winked and took the cycling helmet from where it hung on the handlebars. "You come to slap a bit of paint over De Luca Palace? Watch her, Matt. She's the queen of curtains, don't get between her and her tape measure!"

I hope you get a sodding puncture.

Lizzie pressed her lips tightly together. He had never taken her business seriously, always joking about it, belittling it in public in front of others. To the mayor, at a champagne reception for the team, he had said, *'And my girl Lizzie runs up curtains for celebrities. Don't you, poppet?'* When relatives at Donna and Matt's wedding had pestered her, *'You and Neil are getting married next, aren't you?'*, that line had played endlessly through her head.

I couldn't have spent the rest of my life with this man.

"Still single, gorgeous?" He put the helmet on and clipped it under his chin. "If you ever fancy grabbing some Thai, give me a bell."

"Thanks for the offer, Neil, but I'm busy *'running up curtains for celebrities'* every night of my life until I drop dead aged ninety. So not much time for Thai, with *you*."

A very loud snort escaped Jordan.

"I'm busy being physio for the prem, so it's a win for both of us!" He winked again and Matt pulled the front door open so Neil could wheel the bike towards the threshold. "You enjoy your curtains!"

"Yeah, yeah, laters." Matt nodded casually, slapping his hand to Neil's back as he passed. "Take it easy, yeah?"

As soon as the door closed on her departing ex-lover, Matt strode away, leading them through to a kitchen of gleaming chrome and dark, battleship grey with one entire wall of glass looking out over a vast patio and the lawn beyond. Lights shone in glass-fronted cupboards and he opened one to retrieve two glasses and put them down on the centre island. From the double-fronted fridge, he took out an unlabelled bottle of what was clearly coconut water and filled the glasses, holding one out to her.

Lizzie took it and passed it to Jordan.

"There you go, Jords…your coconut water."

"Cheers, boss!" Jordan took the glass. Matt, after a moment of bewilderment, took another glass from the cupboard and pressed it into a dispenser in the front of the fridge. When it was full, he looked down at it and asked Lizzie, "Just water, yeah? You sure?"

"In lieu of tea…needs must and all that."

"Tea isn't good for you, yeah? It's got the tannins. They're gonna mess with you, bring you down." He shrugged his broad shoulders and pulled the glass free with a metallic click. Another suspicious look at the drink and he held it out to Lizzie as though it were poison. "So, right, here's some water."

She took a small sip. It had a plastic tang, the result of being pumped out from the new fridge. How could a sportsman not drink water?

"But green tea, *that's* good for you. Antioxidant properties, Matt."

"Yeah, yeah, you know that's right." Matt nodded, clearly pleased with her encouragement. "But we're all out. Blame your Neil."

"He's not mine anymore, Matt. Anyway, shall we get on? Jords, you've got the tape measure. Is the camera ready?"

"On it!" Jordan drained the glass, grimaced and put it down before he turned and headed for the door.

"Don't be touching shit, yeah?" Matt called after him before he ran his gaze over Lizzie again. As he spoke, he gestured, his free hand adopting poses that were clearly intended to be street, a little bit gangster, maybe. "So the club's my life, you know? I'm like, Superman out there, and I'm thinking, *sky blues*, right? So that's what I want. Sky blue. Honour the ship, yeah? Donna's not so crazy on the idea, but I've got this vision in my brain. The *dream*, you know?"

He blinked and sucked in his chiselled cheeks, watching her closely, as though that level of profundity might have entirely thrown his newly appointed designer. "Honour the badge. You get me?"

"Yes, yes, indeed. I *get* you. Look… You can have your sky blues, but with those, you'll have complementary colours, too. It'll look lovely. Bronzes…yellows…golds… Golden browns. Did you have any feel for the sort of fabrics you want? And if you want to go ultra-modern or maybe a bit mid-twentieth century retro. Or heck, let's go mad and do antique!"

Matt was confused, rather like a gorilla who had fallen off its tyre at the zoo and couldn't remember how he'd climbed onto it in the first place.

"Yeah, no, no, no." He waved his finger and shook his head. "I say to you, *honour the badge*, yeah? So we got the gold, the blue, but we've got to have red. Red's in the badge, you get me? Gold, blue, red. Like Superman. Like me."

He pressed his hand to his chest and nodded slowly. "And I like what my mum would say is like, you know, like the French and they cut their heads off? So it's all, I like a lot of crowns, you know, like big shields and shit like out on the gate? I want you to bring what's on the gate and make it happen in the house?"

"You want a guillotine as a conversation piece?"

Lizzie realised she was clutching the wooden beads of her necklace. She let go.

"No, no, no!" He laughed, teeth so white they were almost blue. "Like where they lived? They had a lot of gold, big curtains and mirrors and shit? That's what I'm wanting, but honouring the club as well, yeah?"

"Oh, you mean rococo, don't you? Versailles? I would *love* to do that. Matt, this will look fabulous. Let me just show you on my phone, I'll find some pictures for —"

"Rococo?" Matt was back at the fridge and the door was suddenly open. He peered into it and took out the unmarked bottle of coconut water, his brow furrowing deeply. "I'll have to call my cook? I think he said just coconut but, I suppose — What's the *ruh* bit mean?"

"*Rococo*. It's nothing to do with coconuts, Matt." How the hell did he and Donna have a meaningful relationship? Hell, how did they manage to have a meaningful conversation? "Rococo. You know…baroque. Baroque 'n' roll!"

"Yeah, sweet!" He beamed, clearly approving. "And I want skulls and crossbones. I want them wherever you can fit them, yeah? And I'm getting me and your kid painted up like out of film, like a king and queen, and I'm putting it over the pool table, so it's got to look like a king and queen live here?"

"Skulls and crossbones… They're a bit…more *pirate*, perhaps, than Bourbon monarchs. More…poison bottle? I mean, if that's what you want… It's quite Goth actually. A bit Siouxsie Sioux. But, if that's what you want."

"Do you like football, Lizzie?" He blinked, awaiting the response.

"I—I quite like the rugby."

"Skulls and bones, yeah?" He clenched his fist and pounded it against his heart. "Give us life, the twelfth man, you know? Roaring you down, *Matt DL! Matt DL!* You get me?"

"I should be honest with you, shouldn't I? If you're trusting your house to me, I have to say… Actually… I have no idea what you just said."

"Don's got some ideas and I'll have my assistant send you some shit about the club? Give you the vibes?"

Vibes. Oh, God.

"I wonder how Jordan's getting on?"

"I don't know nothing about furniture and all that shit." He leant forward a little, settling his tattooed arms on the counter. "But you know it like I know the game, so this is your Etihad, yeah?"

"I'll consult you every step of the way, and before we even jimmy open a paint can, you get drawings to show you what's what. Yes?"

"Good girl." He nodded, his blond fade not moving at all, thanks to the copious amounts of styling product. Then, to Lizzie's horror, he dragged his T-shirt up and over his head, bunching it in one fist.

"Are you feeling a trifle warm, Matt?"

Lizzie began to edge towards the door. She would bellow until she was hoarse, if he came anywhere near her with that bare torso. It looked like it was moulded out of plastic. Women and men swooned over this man. Women and men would be madly envious of her for seeing this sight. *And I don't want to.*

"I want this on the bedroom ceiling." He turned and she felt her eyes widening. On his back, across the *whole* of his back, was a skull with the wings of an eagle, flames blazing from its eye sockets and blood dripping from fanged teeth. "This is the de Luca devil. This is the brand, yeah?"

The bedroom ceiling? Donna would lie underneath his groaning mass and have to stare up at *that*?

"Right. Who…who designed that?"

"The man himself." He pulled his T-shirt back on and turned to face her, jerking one thumb against his chest. "I drew it on my bedroom wall when I was a kid. It's my totem, yeah? It's spiritual to me."

"A man of many talents, I see. How splendid. So…you want rococo in every room. That's right, isn't it? I'll start getting my ideas together, then we can have another meeting, with Donna here, and I'll have fabric swatches and paint colours and all sorts."

The last thing Lizzie needed was Donna having a meltdown at her for her husband's questionable ideas.

"And get me some zebra skin, leopards, that sort of shit? Not real, yeah, or the feminazis'll be after my dick." He seized her hand and tugged her forwards so he could plant a kiss on her cheek. "And I don't do talking about money, but like, you can probably get that shit sorted with your kid. So we're cool? I respect you, you respect me, we'll be sweet."

"Yes, that sounds marvellous. Right, then... Jordan?"

Her helper stepped into the kitchen so quickly that one might almost suspect he had been lingering on the other side of the door. "Ready, boss!"

"Goodbye, then, Matt."

"Laters, sis, yeah?" He winked then finally acknowledged Jordan too. "And you, little man, you stay cool."

Chapter Seven

Lizzie blinked up at her iMac. Why was it making that noise again? Was it broken? She heaved aside the book on Versailles that she had been working from and spotted an alert on the screen.

Appointment: Ben Finneran 10.30am.

Who? Why doesn't that name not ring any bells at all?
Because she'd been working. Claire or Jordan might have told her, and she could well have forgotten, because all she wanted to do was burrow into her commissions and stop herself from thinking. From feeling.
She couldn't go on in this detached way anymore.
"Ben Finneran, Ben Finneran..." She practiced saying his name under her breath, then she pulled on her jacket from the back of her chair, checked her face very quickly in the mirror she kept in her desk drawer and opened her office door.

She was just in time to hear Jordan say, "The boss is down at the end of the corridor." He'd been told before about speaking like that in front of clients. She sighed. What sort of impression did that give? *'The boss.'* As if her clients were entering the domain of a dominatrix.

The door at the top of the corridor swung open. A dark-haired man in an immaculate greatcoat, the deep blue of midnight, appeared, a red scarf around his neck.

And Lizzie's mouth fell open.

Of course his name wasn't James, just as her name wasn't Louisa. She had known that, really, but she would never have guessed. How long did she have, Lizzie wondered, before he looked up from the screen of the mobile phone he was carrying and saw her? How long before their eyes met as they had across a street in what seemed like another lifetime?

Ben Finneran looked up. He looked straight at her and she saw something flicker across his gaze, something she wasn't sure she wanted to interpret, even if she could have at this distance. For a fleeting moment his pace faltered, then he asked quietly, almost disbelievingly, "Lizzie Aspinall?"

Her real name sounded so odd in his mouth.

"Ben...Finneran?"

She extended her hand to shake, just as she did with all her clients, even though he still had half the length of the corridor to walk. Yet despite that, he put the phone into his pocket and held out his hand in turn before he said, "DCI Finneran. Thanks for agreeing to see me at such short notice."

"Sorry, DCI? You're a detective? A policeman? I..."
I had no bloody idea.

He seized her hand, his grip firm, formal, somehow awkward. "Shall we step into your office?"

"Yes, let's. Sorry. I've just had a new appointment thingy set up on my computer and I'm still getting the hang of it. Pathetic, really! Erm... I'm usually tidier."

She was aware of him stood behind her as she lifted piles of carpet and fabric swatch books from the chaise longue.

"Please, please sit. I... However did you find me?"

But wasn't he here on police business?

James — *Ben* — unfastened his coat and removed it to reveal a suit in the same deep blue, his dark purple, intricately patterned tie a glimpse of a galaxy against a crisp white shirt. He carefully laid the coat on the chaise longue and gestured to Lizzie's own chair, clearly waiting for her to settle at her desk before he took the seat opposite.

"Right... I'll just..." Lizzie hovered, about to take her seat again. "Did Jordan offer you a cup of tea? Do you like tea?"

I know so little about you, but you made my heart dance.

"I'm fine, really." He gestured again, so Lizzie sat. Ben, however, remained standing for a few more seconds, taking in the office. Finally he settled into the chair opposite her and said, "Firstly, I must apologise for last week. I really don't blame you for not replying to my message. Secondly, I hope that we can still discuss this rather more official matter as professionals."

She folded her hands neatly on the surface of the desk, hoping that he would think she was calm. But she wasn't. All that humiliation, all that rage, all her attempts to make herself hate him, to hate herself, and... A message? She shook her head.

"I — I'm sorry, Ja — DCI Finneran. I didn't receive a message."

"I left it at the desk. I described you. I said you'd be alone in the foyer." He frowned as though trying to process this new piece of information. "They didn't pass it on?"

"No!"

Lizzie rushed her hand to her mouth. She was going to laugh, a horrible, grating, hysterical laugh. She could feel it. Her lips were trembling with the promised force of it as it rose up from inside her. But she managed to rein it in.

"It was so busy in the hotel that night. Maybe they didn't see me. I...I thought you'd had enough of me. I nearly left a message for you, but..."

"Well" — he shook his head, humour dancing in his eyes despite the tiredness she could see there now — "that's customer service at its finest."

She allowed herself a smile. The armour she had assumed was beginning to rust and fall away. They had been given another chance.

But it didn't stop the fact that she couldn't have this man. He was wearing his ring. He had a wife.

She folded her hands again.

"Maybe...maybe it was for the best, though. We — We both know it couldn't have lasted." She pressed her fingers to the bridge of her nose. *I want you and I can't have you and it isn't fair.* "And...and here you are, then, on official business."

His lips parted just a little, a small indication of surprise perhaps, from a man who could win that beautiful young wife, let alone summon a lover with just a gesture from his hand. Was he about to cause a scene, to shout and rant and create all sorts of drama? Was he going to bring Jordan and Claire running?

"For the best?" There was no drama though, just a nod that seemed laced with disappointment and the suggestion in his voice that he really hadn't been expecting that. "Okay, yes, official business."

Ben drew in a deep breath, assuming the character of a police officer, just as he had that of *James*, her mysterious lover.

"Ms. Aspinall, I'm DCI Finneran and I'm with the Metropolitan Police. I'm currently working with the Greater Manchester Force on an ongoing investigation." He had successfully donned the mask, it seemed, the words confident and fluent as they left his lips. "We were referred to you by a Professor Grigg at the Fashion Institute?"

"Oh, yes. That'd be Judith."

"Before I go any further, I have to tell you that this is highly confidential, Lou— Miss Aspinall." Yet she could see that he was thrown by his own mistake, even if he wasn't about to admit it. "I must ask you not to discuss it with anyone."

"Of course you can trust me. I often handle confidential matters of a rather sensitive nature. Not exactly in your line, but..." She stopped herself from waffling on. "It's okay. I won't say anything."

"Professor Grigg seemed to think that you might be able to help with some questions we have regarding a length of antique ribbon." He reached into his pocket and took out a pair of spectacles, which he slid onto his nose. Then he dipped into his jacket again and retrieved a small, transparent polythene bag containing a length of material. "We've had a few people look at it so far without any success, so if you can't help, please do say now. Time's of the essence on this one."

With that, Ben set the bag on the desk and pushed it towards her.

Lizzie stared at it. How could the police attach so much importance to such a little thing? She looked up at Ben then, the question in her eyes. She had had no idea that he wore glasses. The simple wire frames gave him such a distinguished, intelligent air. But she couldn't bear to look at him and betray the fact that she still desired him.

She forced her eyes from his, back down at the ribbon, leaning closer. Something...something about this ribbon was familiar.

"Do you know, I'd almost swear... I've seen this before. May I take it out of the bag?"

"Please." She could feel his eyes on her as he knitted his hands in his lap, the gold band on his ring finger catching the light.

Lizzie placed a sheet of white paper in front of her on the desk, then carefully tipped the ribbon onto it. She reached into her drawer, produced a velvet bag and took a magnifying glass from it. She raised and lowered it over the ribbon, focussing on it.

"I realise how silly you must think I look with this, like Sherlock-bloody-Holmes, like I'm taking the proverbial because you're a detective. But..." She met Ben's gaze, but wasn't sure how long she could hold it. She had a horrible feeling that he still wanted her. "I needed a closer look, just to be certain. And this ribbon? I've seen it before, I know I have."

"This is why we need an expert." He blinked, those long eyelashes just as she remembered them. "To me, ribbon is ribbon. I mean, this is pretty ribbon, as far as it goes, but—"

Ben gestured to the short length of silk that was sat atop the paper in front of her, pretty hardly a strong enough word to describe it. It was positively decadent, a jet-black silk of no more than an inch in width, perfect, silvery *fleur-de-lys* embroidered along its length.

"Our chaps have done what they can and they've dated it back to the 1950s, but that's where we go cold." He met her gaze and smiled. "That's hopefully where you come in."

"I'll do what I can." She allowed herself a moment of pride. "I've written a book on vintage textiles." *And I was wearing my favourite vintage dress to go to dinner with you.* "I just… I know I've seen it before. But it can't be in my book, because someone else would've seen it. Judith definitely would've, because she helped me with the photos. Hang on, let's just make absolutely sure it's not in there."

Lizzie pulled out a book from the shelf behind her, a large hardback with a glossy cover. She flicked through to the section on ribbon, shaking her head as she ran through the pages.

"I can't see it in here. So where on earth…?" She drummed her fingers on her desk, and without thinking, handed the book to him. "You know the *lys* is a lily? And it's very big with the French. I mean, this could be French-made, but…"

From the look on Ben's face, she knew that this was nothing he hadn't already heard before, but he politely looked down at the book before returning his gaze to her.

"Really, Ms Aspinall, if you aren't able to help, I *will* understand. I know it's a tall order."

"For goodness' sake, will you please call me Lizzie? And I want to do this. Leave it with me, please. I've seen this ribbon before, I know I have. It makes no sense, it's like seeing the face of a stranger in a crowd but knowing—knowing that they're an old friend."

"Let me leave you my card." *No 'call me Ben',* she noted. His hand slipped into his jacket and withdrew a neat, white business card. He held it out to Lizzie, waiting for her to take it. "And you know where I'm currently based, of course."

Lizzie felt herself blush to the roots of her hair. She took the card from him, and without meaning to, her fingers brushed his. A jolt went through her.

I can't have you and it isn't fair.

"Yes...DCI Finneran. Yes, I do know where you're based. Can you— Are you allowed to tell me why you want to identify it? Have you found a body? Although, how can the ribbon be so well-preserved if it's been buried somewhere?"

"I can't disclose that, Ms. Aspinall, but I can tell you that it's vital to an urgent investigation." He pushed his spectacles up into his hair, that *'Ms. Aspinall'* hanging in the air between them. "Please contact me if you think of anything, no matter how insignificant it seems."

Oh, why won't you call me Lizzie?

"I will. I promise you that I'll do what I can."

"And thank you for being so professional about this." Ben rose to his feet and held out his hand. "I really do appreciate it."

"It's fine." Her voice was high-pitched and unconvincing as she shook. "Well, then... I'll let you know what I can find out."

She wanted to twine her fingers with his, but she chased the thought out of her mind.

Was it her imagination, or did his hand linger, his fingers curled slightly around her own? It was for a second, no more, then he released her and stooped to retrieve his coat and scarf from the chaise longue, about to walk out of her life all over again.

"For what it's worth—" Ben seemed to think better of whatever he was going to say, concentrating instead of preparing to go back out into the cold. He was soon cosy in that well-tailored coat and the bright scarf, his hands encased in black gloves. "I *am* sorry, Lizzie. Anyway, I'll let you get back to work. Thanks for your time."

"I hope…" She couldn't allow herself to hope. She opened the office door for him. "Take care, Ben."

She wondered for a moment if she should place a kiss on his cheek. Wasn't it polite, between friends? But they weren't friends. They were former lovers, who had been brought together for a moment by a length of silk ribbon.

"You too."

And with those last words, he was gone, walking away along the corridor without a glance back.

She watched for as long as she could bear then closed the door. She picked up the ribbon and went to the window, the better to see it in the light.

She *had* seen it before. But where? The answer was just out of Lizzie's grasp.

Chapter Eight

Jordan and Claire had gone home ages ago. But Lizzie couldn't leave. She'd put aside Matt de Luca's grandiose dreams of doomed royalty and had spent the entire day looking at that blasted bit of ribbon. She had combed through all her source books, had flicked through all the photos of her past projects. It wasn't just the appearance of this ribbon that was so familiar to her, but its texture. She must have used it before, but when? Had she trimmed a guitarist's cushions with it? Had it gone round a WAG's pelmet?

"Why do I recognise it?"

Lizzie was staring down at the ribbon in her workroom, wondering if she was wrong. Maybe she didn't recognise it at all. Maybe it was his sudden appearance that had confused her.

But that couldn't be it. She knew her fabrics and her textiles. She knew her jacquards and her damasks.

A breakthrough came when she measured the width. It was exactly an imperial measurement, not metric. It suggested, very strongly, that it was British-made.

She logged into an online resource of scanned textile documents. She kicked off her shoes and took her hair out of its clip. She searched through every query for 'ribbon', throwing up images. Black-and-white photos from long ago featuring models from the past, trapped in their youth, wide-eyed, long-limbed, a ribbon on a cuff or in their hair, an artistic spool on the cover of a magazine.

No sign of the fleur-de-lys.

She got out of her chair and pressed her forehead to the cool glass of the window. She hadn't noticed it getting dark, and now the night-time city was laid out before her again. The shops, the old factories and warehouses turned into flats, cars driving between –

Lizzie picked up the phone.

"Judith…those old catalogues. The agents for the textile companies used to have them. It's just occurred to me that they didn't only include bales of cloth. Didn't you say one of your Ph.D. students was digitising them? I don't suppose you'd let me have access to your online repository?"

Half an hour later, Lizzie sent a text.

DCI Finneran – might have something for you re ribbon. Ms. Aspinall.

Twenty minutes after she pressed send, her phone rang. She breathed deeply before swiping the screen.

"Hello?"

"It's Ben. What've you got for me?" His tone was urgent, full of anticipation.

"I'm fairly sure that ribbon was made in Manchester in 1954. I can even tell you the factory. And I can also tell you that no one's ever stitched it or glued it onto anything. It still has its curl. I can't find any trace of it online, so I doubt it's been sold that way. It's either deadstock that someone's sold at an antique fair or it's been in someone's sewing basket for over sixty years."

"That's not what I wanted to hear," he told her, but there was no annoyance in his voice, just resignation. "You're not still at work, are you?"

"Erm…I am, actually."

"Get yourself off home, get some supper and leave it for tonight. Don't tire yourself out."

"It's all right. I'm not tired. I need to tidy up, anyway. There's books all over the place!"

"I'll let you get back to it." She heard a smile in the words, told herself not to think of the hotel with its crisp linens, his hand gripping her plaited hair. "Goodnight, Ms Aspinall."

"Goodnight, DCI Finneran."

She didn't want to end the call. She held the phone for as long as she could, until it went dead.

So Lizzie went back to her books and away from Ben Finneran, submerging herself once more in the vintage photographs and fabrics, in a world where she was comfortable, a world where she was in charge. Minutes passed and still she turned the pages, seeing and not seeing, the ribbon as familiar to her now as it had been when he'd taken it from his pocket.

The office entry phone shattered the silence and Lizzie ignored it, not in the mood to argue with a drunk looking for mischief. When her phone buzzed, however, a text flashed up on the screen that she *couldn't* ignore.

I'm outside your office. Buzz me in? BF

Lizzie pressed the button. Down in the street, the lock had popped back. Down in the street, a detective was opening the door.

She came tentatively out of her office and crept along the corridor. Framed photos of her past jobs gilded the walls, but she didn't see them. It was dark in reception. She flicked a switch, and as the space was flooded with light, she was just in time to see the man from room 423 arrive on the landing.

What on earth is he doing here? And what does he have in that carrier bag, which really doesn't go with his smart attire?

She unlocked the door and let him in. The room filled rapidly with the smell of fish and chips.

"Good evening, DCI Finneran." Despite herself, Lizzie's tone was vaguely flirty. "And what can I do for you?"

"This isn't quite the supper I promised you last week, Ms Aspinall, but I wonder if you'd join me for fish and chips?" He held up the bag. "And mushy peas, of course."

"Welcome to Manchester! I'll get some plates from the kitchenette. There's even wine in the fridge. White, to go with fish, naturally."

The kitchenette was behind a thick, velvet curtain, which Lizzie swished back with an intentionally theatrical flourish. Ben followed, looking snuggled and cosy in his coat and scarf, the bag of fish and chips hanging at his side. He seemed as confident as ever, filling the space with his presence, his head moving just a little as he took in these new surroundings.

Lizzie loaded a tray with crockery and cutlery, two wine glasses and a bottle.

"Quite the feast! Shall we go to my office?"

"You're the boss. Whatever you say."

"And you're the detective, so I have to behave!"

She led the way down the corridor, rolling her eyes in disbelief at what she had just said.

What's wrong with me, flirting with him?

I can't have you and it isn't fair.

"I didn't manage to tidy up...sorry. I got distracted. But don't worry, the ribbon's safe."

She put the tray on a chair and cleared a space on the desk.

"Plonk the fish supper there, DCI."

Ben did as he was told before removing his coat and scarf again, throwing them with a little less care than before over the chair on which he had sat that afternoon. Beneath, he no longer wore his jacket and tie, and the top buttons of his shirt were unfastened in a nod to a more casual look.

Lizzie tried not to stare. Just a hint of a scattering of dark hair was visible where his shirt was open. She got on with unscrewing the wine and pouring it.

She looked up and caught their reflection in the window. He was almost certainly admiring the view, not of night-time Manchester, but of her bottom, clad in a black velvet pencil skirt.

"So—" He fell silent, and in that reflection, his head remained angled *just* a little down, the path of his gaze *definitely* directed at her clearly very distracting bottom. He blinked and glance up, register the window and their shared reflection in it. He cleared his throat then made a show of turning away, tidying up his coat.

"Here you are." Lizzie waited for him to turn back so that she could pass him his glass. "I feel… Do you know, I feel as if we should toast something. I don't know what, though. Fish and chips?"

"Friendship?"

"That will do as well."

Friends?

But there was an unmistakable smoulder in his eyes, of the kind that had nothing to do with friendship. Lizzie passed her free hand awkwardly through her loose hair.

"Thank you for bringing me dinner, Ben."

"That's what friends do." He clinked his glass to hers. "Now get stuck in before it goes cold."

Lizzie took one of the two wrapped bundles from the bag and laid it on a plate. She passed Ben a knife and fork.

"That chaise longue is upholstered with silk…but I trust you not to get your greasy mitts on it."

She took the last bundle out and opened it onto a plate for herself. The smell of the cod and chips made her groan with hunger. She didn't bother with cutlery, and shoved chips into her mouth as she went to sit on the chaise.

Ben settled beside her, a look of barely concealed amusement on his face. In keeping with his southern roots, Lizzie noted, he was rather more proper, using a knife and fork as though it were normal to eat fish and chips in such a formal manner. He'd probably never eaten it from the wrapper by the seaside, she decided, fending off seagulls and stinging his fingers with the vinegar's sharpness.

"Should've got you a fine linen napkin, sir!"

"*What?*" He looked at her, blinking innocently. "This is how you eat! I swear to God, if I'm not being called out for being from *that Laahndan*, I'm being told it's a brew and not a cuppa or that it's a barm and not a roll. You people are living in another world!"

Lizzie twanged invisible braces. "Aye, Ben, t' would be t' world o' t' North."

"By 'eck, lass, has tha' no manners?" It was a brave effort but hovered somewhere south of the Watford Gap. He assumed his normal voice to sniff, "Bloody heathens."

"I'm disappointed you didn't bring me jellied eels. That's what Michael Caine would've done." Lizzie found a golden chunk of batter and tipped back her head to swallow it one go. "My God, this batter is amazing."

"Michael Caine… Don't get me onto *The Italian Job*, I swear to God, that's perfection." He glanced at her, his smile bright. "I know every single word of it, first to last. I am *obsessed*."

"Is that the one when they mess up the traffic lights? I like *Alfie* myself." She dared a grin at Ben. "I quite fancy him in that, to be honest. Even though he's clearly a bastard. He is, however, a very well-dressed bastard, so I'll forgive him."

"He's horrible." Ben shook his head. "You don't want someone like that."

Too late, Lizzie's brain made the connection. The philanderer, the schemer. And Ben, for some reason, thought that Alfie was contemptible? Ben was a hypocrite. But a well-dressed hypocrite.

"Awright, darlin'?" Lizzie pinched Ben's cheek. "There you go. It was just like being back in that London for a moment, then, wasn't it?"

"Uncanny."

Lizzie reached for a fork so that she could attack the mushy peas. Without looking at him, she said, "I'm glad our paths have crossed again."

"I'm sorry about that message."

She studied his face. There was such sadness in his eyes. She moved a little nearer to him, her voice dropping. "Whatever must you have thought of me these past few days? I only hope you didn't hate me."

"Of course I didn't hate you." Ben chuckled and shook his head, still holding her gaze. "I blew it and I'm not about to make things difficult. We're working together. I'm not that sort of guy."

Lizzie tasted salt as she passed her tongue over her lips. Her voice was barely above a whisper. "You didn't blow it, Ben."

"Let's not go over it." His gaze flitted away and she caught the slight suggestion of his teeth worrying at his lip. "For the best, remember?"

"But perhaps… Look… I do remember what I said this morning. I…"

"What's the value in dissecting it when you made the decision for both of us?" He was looking at her again, his jaw set. "So, we go over it and then what? We both feel crap again?"

"You're the one who turned up here this evening. And what am I supposed to do? I'd have you in a heartbeat, but…but…" She knew the ring was there on his finger without even having to look at it, the ring he had taken off to beckon her, the ring that told her he belonged to someone else, and never to her. "Oh, for God's sake, you used me, you bastard!"

"I came here to make peace with you, to put things right." He set the tray down on the floor and stood. "So

I'm not your *well-dressed bastard* but *I* used *you*? You couldn't get out of that room fast enough once you'd had what you came for!"

"That's right. I know I'm a hussy, a reckless tart who can't get enough cock, who flings herself at strangers who lure her into their hotel rooms. I'm insatiable! You could've beaten me and slit my throat and flung me into a canal. But you...*you*...!" Lizzie glanced at his hand. The gold wedding band was still there on his finger, taunting her. "What about your wife?"

"*Beaten you*? Because that's when men do?" His voice started as a disbelieving whisper, a look of utter bewilderment on his face. Only then did he snatch up his coat and tell her in a firm, furious tone, "And don't you dare bring my wife into this, Lizzie. You know noth — "

He swallowed, shoving his arms into the coat instead of going on.

"I've spent nine years with a man who belittled me every day. To my face, in front of others. He even did it in front of the mayor! And...and I've left him. I've walked away. I was so unhappy, and I couldn't bear it anymore. And you're unhappy, Ben. I can see it in your face. You let your guard slip and I *know*... Let me tell you, as someone who's been there, that you can't go through life just *enduring* when there's someone out there who can make you happier than you can possibly believe."

"Well, thanks for the psychoanalysis." Ben threw the scarf around his neck, making no effort to conceal his annoyance now. "God forbid the *mayor* gets involved, eh? That's the thing with bastards, Liz. They're never as much fun in the flesh as on the cinema screen!"

"Oh, do sod off then, you philandering shit! You've hurt me just like everyone else has, and the moment I have the temerity to be upset, I'm just shoved aside again. Fine, great!" She inhaled, and when she opened her mouth again, it was a roar. *"Why don't you just bugger off!"*

"Let's cut to the chase, shall we? Slap me, I'll catch your hand and then we'll fuck each other senseless over your bloody desk?" He was furious, she realised, his voice no longer calm. "You were *used*? That's rubbish and you know it."

Lizzie's voice was cold with rage. "I'm not *the other woman*. I have more respect for myself than — Oh, God! I thought I did, but I saw your ring in the bathroom, and I still came back to you! What does that make *me*?"

"You weren't used, you weren't beaten and you weren't *lured* anywhere, so stop playing the victim. It doesn't suit you." He seized the door handle and wrenched the door open. "And if it makes you feel better, Liz, you're *not* the other woman. Happy now?"

"I don't understand."

"Get ready to pop the champagne, because my wife's dead." He gave a theatrical shrug, but she saw the change in his face, the desolation writ across him. "And she died a lingering, painful death. But at least Lizzie Aspinall gets to feel superior, so there's that."

And with that final full stop, he turned and left the office.

His feet retreated down the corridor. Soon, those same footsteps would echo down the stairs and be lost in the street.

Dead? She'd had no idea. But it all made sense now. Everything. Each time she had seen his mask slip, she had seen it but not understood.

"Ben?"

She said his name, but she didn't think it was loud enough for him to hear. She followed him into the corridor. He was almost at the top of it. And she ran to him, shoeless, over the wooden floor, almost losing her footing, hobbled by her pencil skirt.

"Ben, please. I'm so sorry!"

"I'm sorry you felt used." He turned, the anger in his voice replaced by defeat and regret. "I'm sorry you felt lured, I'm sorry your husband was a bastard but I'm not sorry that I met you. I'm just sorry it ended up like this."

"Ben, let me speak…please. When you didn't turn up, I thought you'd come to your senses and gone back to your wife. That's why I felt used. I'm so sorry I thought that of you. I had no idea that she— Oh, God, everything I try to say just seems so inadequate. I've spent the last few days missing you more than I ever thought it possible to miss anyone. I wanted to hate you, because that would've made it easier to bear. But…I couldn't."

She looked down at the shape of her toes, encased in thick black tights. She swung her arms awkwardly at her sides.

"I'm sorry I shouted at you. I'm angry with myself, Ben. Not you."

"I came here tonight because I wanted to be with you, even if all that meant was eating fish and chips, because all I can think about is you." Ben pushed his hands back through his hair, his eyes fixed on a point somewhere over her shoulder. "The nights I wasn't at the station, I waited in the lobby at seven, just in case you—"

"We're a right pair of silly sods, aren't we? Because while you were stood in the hotel lobby, I was stood in the side street, looking up at your window and thinking, *It's too late, the curtain's open, the light's off and he's not there.*"

She bit her lip, stifling an awkward laugh.

"Thank you for bringing dinner, Ben. It was so sweet of you. I was ravenous. You're so kind, and I'm just a harridan who shouts a lot."

Lizzie extended her hand to shake his. He caught it but, rather than shaking, drew her closer and replied mischievously, "You're right, you are."

"Ben! There's something else, too. In case you were wondering. My ex... We weren't married. I—I just wanted to tell you, seeing as we're being honest with each other." She took a deep breath. "So let's start again. My name is Lizzie, I'm an interior designer, I currently live in a ridiculous show flat and I'm recently single. I've written a book about vintage textiles, and some people think I'm an expert on such things. And you, Ben?"

"My name is Ben, and I'm an alcoholic."

"Almost as bad as an interior designer! Can I... Would it be inappropriate if I asked you for a hug?"

"Honestly, now that you're involved in a case? Yes." Despite that, he enfolded her in his embrace, holding her close. "I'm not an alcoholic really. I'm a copper, I have an amazing kid and I just flogged a house down south. I drink a lot of tea, don't get nearly enough sleep and swim every morning, even if it means getting up at the crack."

Lizzie rested her cheek to his. They weren't supposed to be doing this, but he didn't show any sign of letting her go. "You have a daughter, don't you? A very beautiful daughter."

"She looks like her mum," he murmured wistfully. "And I was eating breakfast with her when your *lingerie* fell out of my pocket."

"That must've been a bit awkward! I didn't mean for that to happen." Lizzie pressed her lips against his neck for the briefest moment. "I'll be more careful where I leave my undies in future, I promise."

His neck arched even as he murmured, "You know we can't, Lizzie…"

"Yes, you said. Only…I can't stop thinking about what we did together. It sometimes feels as if you're still touching me. I smell that divine aftershave of yours when you're not there." She moaned his name as she held him closer and danced her fingertips up his spine. Even through several layers of clothes, she felt him respond with a tremor.

"We shouldn't—" Yet he slid his hands down her back to rest on her buttocks, his breath warm on her skin where his lips traced kisses across her jaw.

Her hips moved closer to his. Even through that big coat of his, she knew he was aroused. She reached between them and, as he kissed her jaw, she unbuttoned his coat.

"We need each other, Ben…"

"You're working on the case," he reminded her in between kisses, even as his body pressed to her. "I've not stopped thinking about you…"

"Nor I you…"

"That bloody rose perfume of yours…" His hand massaged over her buttock, caressing appreciatively. "It's everywhere I go. *You're* everywhere I go."

Lizzie ran her hand over his erection, through his trousers.

"I want to touch you again. Will you let me?"

"We shou—" Ben breathed into another kiss, his hips circling against hers. Then he whispered her name and gasped, "Touch me."

Lizzie sank her fingers into his thick hair, sighing against Ben's mouth at the feel of him and the memories it stirred. She fumbled to open his fly with her other hand, but once the fabric had parted, once she had slipped her hand inside the waistband of his shorts, she found her confidence. She encircled his erection with a delicate grip and slid her hand up and down its length. His breaths were harder, in time with her hand.

Her name left his lips as a moan, then his mouth was hungry on her, kissing her as though she might be about to disappear. He claimed her with his lips and tongue, one hand squeezing her bottom roughly, the other beneath her sweater to spread that same delicious heat through her skin. His touch was as soft as his body was hard where it was pressed to her, and he breathed, "I need you."

Lizzie gasped between kisses. "Back to my office?"

Ben lifted her effortlessly clear of the floor, nestling her safely in the protection of his arms. Then he carried her back along the hallway where, just minutes before, the air had crackled with anger. It was a different kind of electricity that buzzed there now, and Lizzie clung to Ben as they went, the heat in their kisses building with each step towards her office.

Lizzie barely noticed that Ben had shoved the office door open or that he had shielded her head with his hand as he carried her through the doorway. He laid her down on the chaise as though she were the most precious thing in the world, shrugging off his heavy coat and scarf as soon as his arms were freed. Then he settled beside her, their mouths meeting as his hands moved over her body, and Lizzie revelled once more in that assured touch that she had never thought to feel again.

She skimmed her fingers down his shirt, exploring the warmth of his skin underneath as each button came undone. He responded, sighing her name—her real name— sliding his hand up the hem of her skirt with a firmness that made her gasp. Despite the thick tights Lizzie wore, Ben easily navigated her body.

Still caressing Ben's revealed skin, Lizzie whispered, "Will you get in trouble if they find us out?"

"They probably won't pin a medal on me," he replied, breathless. "You really think you can make something of that bit of ribbon?"

Lizzie combed her hands through Ben's hair, gazing at his expression of professional determination and searing desire.

"Can I show it to—" Lizzie was incapable of speech for a moment when her back arched as Ben's fingers moved against her. She caught her breath and finished her sentence. "A—a couple of dealers I know?"

"Show it to anyone who might know." His hand was at the waistband of her tights, encouraging Lizzie to lift her hips. As soon as she did, he began to roll the tights lower, bringing her underwear with them.

"I will. I know who I can trust. I'll be careful, I promise." Lizzie nudged his trousers down along with his shorts and clutched his erection as his fingers entered her. "Oh, Ben, you're so hard…"

"I want you." It was somewhere between a gasp and a growl, low in his throat. He stroked deep within her core, drawing her pleasure out whilst his free hand pushed her sweater higher and moved over her exposed bra, his fingers seeking out her hardening nipple.

Shivers of pleasure began to tremble through her as she was drawn into the penumbra of bliss. She pressed her mouth to his ear. "You're— You're making me come again... Oh, Ben!"

She felt the cool air on her breast as he eased it free of her bra, then it was replaced by the heat of his breath when he took her nipple between his lips, the very tip of his tongue flicking deftly over the tight bud.

Lizzie was helpless under his mouth and his hands, the slow burn of her pleasure building and building.

"I need you, Ben! I need your touch, I need your smile, I need the way you look at me, I need your body and I need to make you happy!"

Ben lifted his head and met her gaze. In those dark eyes, she saw desire and lust and, somewhere, sadness warring. He blinked and whispered, "I need to catch this bastard, Liz."

"You will..."

Pity the criminal who this man goes after. Whoever it is, whatever they'd done.

"Ben...DCI Finneran, is it inappropriate that I found that"—Lizzie's back arched again as he grazed her nipple with his teeth—"I found that really sexy?"

His only reply was to move his fingers harder than ever, and with her eyes closed she heard him turn over his coat as he sought out the wallet it must contain.

"Do you...in that wallet of yours... Do you have your warrant card?"

His response was to press his wallet into her hand without lifting his head from her breast. Then he closed his fingers around her hip, holding their bodies tight together.

Lizzie, her hand shaking, unzipped his wallet and saw his bank cards, the top of a photobooth picture, some receipts, some foil packages and the crowned six-pointed silver star on the front of his warrant card.

Still his fingers thrust inside her, his thumb pressed to her clit whilst his lips roamed her exposed breast, nuzzling and kissing the soft skin.

Even whilst her body thrilled to his caress, she managed to take the warrant card out of his wallet and flip it open. There was Ben, a slightly younger version, but no less handsome His set expression was almost neutral, but there was determination in his face and just the hint of a grin at the corners of his mouth.

"Have you always been extremely handsome, DCI Finneran?" She showed him the photo and tried to mimic the opening gambit in a courtroom cross-examination, despite the undercurrent of her desirous moans.

"No comment," he murmured, his voice low and muffled by her body.

"Where — oh, Ben! — were you on the evening of the seventh?"

"I would've been in my hotel room." His kisses trailed up to her shoulder. "I'd met my daughter for supper before going back there alone. I intended to go for a swim, but…"

"But…?" Lizzie's free hand tangled in his hair. His erection was pressing her bare thigh.

"But I decided to take a shower instead."

"A shower, eh?"

"I saw this beautiful woman, and she saw me too." He nuzzled at her throat. "The way she looked at me was— It made me hard. I was so turned on..."

"Made you hard? From across the street?"

"Because I wanted her, and when she looked at me, I knew she wanted me too."

A wave of pleasure trembled through Lizzie.

"So I took a shower and I thought of her." He brushed a kiss to her lips. "And I touched myself."

"You—? Did you make yourself come, DCI Finneran?"

"I came," he whispered, catching her lip gently in his teeth. "Hard."

Lizzie moaned at his words, at the thought of him in that shower alone, thinking of her, his hands on himself. She dropped the warrant card and held his erection again. So that was how he'd managed it on their first evening together. That iron self-control up until Lizzie had said... She would say it again, now.

"I want your cock inside me."

And he repeated his first words to her, his voice as thick with desire now as it had been then.

"Let me fuck you."

She let go of his erection. Having managed to hold on to his wallet, she teased a sealed condom out of it.

"Let me put this on you."

She carefully tore the corner of the foil packet with her teeth.

"Are you ready, Ben?" It was a silly question, as he was clearly aroused, but it seemed only polite.

"I'm ready."

She closed her eyes and brought her mouth to his, kissing him deeply as she slid the condom on. He withdrew his fingers from her, and for a few fleeting seconds, his hands left her body completely. Then he took hold of her tights and drew them farther down, slipping one leg between hers.

Lizzie held his face in her trembling hands and gazed into his dark, glittering eyes. He grasped her hips and guided the tip of his cock inside her. He seemed to be holding himself back, but with a groan, he entered her. For a moment they simply gazed at each other, then he began to move, pressing into her with hard, deep strokes.

And Lizzie knew they shouldn't be doing this, now that she was his expert witness. But nothing in the world seemed able to keep them apart. The width of a night-time street, a missed message… The thread hadn't broken, it had become only stronger.

He clung to her, their bodies joined, their lives entwined by that unseen thread. With each long thrust he gave a groan of pleasure and exertion and she could feel the tightening of the muscles in his arms, the way his embrace grew stronger than ever with each passing moment.

"Say my name," Lizzie whispered.

"Ms."—he punctuated the words with kisses—"Lizzie. Aspinall."

The pleasure that had been building in her was increasing again, sparked by the sound of her name being spoken in Ben's southern tones.

"Make me come, Ben Finneran…!"

"All night long," he replied huskily, echoing that first night once more. Then his hips were moving hard and fast, his mouth dropping to her breast.

Lizzie's hips bucked as, once again, the man from room 423 brought her to bliss. As she soared, aware only of intense pleasure and the touch of her lover, she shouted his name — his real name. And at her cries, she heard Ben reply with her own name, felt the final hard push, the tensing muscles as he surrendered to his orgasm.

Lizzie held him tenderly as the last shudders of their orgasms trembled through them.

Time passed. She had no idea how long. All she knew was that they were together. She smiled just to see him there in her arms.

But eventually, Lizzie would have to survey the wreckage. Her bra was half off and so were her tights, her skirt was pushed up to her middle, her tights were dangling from one foot, and somehow Ben's leg had got twisted up in them. And he hadn't removed one solitary cufflink, but what she could see of his chest was sheened with perspiration. His trousers and shorts had only managed to get to the tops of his thighs. One foot was on the chaise, the hint of a footprint where he had gained purchased against the chair's arm. The remains of their fish and chip supper were strewn across the floor, and one of the wine glasses had been knocked over. It wasn't as if the room had been tidy to start with, with Lizzie's source books on every other available surface.

She would have stayed here like this all night with him, but it was late now, and the chaise longue wouldn't accommodate two sleepers. Had he dozed for a moment? His dark eyes opened, large and sleepy.

"Who knew fish and chips could be so irresistible?" He gave a cheeky smile before settling his head on her shoulder again. "I missed you so much…"

"I couldn't bear it when I thought I'd lost you. Let's promise each other something?"

"Go on," he murmured contentedly.

"Let's not have any more misunderstandings. No more missed messages, no more—" Lizzie had caught sight of his hand. He'd taken off the ring again. "No more confusion. Let's be honest with each other."

"It's a deal." Ben lifted his head and kissed the tip of her nose.

"Good!" Lizzie ruffled his hair. It was so luxuriant and thick. She could happily get tangled in it and not escape for days. "By the way, I want to give you a present."

"Another one? Will it match the undies you already gave me?"

"Dare I ask what you did with them? When you turned up here and announced you're in the bizzies, I thought for one stupid moment that you'd traced my DNA! For a millisecond, I might add, because that really *would* be ridiculous."

"I did when any gentleman would, Ms Aspinall. I had them laundered and kept them safe, ready to return them to their rightful owner."

"Aren't you a gentleman?" Lizzie gave him a quick kiss. "Now…let me just…"

"Do you have a bathroom I can use?" Ben sat up, perching on the edge of the chaise.

"Of course. Just turn right outside this door."

"Two minutes," he told her, zipping his trousers as he stood and ambled from the room.

Lizzie manoeuvred herself from the chaise and rearranged her clothes. She went to her desk, where an unsteady pile of books was waiting for a sudden draught to send them flying, and then returned to the chaise with one of the books cradled in her arms.

When Ben returned, he looked wonderfully ruffled. Though his trousers were now fastened, his shirt hung open, his hair in complete disarray thanks to her fingers. He greeted her with a smile and sat on the floor beside the chaise to retrieve the forgotten wine bottle and glasses. Once they were full again, he handed one up to Lizzie and told her, "Here's to ladies who know their ribbon."

Lizzie balanced the book on her knee, sipping the wine while ruffling Ben's hair even more. She put the glass down beside the chair and passed him the book.

"Here — for you. I want you to have this. It's the book I wrote. It's the reason you're here again now. Vintage textiles expert witness."

"That's… Thank you." Ben reached up and took the book from her, his face lit by a smile. "I hope you signed it, Ms Aspinall?"

"Open the cover and find out."

Ben ran his fingertips across the cover, a photograph of a rainbow of fabrics. Then he opened it. While he had been in the bathroom, Lizzie had written a dedication on the title page.

To B, from L xxx PS: turn to page 72!

"I wrote the kisses, then thought…if one of your police friends finds that, they'll wonder what's going on! But they won't necessarily know it was from me, will they?" Lizzie winked. "It could've been from…Louisa."

"Page seventy-two," he murmured, and flipped through the glossy paper to find it.

"Your mate Michael. The scene from *The Italian Job*, when he goes to the tailors and gets mocked for his clothes being out of date!"

"I know it well!" He sat back, resting his head against Lizzie's knee.

"I thought that illustrated how menswear evolved in the 1960s. Erm…anyway. You'll have to excuse my sister's influence. She made the publisher put in pictures of me in my workroom, fondling fabric. It was very weird! *'It's all about the brand!'* she'd said. My brand is… awkward woman rubbing velvet, apparently."

"In case you're wondering, I don't always wear suits, by the way." Ben peered at the book then blinked and turned to look at her over his shoulder. "How did you know I have a daughter?"

"The second time we met… You were in the bathroom, and I hid my knickers in your pocket. And you see, I moved the chair, it nudged the table, and it made the screen of your phone come on. And there you were, with a woman I took to be your extremely young wife. But then when you said that you have a kid, I thought, *Idiot, they've got the same smile. That's his daughter!*"

"She's only just turned twenty!" Ben grimaced and shook his head. "Definitely not my wife, but the world's greatest-ever daughter."

Lizzie rubbed his shoulder and half-laughed.

"I'm so sorry! I'm not doing very well, am I? I assume she's your wife, then frighten her with my undies and I've not even met—"

Meet his daughter? Was that possible now? And could she become part of his life, and he part of hers?

"When the case is over—" He still gazed at her, his expression gentle. "We really shouldn't be doing this, Liz, but the thought of not being with you… We just have to be careful while you're involved in the investigation."

Lizzie nodded. "Don't worry. I won't turn up at the police station and ravish you over your desk."

"I wish you would." He laughed. "But I'm not using you. I promise that."

"I'm sorry I said all those things. Do you forgive me? I had *drastically* got hold of the wrong end of the stick. I'd be a pretty crap copper, wouldn't I!"

"We were both angry. There's nothing to forgive." Ben put the book down and reached up for her hand. "I just don't want you to wonder why we're creeping about, that's all. I *need* to wrap this case up. I feel like I'll never rest until it's done. After that, *anything* you want from me, it's yours."

"A case wrapped up with ribbon?" Lizzie yawned. "I'll get onto it as soon as I can tomorrow morning."

"Let me tidy up this mess of ours then we'll get you home. You look exhausted."

"So do you! Don't worry, really. I have a *very* understanding cleaner."

"No way... That's above and beyond the call of duty." Ben kissed Lizzie's hand then went to work collecting the discarded crockery and wrappers, bundling the rubbish into her wastepaper bin and the empty bottle after it. "How far do you have to go tonight?"

"If I tell you the flat's on Princess Street, I'm going to take a wild guess that it might not mean very much to you."

"You'd be dead wrong. My girl's got a bar she goes to along there." He put the plates on Lizzie's desk and began to button his shirt. "I'm a copper. I don't miss much. "

Ben was silent then, concentrating on making himself look halfway respectable. He scooped up his scarf and coat and, from within the pocket, retrieved his wedding band and put it back onto his finger.

Lizzie tried to pretend she hadn't noticed. She began to re-shelve the books that were scattered about.

"Okay, then. It's in an old cotton warehouse. A ridiculous show flat which isn't really meant for anyone to live in, but…needs must and all that. It's mine, at least. It's not far at all from your hotel, in fact. Just a few minutes' walk."

"You look all in, Liz. Leave the books until tomorrow and let me get you home?" Ben put on his coat, retrieved his wallet and warrant card then crossed the office to loop his red scarf gently around her neck. It was even softer than she had expected, the wool cosy on her skin.

And it had his scent.

Lizzie took her coat from the armchair under the window and buttoned herself into it. He was smiling at her so sweetly, and she realised it was the first thing he had undressed her of. The very coat she had worn as she'd run to him through the night.

"Off we go then, and don't forget your present!"

"Not a chance of that!" Ben tucked the book under his arm and, foregoing gloves, held out his hand to her. "Come on. Bedtime."

Chapter Nine

Although it was late, Manchester was still busy, with its collection of partiers, drunks and those people who were always striding purposefully somewhere. Maybe the destination was a mystery, even to them.

Ben laughed as Lizzie pointed up to his hotel.

"It's on my route!"

They crossed the square, glittering with Christmas lights, and were on Princess Street. Not far from the front door of Lizzie's apartment building, she noticed Ben bristle, suddenly alert.

She squeezed his hand, turning her head.

"What is it?"

He held up his hand and shook his head almost imperceptibly. Then he turned to look back along the road, scrutinising every doorway, every shadow. His fingers tightened around hers and she saw his attention settle on the narrow opening of an alleyway that ran between the buildings about twenty feet from where they now stood. Lizzie peered along the path of his gaze but saw nothing in the sodium streetlight.

Then, with a shiver, she *did*.

From between the buildings, a long shadow fell across the orange-tinted pavement as though someone were standing just beyond the mouth of the alleyway. The shadow moved, suggesting its owner had taken a step forward. Whoever it was might be peering around the brickwork at them even now, unseen yet seeing. Ben started towards the alley and the shadow disappeared back into the darkness from which it had seeped, accompanied by the sound of footsteps running into the night.

Lizzie's spine locked solid with fear.

"Was it just some random drunk person? Ben?"

"Probably just someone wondering whether we were worth mugging." He slipped his arm around her shoulders, drawing her closer as they walked on. "Luckily for them, they thought better of it."

"Maybe…" Lizzie breathed in a lungful of the freezing night air. She had to say something, even if it made her sound paranoid. "Have you — Have you ever heard of a footballer called Matt de Luca? Plays for City?"

"Don't talk to me about that bloody man!" Ben pulled a face of mock outrage. "Slotted away an injury time winner—from a *foul*, by the way—last year. Should've been sent off and instead he's man of the damned match. Cost us the top four, got that bunch of cheating toerags up there instead!"

"That's a yes, then?" Lizzie was astounded, and almost laughed. She was about to ask him which team he supported, but that shadow in the alleyway, so close

to her makeshift home, had unsettled her. "Look, Ben…
Matt de Luca has a stalker."

"Yeah, I know. Every Gooner in London'd like to
knock his head off." He seemed to realise that she was
being serious then, and said, "Why would Matt de
Luca's stalker be interested in us?"

Lizzie pressed her fingertips to her forehead.
Something lurched inside her. She was scared, a
visceral terror that there was someone out there in the
night, who wished her family harm.

"Because Matt de Luca is married to my sister."

"Was that your sister in the Mezz that night?" He
gestured to his head with his hand as though flouncing
a magnificent coiffure. "With the hair?"

"No wonder you wear glasses. How long-sighted
are you, for heaven's sake? Yes, that's her. Donna de
Luca, née Aspinall. They were only married in June."

"Oh, come on. No offence to your sister, but you
couldn't miss that hair, that luminous blonde
footballers seem to go for." He kissed Lizzie's forehead.
"I'll mention all this at the station in the morning. You
never know what might turn out to be a lead. I need to
know though. Do you think you've been followed
before or is this strictly de Luca?"

"I don't know. The thing is, I do work with
celebrities. Could someone's stalker become so
obsessed that they'd stalk me too because I made their
mansion in Alderley Edge look like a market in
Marrakesh? I was only at Casa de Luca — sorry…my
silly name for it — yesterday, over in Altrincham. Matt
wants me to turn it into Versailles. Could that be a
connection?"

"Don't worry about that tonight. Just get a good sleep?" He looked along the street. "Which one is yours?"

"Just along here."

The entrance was almost as grand as Ben's hotel, with stone steps leading up to an enormous pair of original nineteenth-century doors.

"Fancy for a warehouse, isn't it! I'd invite you in, but if we end up in bed together, we won't get any sleep. And you haven't brought your toothbrush, either."

"I'm not here for that. I'm strictly here to make sure you're safely through that door." Ben smiled gently. "Now get to bed, Ms. Aspinall."

"Night-night, darling Ben." Lizzie pressed her lips to his.

"If you need me, you've got my number." He returned the kiss. "Sweet dreams."

As Lizzie walked up the steps, she grinned over her shoulder at Ben. At the doors, she blew him a kiss. He answered with a smart salute before returning the kiss with one of his own and calling, "Sleep tight!"

"And you!"

Lizzie waved to him as she closed herself behind the heavy wooden doors.

Chapter Ten

Lizzie put the phone down. She'd spoken to another textiles dealer, another person who hadn't had any ribbon pass through their hands recently that resembled Ben's evidence. Lizzie's contacts were thorough. They didn't miss a thing, in case somewhere in a crate of otherwise unremarkable fabric, something rare might be hiding.

But she had definitely seen that ribbon somewhere before.

She stretched her arms and smiled again as she saw the chaise longue, his footprint still visible on its arm. She took a photo of it on her phone, grinning as she texted it to Ben. She artfully hid the footprint behind a cushion then headed off to get a cup of tea. She had some more textile dealers to talk to, but she needed caffeine first.

Claire and Jordan were in reception, leaning over the computer together. The last time she'd found them huddled like that, they'd been creating an online farm.

"Come on, guys! We've got loads to do before we shut for Chrimbo. Turn that off, and—" She was silenced by a familiar voice from the television.

Her colleagues lifted their heads in unison and looked up at her.

"Press conference about the poisonings," Claire told her.

Lizzie didn't say anything else. She came round behind the desk and stood beside them to watch. She blinked in mute amazement.

It was Ben.

DCI Ben Finneran was sat at the centre of a long table, immaculate in a dark grey suit and white shirt, dimples pressed in at either side of the knot in his silk tie. His hands were neatly clasped before him on the table, his dark hair combed back from his face.

A woman in plain clothes sat beside him, who was presumably another detective, and the rest of the table was taken up with high-ranking police in uniform. Camera flashes went off in their faces, flaring off the lenses of Ben's glasses. Journalists shoved microphones and recording machines towards Ben, the air confused with their bombardment of questions.

"And now we're live in Manchester at the press conference concerning the spate of poisonings that have been happening across the city…"

The camera swayed a little unsteadily, as if someone in the throng had bumped into it. At some sign, invisible to the viewers at home, there was silence, and Ben looked into the camera.

"So is that what he wanted when he came over?" Jordan looked to Lizzie. Claire tried to shush him as Ben began to speak, but Jordan kept talking. "I wouldn't mind him taking down my particulars!"

Ben's name and title appeared in the bottom of the screen now as he shuffled a pile of paper.

"Recently there has been speculation regarding the tragic deaths of Manoor Barsar, Jennifer Hopkins and Ian Mountford. This has been a delicate and complex investigation but we are now in a position to confirm that Mansoor, Jennifer and Ian were killed by ingesting antifreeze that had been poured into their drinks during nights out. In addition, we're investigating several other possible attempts on the lives of people who received medical attention and have since been released from hospital. These assaults and murders have all taken place during the past eight-week period."

A buzz ran through the journalists, flashbulbs popping once more.

"None of the victims were known to one another, and these assaults appear to have been carried out at random." Ben drew in a breath and his throat moved as he swallowed, the sadness in his eyes once more. "I've spoken to the families of Mansoor, Ian and Jennifer and assured them that we *will* catch the person responsible for the death of their loved ones."

He blinked, more cameras clicking, and Jordan muttered, "That's Christmas drinkies up the spout."

"It's important to reiterate that these are isolated incidents and there's no need to panic." Ben's voice was measured, even as his words were serious. "People should continue to enjoy the season but remain vigilant. Look out for yourselves and your friends when visiting pubs and bars. We're following up a number of leads, but we ask, if anyone has anything they would like to tell us, please contact our incident room.

"If anyone has seen anything that's given them cause for concern" — he looked into the camera — "that's why we're here."

Lizzie saw the tender solicitude in his eyes and knew it was genuinely felt. He really did care.

But poisonings? What on Earth could that piece of ribbon have to do with that? She stared at the screen, as if Ben would yield his secret.

"Do you think they've got a clue?" Jordan looked to Claire for an answer. "I mean, he's cute and he gives good police but...he doesn't know, does he? Not. A. Clue."

"Be quiet, Jordan. This is serious!" Lizzie kept her eyes on the screen. Cameras clicked and whirred and someone off camera could be heard asking if there were any questions.

"DCI Finneran, isn't it true that you were investigating similar cases ten years ago in London with the Metropolitan Police? They were never solved and the Met's admitted this could be the same person. What do you have to say to the widower and family of Susan Burns, the pregnant victim of the poisoner?"

Lizzie gasped and covered her mouth with her hand.

Ben showed no sign of discomfort or awkwardness, remaining as still and collected as ever, his hands still knitted on the desk. "Everything I had to say to the family of Mrs. Burns has been said in private. I continue to seek justice for Mrs. Burns and each of the other victims of the attacker and the families of those who passed away. I won't rest until they know that justice has been done."

Another question from the floor.

"Are you sure it's the same person? Could it be a copycat killer?"

"We are absolutely sure this is the same person." He unknitted his hands and lifted one palm. "And before you ask me, I can't confirm *how* we know this."

A journalist with a large sponge microphone decorated with a gaudy logo was next.

"How close are you to catching the Christmas Cocktail Killer? Are you going to get them before Christmas?"

"The Christmas Cocktail Killer?" Ben's eyes narrowed just a little behind his spectacles, and though he remained composed, Lizzie sensed the annoyance in him. "That's incorrect, disrespectful and unhelpful. Do we have any more questions?"

Someone raised a hand and a question followed.

"Can you confirm, then, that the poisonous substance used ten years ago in London is the same one that's been used here?"

"Antifreeze was the substance used in the south, but there are other points of correlation that lead us to believe that we're dealing with the same perpetrator." Ben blinked and shifted very slightly in his seat to look out across the sea of microphones and cameras. "We aren't in a position to say anything further than that at this stage."

Feedback screeched from the speakers as the journalists rushed at the police with questions and microphones. But they were pushing back their chairs, shaking their heads at the demand for more questions. The camera fell on Ben as he leant in to talk to a colleague, nodding, his face serious. Then he adjusted his tie, tucked the papers beneath his arm and walked out of the camera's scope.

Lizzie, her phone still clutched in her hand, was dumbfounded. And that photo of the chaise longue! Ben, conducting himself with such professional calm, so solicitous about the victims, so coolly assertive when dealing with the journalists, then there was Lizzie, texting him a photo of a sofa. Sometimes, she was as vacuous as her sister.

She sent him a text.

Just saw you on TV. Well done L xxx

"Top quality bullshitting," Jordan decided, "apart from that business with the antifreeze. It's horrible!"

Lizzie looked up from her phone.

"Just be vigilant, you two. That's all you have to do. And you'll be fine. Ben's watching over you."

"Ben?" Claire nudged Jordan and gave an insinuating wink. Lizzie chose to ignore it.

"How can you be vigilant when you're out on the lash?" Jordan opened his arms wide, questioning. "He says keep an eye on your drink. Well, *helloooo*, I don't bring my drink onto the dance floor. I don't keep one eye on vino when I'm getting hot and heavy, do I? Coppers don't go out boozing and they definitely don't do *hot 'n' heavy*, so maybe they can stare at the cocktails all night, but I can't! Anyway, *Ben*, as you call him, hasn't got a clue. I'm sticking to that, boss, whatever you say!"

The ribbon, safe in her desk drawer, loomed in her mind.

"They can't give away too much. There'll be things they're keeping back. If they're getting closer, they'd only scare the killer off then they'd never catch them." Lizzie was on her phone again, scrolling through her contacts for any other dealers she might have overlooked.

There was a tap on the office door, someone having got as far as the entrance hall without ringing the intercom. Jordan trotted over to open it and admitted the smiling girl who worked on the floor below, answering phones for a shoe designer who specialised in drag queens. She waved her hand at the gathered office and held up a white envelope, the sort that might contain a greeting card. On the front, someone had glued one of Lizzie's business cards, but there was no stamp.

"Someone must've pushed this under the door last night," she told them apologetically. "I picked it up in our post this morning. Sorry!"

"Not to worry, love." Jordan took it from her and she waved again before he closed the door gently. As he crossed the office back to the desk, he was already tearing open the envelope. "Another Christmas card for the lovely Lizzie Aspinall. My money's on... Well, we got an actress yesterday and two models this morning. I'm going to guess...that singer who had her place all done out in neon for the summer."

"Her? My eyes still ache!" Claire laughed.

Jordan's smile faded into a frown as he looked at the front of the card. He opened it and the frown deepened further as he said, "This can't be for us."

Lizzie had found two more dealers who she would ring, just as soon as she had that cup of tea inside her. She put her phone in her pocket. She finally tuned in to what Jordan had said.

"That doesn't even look like a Christmas card! It's a..." Lizzie's mouth fell open. The card depicted a bunch of lilies laid in sunlight cast through a church window. *With sympathy,* it said in silver writing printed across the front. Nausea began to rise inside her.

Lilies. The fleur-de-lys.

She opened it to see a printout glued inside.

I'm in every shadow.

And there, beneath, crudely scrawled in biro, a fleur-de-lys.

"Oh, my God… Oh God."

Lizzie's legs nearly gave way beneath her. Claire and Jordan held her up and helped her to the plush sofa in front of the reception desk. She sank into it, barely aware of the voices in the room, the sofa beneath her, the sound of someone swishing through the curtain into the kitchenette. She was aware only of darkness encroaching at the edges of her vision, and that same fear she had felt last night, as the footsteps echoed away.

In Lizzie's pocket, her phone buzzed with a text. She swallowed, her hand shaking as she pulled out her phone. Such a normal thing. She looked at phone countless times a day. Why couldn't she do it without fearing some new terror?

She stilled her shaking enough to swipe the screen.

Thinking of you and that photo. B x

Tears pricked at her eyes, but she held them back.

If Ben could be so collected at that press conference, then she could deal with this.

Lizzie dragged herself off the sofa and stumbled down the corridor, the same one that Ben had carried her along only a few hours before. The card felt like a lead weight in her hand. She nudged open the door and dug Ben's card out of her purse. The loop of thread that he had tied around her plait fell out with it.

With new purpose, Lizzie put on her coat. She made sure the ribbon was safely locked in her desk drawer, then she put the card and the torn envelope carefully inside a new A4 envelope.

She brought up Ben's number as she walked back to reception and it rang.

"Going to the police station!" she called over her shoulder as she went through reception and pattered down the stairs.

"Hello." Ben's voice was a welcome note of safety, as calm and friendly as it ever was. "What's going on?"

Her footsteps echoed down the stairwell as she ran.

"Ben, I'm coming in. I've got something you need to see."

"Tell me?" Now he sounded more urgent. "Is it the ribbon?"

"It's a *'with sympathy'* card."

There was silence between them for a second, then another, before Ben told her, "Are you at the office? I'm sending a car over. Wait there."

"Yes, I'm just coming downstairs. What's going on, Ben? Will Claire and Jordan be okay? Should I send them home?"

"They'll be fine. Just wait outside your building. We'll be there."

"Okay…okay… Bye, then."

As Lizzie rounded the last corner of the stairs, the ground seemed to trombone up towards her. She clutched the banister and heaved for breath before slowly taking the last few steps. She opened the door and fear struck her anew.

What if I open the door and the stalker is there?

She closed the door again and sent a text to Ben.

Am waiting in lobby. Can't go outside.

And she waited.

Black beamer, his reply said. *Ten minutes.*

Lizzie crouched down on the floor, in the corner, just as she had when she had been afraid as a child. If she made herself as small as she possibly could, then the ghost in the wardrobe, the witch in the chimney-breast and the vampire in the attic couldn't see her, couldn't reach her.

When she'd been a child and she'd had her rag doll clutched tightly in her hands…

She closed her eyes and thought only of that.

A car horn sounded outside, then someone was buzzing the door. Lizzie fought off her terror and pulled herself to her feet. She called through the crack in the door, "Who's there?"

"It's DCI Finneran, Ms. Aspinall. Can you open the door, please?"

Lizzie yanked it open and reached for Ben's arm.

"Ben, oh, Ben!"

"It's all right." He stepped into the empty foyer and closed the door behind them. "It's okay, Lizzie. I'm here."

"We thought it was a Christmas card."

She held out the envelope, only now noticing that his face was as white as the wall behind him. He patted his pockets for something, eventually murmuring, "No bloody gloves. Give me a second?"

With a kiss to Lizzie's cheek, Ben opened the door, setting it on the latch. She heard the car door open and close before he was with her and the door was closed again. Ben pulled a pair of latex gloves over his hands and took the card, his gaze meeting Lizzie's.

"I'm going to take care of you, Lizzie. I swear it."

His face, already white as snow, seemed to lose what little blood remained when he took the card out of its envelope. He studied the front then read the inscription inside. She saw a muscle in his jaw tighten as he put the card back into its envelope, his full lips growing thinner.

"We need to take this seriously. Can we go up to the office or would you rather come down to the station?"

"Please take me away from here. This is where they left the card. I can't— Please, Ben... That *thing* is addressed to *me*."

"Lizzie" — Ben's gloved hand closed over her upper arm—"Come on. Where's that girl who almost kicked my arse out of here last night? You're safe. I promise it."

Lizzie almost smiled. "I'm scared, Ben."

"We've got a car outside." He pressed a kiss to her lips. "Let's go."

Lizzie pushed the door then peered around it. People milled about in the street, but every face was a threat.

"Quickly, please. They might be here even now, watching."

"They're not." He was so sure, so certain of it. Ben's hand came to rest on Lizzie's elbow, then he escorted her down to the black car that was waiting and opened the back door. "In you get. It's all right."

Lizzie climbed in. The coolness of the leather upholstery seemed to calm her, even as an uncontrollable shiver went through her, her teeth chattering as she pulled her coat around her.

How can he be so sure?

Just a normal thing. Get in the car, put on a seat belt. So normal, nothing to fear.

Ben was at the boot, and when he returned to the car and opened the passenger door, his hands were bare once more. The card was in a clear, sealed bag, and he threw it onto the dashboard and climbed in. He looked over his shoulder to meet Lizzie's gaze but addressed the young, uniformed driver.

"PC Choudary, get us back to the station as quick as you can."

He's not driving.

Instead, the driver's seat was occupied by a young woman with short, dark, cropped hair. She looked at Lizzie for a moment in the rear-view mirror, her large brown eyes ringed with kohl.

The car pulled smoothly out into the flow of traffic, the tick of the indicator as reassuring as a heartbeat. The familiar streets skimmed by, and Lizzie clung to that. How could she be unsafe in the city she called home?

Ben was still watching her, even as he reached out and took the bagged card in his hand, settling it on his lap and away from her line of sight.

"Ms. Aspinall, are you all right?" He was formal, polite, professional.

"I…I think so. Are you sure Jordan and Claire — only I've run off and left them, and the ribbon — "

Lizzie inhaled deeply. It was only then that she realised she hadn't been breathing properly at all, only little, light breaths that hadn't cleared through her lungs. With a rush, she caught at the oxygen and immediately felt calmer.

"You can call your office from the station if you need to." He addressed the driver then, his voice lower.

"Anj, can you stick the blues on and get us there a bit quicker?"

The driver nodded, and suddenly the car accelerated, the yell of a siren all around them, echoing off the tall frontages of the buildings that crowded along the streets like cliffs. *What the hell is going on? What does Ben know?*

Lizzie's voice was robotically calm.

"I told them where I was going. It's all right. I was supposed to be designing Versailles."

The car drew to a smooth halt in front of a gleaming building of chrome and glass, an enormous police badge shining on the side in the cold winter sun. Ben was out of the vehicle almost before it had stopped, and he opened the door for Lizzie and stepped back to allow her to join him.

Lizzie had never been here before. Why on earth would she have? She pushed herself out of the seat and snuggled into her coat against the cold wind that whipped around the building. Whoever had sent the card wouldn't be here. Couldn't be. Could they?

Still Ben carried the card in its bag, such a small, insignificant thing to cause so much terror. He didn't even have a coat, Lizzie vaguely noticed, just the carefully cut grey suit that he had worn on TV less than an hour earlier. She followed him up a set of wide steps and into the bustling foyer, the sound bewildering after the wild journey in the car.

Ben spoke briefly to the uniformed man behind the gleaming reception desk, then he turned back to Lizzie and said, "Can I get you anything before we go through? Cup of tea?"

"If you could get me a cup of tea, I will love you forever." Too late, Lizzie realised what she'd said. "So to speak…"

Ben chuckled and replied, "In that case, I'll get you a *great* cup of tea. Grab a seat, and give me two minutes?"

Lizzie nodded as Ben headed off. She dropped into a plastic chair and tapped out a text, sending it to both Jordan and Claire at once.

If anything else weird happens, ring me ASAP.

"All sorted?" Ben was standing beside the chair, holding two steaming paper cups and no bagged sympathy card. He held one out to her and smiled. "Let's go somewhere more private."

"Thank you." She took the cup and swallowed a mouthful of the hot tea before following Ben through the labyrinthine corridors of the police station. He strode just far enough ahead to look formal, just close enough to let her know she was safe, until they were passing identical grey doors, dulled chrome panels on each, indicating if they were occupied. He opened one of those that appeared to be empty and, after confirming that it was, ushered Lizzie into the room.

The interview room was far from being welcoming, but that was possibly the point. It contained a table and four chairs, two either side. Weak light came in through a barred, frosted-glass window.

"You could do with some nice curtains in here." Lizzie attempted a smile and drank more of her sweet, milky tea. Her nan had always said, *'sugary tea for a shock'*, and Ben had apparently heeded her advice, without even having met the woman.

"We'll do the formal bit in a moment." The professional façade was gone, his face drawn with concern. Ben put his tea on the table and curled his fingers around hers, holding her hand tenderly. "You looked so bloody scared."

"After that person last night… I could've just dismissed it, but not with that message. *I'm in every shadow*. Ben, it's so horrible! What's happening?"

"Do you trust me?"

"Of course I do."

"Then trust me to keep you safe." He squeezed her fingers and placed a gentle kiss on her lips. "Drink your tea and relax. There's no safer place to be than here. Let me take your coat?"

Lizzie began to unbutton it. It was very odd taking off anything in front of him without being in the heat of passion. But she had to put all that aside. They were not meant to be carrying on with each other, and even thinking about such things in a building full of police seemed to be asking for trouble.

With great care, Ben helped her to slide the coat down her arms. He laid it down across the width of the table then moved to stand in front of her again, studying her face.

"Were you all right last night after I'd gone?"

"Yes. I went to bed and fell asleep. And…that was all. Well, apart from a bin getting knocked over in the alleyway in the middle of the night, but I heard someone shout, and… It must've been a fox or a cat. It did make me jump, though!"

"Can I—" He blinked, reaching for her hand again. "Would it be crossing a professional line if I hugged you?"

"Oh, Ben…" Lizzie looked over at the door. "What if someone came in? Do they have cameras in here?"

"There're no cameras and no one's going to come in." He glanced towards the table where the recording equipment sat silent, unused. "Sorry, I— Let's get on."

Lizzie's gaze switched from Ben to the dismal window. She would have hugged him, but she couldn't bear the thought of getting him into trouble. He followed her lead and glanced to the window, murmuring, "That photo was just the tonic I needed."

Lizzie twitched her eyes back to Ben. She couldn't have repressed her grin if she had tried. She laid her head on his shoulder and she was once more in his firm embrace.

"Sorry. I sent the photo just before you were on the telly. I was worried you'd think I was a vacuous hussy when you saw it. You, so intent and serious, then you look at your phone and see *that*."

"Last night—" He sighed contentedly, holding her close. "It was perfect."

"Wasn't it just?" She brushed her lips over his neck and whispered, "Is this what they mean by *helping the police with their enquiries*?"

His laugh was soft but she could feel the tension in him despite it, and as if he had realised, he tightened his arms around her. For what seemed like a long time they stood there, unmoving, needing nothing but each other.

Lizzie's fear didn't ebb entirely. She would still be on her guard. But it was easier to be cautious knowing that Ben—and an entire police station of coppers— would protect her if, God forbid, that figure in the shadows came any closer.

"I need to take a statement," Ben eventually told her, his voice muffled against her hair. "We'll have to start with last night, then we'll get on to— I promise you we'll get him, Lizzie. All of this *shit*... he's just bringing us closer."

"If something good can come out of something so— What's going on, Ben? Stalking, poisonings... Is it all the same person?"

"Grab a seat." Ben kissed her forehead with utmost tenderness. "We'll go through it all."

"Can I sit next to you? That's not breaking the rules too much, is it?"

"You can sit wherever you like," he assured her. "Make yourself comfy. I just need to grab a few bits of official paper."

Lizzie checked her phone while Ben was gone from the room. Jordan had sent her a text.

You ok, Boss? Has he taken down your particulars yet? ;)
J

Lizzie sighed. His heart was in the right place, at least.

Ben arrived with a folder tucked under his arm, his spectacles on his nose and two fresh cups of tea. This time, though, there was no paper cup, but a chipped white mug that carried the legend, *Dad, You Are Epic*, and another decorated with the fading image of the cast of *Rainbow*. He put both down on the table and told her, "You're *Rainbow*. Tell me you don't take sugar, though, because I didn't put any in it this time."

"It's fine, thank you." Lizzie grinned at the mug. "I always wondered about Rod, Jane and Freddie. Didn't you? A *ménage a trois* on children's telly."

"I think they've all been married to each other in various combinations." Ben threw the folder down onto the tabletop and stripped off his dark grey jacket. With a little more care, he put it on the back of one of the plastic chairs, the harsh light reflecting from the silken maroon back of his waistcoat. Then he lifted the second chair and put it next to his own before he told her, "As close as you can get."

Lizzie held the warm cup on her knee. She wanted more than anything to run her hand down that satin back, but entertained herself with the thought of it, rather than executing the reality.

"I've never done this before. It would almost be exciting, if it wasn't so —" *Grim. There, that's the word.* The sun brightened beyond the window for a moment, casting a beam across the table, just like the sunlight depicted on the card. Lizzie shuddered.

Ben took his seat beside her and opened the folder. Inside was a small sheaf of paper and a biro, clipped to the cover. He began to fill in the top of what she realised was to become her statement, pausing only to confirm her name.

"So, we need to record what happened this morning and last night —" Ben fell silent as he considered that. "That shouldn't be too much of a problem. No decent copper would let his expert witness walk home alone after meeting to discuss her part in the case."

"You might want to delete that photo from your phone. That footprint could be quite incriminating."

"You're not going to make this easy, are you?" He glanced at her with a devilish smirk. "So, Ms. Aspinall, let's start with your walk home last night."

"I was walking home from my office on Deansgate. I came alongside the hotel, then through the square, and at the top of Princess Street, I turned right. I didn't notice anything untoward, until —" Lizzie patted Ben's knee. She was tempted to leave her hand there but didn't. "Should I have added, *I was being accompanied home by DCI Finneran?*"

"We probably should mention it." He smiled. "Keep going. We'll add that in here."

"I didn't notice anything untoward until DCI Finneran, who was accompanying me home… That is, was walking me home — noticed someone in an alleyway. It runs beside the next apartment building from mine. I could see a shadow, so they must have been stood just at the top of the alley, maybe just slightly outside it. Finneran thought it was a would-be mugger, but because my sister had told me about the stalker that she and her husband have, I was alarmed. Finneran began to walk towards the alley, but whoever it was ran off. That was all. I said goodbye to Finneran and went up to my flat."

Lizzie puffed out her cheeks.

"Should I mention the urban fox and the bin?"

"Just for the record, can you confirm your sister's identity, then we can get onto the fox?"

"Sorry. My sister's name is Donna Marie de Luca. She's married to Matt de Luca, who plays for City. They got married in the summer in the Maldives. Then came home for a — I'm sure you don't need to know about her wedding reception, do you? In fact, she sold the magazine rights, so there's plenty of photos if you need to see her arrive in a crystal carriage with pale blue cushions. It was so unbelievably naff."

Thinking about the de Luca nuptials was a pleasing distraction.

Ben's pen paused on the page and he looked at her. "Do you want me to write that bit down? I should, by rights."

"Possibly not the bit about it being naff." She laughed awkwardly. "Erm...and nothing else happened last night, although... My flat is at the corner of the building, so the living area looks out over Princess Street, but the main bedroom is over a side street. Another alley, really. I was woken by a shout and heard a bin go over, and... I've heard that happen before. It's probably just an urban fox looking for pizza. But it did make me jump after that business with the person in the alleyway. I didn't check the time. I know I should've, but...I just lay there very still because I was scared. And it was so quiet, and I told myself not to be silly, then I fell asleep."

"You should've rung me." He laid the pen atop the paper and reached to take her hand. "The thought of you alone and afraid—"

"I didn't want you to worry. And it was only a bin getting knocked over. It happens all the time."

Lizzie looked up at Ben, realisation dawning in her eyes. She held his hand tightly.

"Once or twice a week, sometimes three times a week. Is that a coincidence? Perhaps I should've looked out of the window? Or not."

"Let's say *not*." His jaw tightened and he asked, "Has this been happening since you moved into the flat or is it a recent occurrence?"

"Possibly..." Lizzie rolled her eyes to the ceiling as she thought. "Possibly...about a week after I moved in? Because I remember thinking the first few nights I was there, *This really is nice and quiet for the city centre. I* wasn't sleeping very well anyway. But then, not long after that, I'd hear the bin go over. Not every night, but... It was annoying, because I'd finally get to sleep, then I'd be awake again."

Ben picked up his biro and started to write again, his hand moving swiftly across the page as he recorded her words faithfully. Yet she could see that his jaw hadn't unclenched, could read in his stern expression all manner of things, and none of them were good.

"Let's move on to today. Take me through what happened when you received the card?"

"I was in reception, in my office. We'd just finished watching your press conference, in fact. Then Abigail, who works in one of the offices downstairs, turned up with an envelope. She said she'd picked it up by accident with their post. I wasn't really listening, and Jordan took the envelope and started to open it. We assumed it was a Christmas card. The envelope just had my business card stuck onto the front. Then Jordan realised that— Well, it certainly wasn't a Christmas card. He was stunned. I took it from him and looked at the front, then looked inside. It was bad enough receiving a sympathy card, like some sick joke, but the thing about shadows and the fleur-de-lys inside. I knew I had to come and see you right away."

Ben wrote the names *Jordan* and *Abigail* on another piece of paper, drawing a square around the second.

"And is there anything else you'd like to add?"

"You don't think... You don't think this is my ex, do you? He's not a violent man. We split up quite amicably, really. But still... I thought I should mention that. It is, after all, why I've ended up living in that flat."

"Okay." He nodded, the conflict of interest becoming deeper with every new word. "Tell me about him?"

"He's one of the physios at City. Erm... He's called" — Lizzie swallowed — "Neil Mellor."

The name hung in the air between them like a bad smell that wouldn't disperse.

"We... We were living together. Had been for a while. Look, you don't need all the ins and outs of it. It's because of him that my sister met Matt, and she's happy, so...I moved out in August."

And now Neil's involvement seemed suddenly very official. His name was added to the list and an even thicker box drawn around him. Ben took his mobile number from Lizzie, writing it alongside the box and underlining it twice.

"Anything else?"

"Matt and Donna hired me to do their house. I mean, that connects me, my job, doesn't it, to them? Not just because I'm her sister."

"To decorate it?"

"*Design* it." Lizzie patted Ben's knee again, grinning, and this time kept her hand there. His leg twitched for a second at her caress. "Matt wants Versailles, so I've got to come up with a colour scheme and source all the carpets, furniture, hire decorators... For some reason he also wants this skull-thing he's drawn on the bedroom ceiling, but he's the client and has to live with it, so it's up to him."

She felt so much happier talking about her work, a world that she could control, a place of swatches and colour charts, without figures in shadows or sick jokes. She wouldn't let it encroach.

"Design it, I apologise."

Ben leant forward just enough to kiss her, his lips reassuring along all this soulless steel and glass. The kiss lingered, his hand coming to rest on her arm.

Lizzie leant in to his kiss, trailing her hand up from his knee to his thigh. The muscles tensed for a moment, then released. The very fact that they were not supposed to be doing this only stoked the desire that was burning inside her, desire which had transmuted from fear.

"I'll need you to read through this and sign it." His efforts at formality were laudable but failing. She could sense that from the catch in his breath, the tightening of his hand on hers.

"I'll need my hand back, please, DCI Finneran."

"In a moment." The words were a breath into another kiss, his free hand moving to caress her face.

Lizzie reached her other arm around him and ran her hand up the satin back of his waistcoat. Their tongues darted into each other's mouths as Lizzie drew her fingertips higher up Ben's leg. He made no attempt to stop her.

He did release her hand then, but only so he could slip his arm around her waist. He had been wrong to say she was as close as she could get because now, his arm around her, he lifted her across into his lap.

Their kiss became even deeper, more passionate. Lizzie ran her hand through Ben's hair. She could feel his erection against her thigh, and it aroused her even more.

"I want you, Ben…"

"We can't—" Even as he said it though, his mouth was on her throat, his hips pressed to hers.

With one hand, Lizzie unknotted his tie and dropped it onto the floor. Sighing his name, she haphazardly unbuttoned his shirt as far as his waistcoat, then brushed at his nipples. He moaned at her touch.

"Have me, Ben," Lizzie whispered.

His back arched towards her, his hands roaming over her back as he groaned. "Don't stop—"

She unfastened his waistcoat with her free hand. It fitted him so perfectly but when it was undone, its sides fell open and she unbuttoned the shirt that was revealed. She pushed it back to expose his torso and cupped and squeezed his nipples all the more. She trailed one hand lower, following the hair that descended from his navel, and stopped at the top of his trousers.

"Shall I unfasten you? I know we should stop, but I—"

"Do it," he gasped, his fingers already on the buttons of her blouse, unfastening them to reveal the pale skin beneath. He ducked his head and pressed his lips to the swell of her breasts, breathing her in as though she were his oxygen.

She sighed his name, or as close as she could manage, and shifted slightly so that she could reach his belt. She unbuckled it quickly, then undid the top button of his trousers. But she couldn't unfasten anything more as her own body was in the way.

"I—I can't reach your zip..."

In reply Ben took his wallet from his pocket and threw it onto the table. Then he stood and lifted Lizzie with him. He laid her down along the table so her head was pillowed on her coat, her blouse spilling open on either side of her body. His gaze swept over her hungrily then he kissed her again, his hands at the button of her trousers. Lizzie lifted her hips off the table, long enough for him to pull down her trousers and knickers, and they dropped onto the floor.

Lizzie didn't feel exposed or embarrassed, lying before his gaze in such a wanton, naked state.

"Your turn next, Detective."

She pushed herself up so that she could reach his zip and tugged it, pulling his trousers and his shorts down together. Then she lay back on the table and gazed at the naked glory of the man who desired her. He knelt with one knee between hers and leant down to kiss Lizzie, one hand resting on either side of her face. The kiss went on and on, their tongues exploring, his chest just brushing her breasts, the fabric of his open shirt teasing her naked skin.

Lizzie swept her hands down to his buttocks, enjoying their strong, muscular curve. He made little thrusts, as if encouraging her caresses, knowing that she admired his toned form. His bare erection brushed the soft skin at the inside of her thigh, making Lizzie's hips stir beneath him.

Lizzie felt one of Ben's hands leave the table and heard the sound of crockery as he set the mugs down on the chair. She had a fleeting thought of the daughter he had mentioned then, as his other hand lifted too, of the wedding ring that she guessed he was about to remove.

Lizzie gently took his left hand in hers.

"Ben...you don't have to take it off."

She met his dark eyes through the lenses of the glasses that he hadn't had time to remove.

His gaze flitted down to their linked hands. Lizzie felt his fingers start to clench, saw his lips part as though he was about to speak, but he didn't. Instead he lifted her hand and kissed it in one of the most tender gestures she could imagine.

"It's part of you, Ben."

"Lizzie," he sighed in the moments before their lips met. "Ms. Lizzie Aspinall."

She caressed his erection as his mouth fell hungrily to hers. She felt the air on her shoulders as he pulled down her blouse, and his lips moved from hers to kiss her bra straps down to her arms. The tip of his tongue was hot on her skin, the familiar sounds of him tearing open the wrapper and rolling on a condom seemingly in another world. Here it was all touch and sensation, her head filled with the exotic scent of his skin, the hunger of his kisses.

She guided his hand to her tender flesh as she caressed his sheathed erection. His fingers rubbed and circled against her as his lips traced her half-revealed breasts.

We shouldn't do this.

Yet they were.

"And where were you," he teased, lifting his head to meet her gaze, "last Tuesday night?"

Ben's hand smoothed over Lizzie's bra, gentle and light before he tugged sharply, freeing her breasts. Her hand was tangling in his hair again, bringing his lips to her skin as she arched towards him.

"I was with the most handsome man I've ever seen...I didn't even know his name...and we had the most incredible sex of my entire life."

"I won't put that in your statement," Ben whispered. He shifted his hand to Lizzie's hip and eased her higher. Then, with the slightest thrust, he entered her.

Lizzie wrapped her legs around him. His movements were swift, deep, urgent.

We shouldn't, we mustn't, we can't stop.

Warmth swept through Lizzie's body. She needed this man, her Ben. She craved him deep in her bones.

His touch, his skin, his cock, his voice, his breath, his scent.

"Lizzie," Ben gasped fiercely, his grip on her hips holding her tightly. He pressed his body down to hers as he filled her, making her his. Anyone could walk through that door at any moment, so why did the thought of it make her even warmer, her fingers tangling in his dark hair as she urged him still deeper?

Ben gripped the table edge, and Lizzie covered his hand with hers. She could feel his ring on her skin, but it only made him feel closer to her. The two of them had come from a sad region of grey to connect with such intense passion, to be drawn together by a thread, a ribbon.

And he would keep her safe. She believed it as she never had of anyone else, believed that no matter what enemies were out there, her lover would be at her side.

She didn't want it to end, but he was taking her higher and higher, his own impassioned moans signalling that he too was nearing his peak of pleasure. And it wouldn't end. Beyond this room there was a whole city, a whole world where they could be together.

He cared for her, he needed her. But this wasn't allowed.

Ben muffled his groans against her neck and Lizzie closed her eyes, breathing in the scent of his hair, feeling every part of their bodies where they met. It was bewitching, two strangers with their unseen thread, bound together by fate.

Lizzie trembled as bliss poured through her, her body straining with the extraordinary force of her orgasm. A cry began to build in her throat and she deliberately put her lips to Ben's in order to stifle it as his own groans grew louder.

Perhaps he had the same thought, because he kissed her hungrily, catching his cries of pleasure against her mouth. She felt the surge of power run through his core as his climax claimed him, felt the jerk of his hips, the renewed urgency of the kisses at the moment when he would usually be making enough noise to wake the neighbours.

The beat of answered desire thrummed in Lizzie's body. She held Ben's face and tenderly kissed every inch. He sighed, Lizzie's name a tired murmur on his lips.

Her lover sank down onto her, his body a gentle pleasure atop hers. His breath was hoarse with exertion and she ran her hand down the silken back of his waistcoat, feeling it cool and smooth beneath her palm.

His sweat cooled on her body. The air was alive with his scent and her rose perfume combined. Lizzie laughed gently at the decidedly disordered state of his hair. But how on Earth could they leave this room without someone intuiting what they had been doing? Was she really going to get him trouble?

"You still need to sign your statement, Ms Aspinall." He lifted his head and smiled. "If you'd be so kind."

Chapter Eleven

Enlarged photographs of the ribbon, taken in the forensics lab, were laid on the desk in front of Lizzie. The sounds of the police station echoed outside the small office. Purposeful footsteps, ringing phones, a siren as a police car pulled away from the car park. Lizzie had been given a bolthole at the station, afforded special privilege as DCI Finneran's expert witness.

There had been two last people to contact.

And neither of them had seen hide nor hair of such a ribbon.

She stared at the tired, forgotten spider plant that was dying slowly on the windowsill. That was it. That was the limit of what she could do. And it wasn't enough.

Lizzie needed air. She sent Ben a text, not wanting to interrupt him in the incident room.

I'm all out of contacts and none of them have seen the ribbon. I'm so sorry. Popping outside for a mo' – I need fresh air. L xxx

She was swiped through a succession of security doors by police who each checked the temporary badge she wore on a lanyard. Once she was out through the front doors, she closed her eyes and drank in the cold December air.

There were some uniformed and non-uniformed officers smoking at a regulation distance from the building and Lizzie noticed a tall young woman with glossy, dark brown hair huddled into a parka. She was vaping, with elaborate movements of her wrist, the worn *Rainbow* mug that Lizzie had drunk from earlier in her hand.

It couldn't be. But Lizzie realised that it must be, because there was something oddly familiar about her. Not just from the photo that she had accidentally seen on Ben's phone, but for the very fact that there was something rather Ben-like about her.

Lizzie was standing only metres from Ben's daughter.

Lizzie watched her, wondering if she should approach. It should be up to Ben to introduce them, but Lizzie couldn't help it. The girl didn't seem to notice her to start with, but eventually gave her an intrigued side-eye stare.

Lizzie smiled and took a step towards her.

"Sorry, I didn't know if I should say hello or not. But are you Ben Finneran's daughter, by any chance?"

If she's not, I'll feel very silly.

"I might be," she replied with just a hint of amused suspicion. "Depending on who might be asking."

"This is a bit awkward, isn't it?" Lizzie grinned. "I'm Lizzie. Your father and I are — friends."

"Are you —" The young woman's face brightened with a knowing smile. "You're the lady with the pocket?"

"The pocket?"

"You left a little something in dad's jacket?"

Lizzie knew her face was turning crimson. She sputtered with laughter.

"Sorry about that! Imagine seeing my undies before you'd even seen my face!"

"That man's like granite when you're trying to get something out of him. He wasn't giving up your name for anything!" She took a drink from the steaming mug and stamped her booted feet against the cold. Then she slipped the electronic cigarette into her pocket and held out her hand. "Hello, Lizzie, I'm Sam!"

"Hello, Sam." Lizzie pulled her hand out of her coat pocket, careful not to trail anything with it, and took Sam's hand. Poor Ben, on the spot because his nameless lover had hidden her knickers in his pocket. Lizzie tugged at the card on her lanyard. "I'm just — I've been helping with something. I'm not a copper."

"Yeah, me neither, if you hadn't already guessed. I'm waiting for a mate who works here, so I blagged a brew from Dad." She lifted the mug. "You've made a really serious copper into a really smiley bloke, Lizzie with the undies, so thank you."

"I have? Well, he's made me very happy too." Was that too much to say to the girl? Lizzie scuffed her foot over the ground. She noticed a rucksack at Sam's feet, a textbook just visible. "So you're twenty, then, your dad said. Are you a student?"

"Chemistry," Sam informed her. "A proper subject, as Dad would say."

In a stage whisper, Lizzie said, "Don't tell him I did History of Art!"

"Too late!" Ben told them from where he stood just behind the women. "This huddle looks like trouble."

Lizzie turned to him. "Sam tells me she studies Chemistry." As if he didn't know. What sort of a thing was that to say? But would *Your daughter has already mentioned my undies* be any better?

"And Lizzie told me her name was Lizzie." Sam grinned.

"Ms Aspinall," Ben replied, "is assisting with an investigation, Samantha, so we'll have a bit less cheek."

"I did what I could. I'm not very good at playing detective."

"It was lovely to meet you, *Ms Aspinall*." Sam looked at her phone and planted a kiss on her father's cheek before she pressed the cup into his hand. "See you later, I'm meeting someone."

Sam pushed open the gleaming glass door and disappeared into the building, leaving Ben and Lizzie alone. Dapper, professional and *DCI Finneran* once more, Ben slipped his free hand into his pocket and asked Lizzie, "No joy?"

"None, I'm afraid. I'm so sorry." Her hand dangled loose at her side. She screwed her eyes up and peered at the colourless sky. "So perhaps it has been in someone's sewing basket for years after all."

"It was a long shot." He let his hand brush her shoulder for a second. "I'm going to be here until late. Do you want to hang around? You're welcome to if you don't want to shoot off on your own."

"I wouldn't want to get under your feet." But Lizzie didn't want to leave. She felt safe here. "I could have another think about the ribbon, maybe? Try some museum curators I know. I just can't get over the fact that I recognise it. How come I can, and yet all those dealers, and all those experts you've spoken to, don't?"

"Look, don't think I'm being pushy, and I'm pretty bloody sure that you can look after yourself—" Ben ruffled his hand through his hair and dropped his voice. "Tonight. Will you be all right on you own or—"

He let the offer hang between them, the decision Lizzie's to make.

Lizzie whispered her reply, all too aware that the denizens of Smokers' Corner found their conversation interesting, even if they were too far away to hear. "Of course you can. Stay at mine tonight, if that's what you're asking."

"Thank you." Ben smiled, affection shining in his eyes. "And if you *do* want to wait here until I'm done, we can grab some takeaway on the way out?"

"That sounds like a plan."

"I'll put Sam to work, she can pick up my toothbrush." He grinned. "Did you know I was in a hotel?"

Lizzie dimpled at him. "I had no idea."

Chapter Twelve

"So the black BMW wasn't yours, then?"

"Do I *look* like I'd drive a Beamer?" Ben opened the rear door of a deep blue Audi and slung in the bag Sam had packed for him. Then, a gentleman as ever, he opened the passenger door for Lizzie.

She climbed in and waited for him to get into the driver's seat.

"Well, my sister drives a convertible BMW, so I can't really comment! But seeing as you don't have hair extensions or a St Tropez spray-tan, then—no, you don't look like the sort of person to drive a BMW."

Ben gave a comical grimace as he fired up the engine. "Whoops."

Lizzie laughed, resting her arm on the car door. The clock on the dash showed it was just after half-past nine.

"What do you fancy for dinner, then?" It was such a pedestrian thing to ask the man who had once been her nameless lover. Then again, she had only recently seen him drink out of a mug that had *Dad, You Are Epic* printed on it.

"I know I said a takeaway" — he hit a button on the steering wheel a second too late to stop George Harrison's voice from thundering from the speakers to almost deafen them both — "but depending on what you've got in, I could knock us something together."

"Really? That would be lovely. There's pasta in the cupboard and God knows what in the fridge. I keep buying too much because I haven't got used to — well."

Lizzie stared out of the window and only found herself seeing her own reflection.

* * * *

"I knew you'd live somewhere plush," Ben decided as he stood in the entrance hall of Lizzie's flat, his bag over his shoulder and a suit bag in his hand. "But I didn't think it'd be a castle."

"You have to be prepared for a distinct shift in styles from room to room! This is supposed to be Mediaeval, sort of baronial."

They passed through the jewel-coloured light cast by the stained-glass panels in the ceiling, lit at night by spotlights.

Lizzie shook with silent laughter when she saw how wide Ben's mouth had dropped open. "Some of the footballers are really into it. Do you like my sword?"

Over a large, antique table was a shield with a sword tucked behind it. A panel in the shield's coat of arms doubled as a mirror. The hallway itself was so big that it had room for a wooden throne, upholstered with velvet and tasselled cushions.

"Don't worry, the living area is more minimal!"

"It's showy but…" Ben sank decadently down to sit on the throne and pouted. "Do I look regal?"

"Yes, my liege." Lizzie grinned at him and curtseyed.

"Come on, gorgeous!" He stood again and patted her bottom. "Show me to the kitchen!"

Lizzie pushed open one of the large oak doors leading off the hallway to reveal an open-plan living area that had been teleported from Copenhagen in the 1950s. Everything just so, nothing cluttered, all the woods and the fabrics and the paint and wallpaper chiming together to hit just the right note, the mid-century design cool and inviting.

"This looks a bit more comfy." Ben put down his bag and draped the suit he carried over a chair. "Now, how hungry are you, because I'm thinking a *massive* pile of food?"

Lizzie took him over to the kitchen area, which was separated from the lounge and the dining table by a breakfast bar.

"Go on, then. It's surprising how hungry ribbon-hunting can make a girl." She opened the door of the huge fridge and pulled out a bottle of wine. "Drink?"

Ben peered over Lizzie's shoulder into the fridge, clearly looking for *something* before he said, "I'd love one."

"I'm sure you're manly enough to drink rosé without it impinging on your masculinity. Anyway, Chef Finneran, the fridge is all yours."

"I am *that* manly." Ben pecked a kiss to her cheek. Then he began to shed layers, losing his coat, jacket and waistcoat one after the other. Next went his tie until, finally, he decided, "Make yourself comfy, Ms Aspinall, and leave the hard work to me."

"Do you mind if I dress for dinner?"

"Please do." Ben slid his glasses onto his nose. "Does that mean I have to put my tie on again?"

Lizzie ran her finger from his belt buckle, up the crisp white cotton of his shirt, over the exposed skin at his neck, and danced her fingertips across his jaw.

"Not at all. You're fine just as you are. But go on, indulge me."

"I fully," he kissed her hand, "intend to."

"I won't be long." Lizzie winked and took a mouthful of her wine. Leaving Ben busy in the kitchen, she went off to change.

Ten minutes later, Lizzie returned to the smell of something delicious in the kitchen.

"Chef Finneran's been busy!" She clicked across the wooden floor to the kitchen in a pair of kitten heels, and leant against the worktop. He turned from the pan he was stirring and his eyes popped wide open as he swept his gaze over the shimmering green silk dress that Lizzie was wearing. She saw the smile in his eyes before it reached his lips and he gave a very appreciative nod.

"Chef Finneran's now cursing his garlicky hands! You look beautiful. Well, you always do, but you look all vintage and beautiful."

Lizzie grinned and picked up her glass of wine.

"It's nice to match the decor. It's just as well this part of the flat isn't Mediaeval, or I'd be stood here in a wimple."

"And me in shining armour?"

Lizzie caught her arm around his waist and pressed her lips to his neck.

"*Always*. Thank you for rescuing me earlier, by the way. And thank you for cooking me dinner."

"I should warn you, it's hard to keep me out of the kitchen. I learned pretty fast when I had a little girl to look after." He kissed her hair. "Why don't you choose some music for us while we eat?"

Lizzie wandered off to the sitting room area and fiddled with the unnecessarily complicated sound system. Finally, she convinced it to play some lounge music, which filled the mid-century room with mid-century music.

"I hope you like Frank Sinatra and his pals."

"Perfect." Ben went back to the stove, one bare foot tapping. "You actually had pine nuts, which is unheard of, so you now have pesto! I know you're northern, but at least give it a try."

"And you're a cheeky southern git!" She came back into the kitchen and stuck her finger into the bowl of pesto. Ben was watching her with ill-suppressed eagerness as she brought it to her mouth. "Mmmm... Very good, Chef Finneran, very good indeed."

He beamed and told her, "And it'll be better than the meal we *didn't* have last week, I promise."

"I had this dress on, you know. It's reproached me every day from the wardrobe, so I *had* to wear it this evening for you."

"I had this suit on," Ben admitted. "So it was meant to be."

Lizzie kissed him, but broke away just before it could become heated.

"Shall I lay the table?"

"Your house, your rules!"

"I think we'd be more comfy on the sofa, though, don't you?"

"If that's what my lady wants," Ben replied happily, occupied with the cooking once more.

Chapter Thirteen

Lizzie put her empty bowl on the coffee table and stretched her arms above her head.

"That, Chef Finneran, was delicious. You can cook for me again."

She draped her arm around Ben's shoulder and snuggled into him. He cuddled against her, his hand raising to his mouth to stifle a deep yawn.

"I haven't had a chance to cook a special meal for a while, Liz. Thanks for letting me loose in your kitchen."

"Poor old Ben. You need a good kip. I should warn you, though, I have an utterly ridiculous bedroom."

"Are you going to trade me in for a younger model if the best I can do tonight is fall asleep in your arms?" He yawned again, nuzzling her hair.

"After what we got up to in the interview room earlier? No way. Come on, let's get you to bed."

Ben rose to his feet and stooped to lift Lizzie into his arms. He kissed her and whispered, "By the way, I have no idea where I'm going."

"Leave 1950s Denmark, go back into the Mediaeval castle, turn left, and you'll find yourself in a *fin de siècle* bordello. You can't miss it."

"Bloody hell, what did I do to deserve you?" The next kiss was deeper, more lingering. "A bordello and *those* dimples... I can see I'll have to convince you to invite me back!"

Following Lizzie's directions, Ben pushed open the bedroom door. "Lights, Ms A?"

"Promise not to laugh?"

"I swear it."

Lizzie stretched out her leg and turned on the light switch with her bare toe.

Red, gold. Cherubs. Cushions. An enormous bed with an elaborate gold frame and a mountain of pillows. A dressing table fit for the star of the Moulin Rouge. Swathes of dark crimson. Crystal beads hanging from the chandelier. Velvet, satin. Posters advertising *Le Chat Noir, Folies Bergère, Moët et Chandon* covering the walls where the velvet damask couldn't reach.

"I do wonder if it's a little...overwhelming."

"Stop putting yourself down. That ex of yours isn't here and I'm not going to put up with it, Ms Aspinall." He laid her gently atop the bedcovers. "Now get into that bed and tell me why this flat hasn't got a Christmas tree?"

"Christmas! I can't even think about Christmas yet. I'll just stay here, I think. Watch *Raiders of the Lost Ark* and drink Bailey's until I pass out. Which will be preferable to visiting my parents, where Donna and Matt will coo over each other and my mother will berate me for not having a hubby of my own."

Lizzie stared across at one of the gaudy posters on the wall. She felt awkward for having told Ben that. He didn't seem to notice though, too busy undressing with that casual confidence of his. This time she knew it wasn't a seduction, but a man at the end of a long day who was looking forward to tumbling into bed with the woman he— Well, they thought very fondly of each other.

"You could come to Sam's place if you like." His tone was so carefree, as though this was a perfectly everyday suggestion. "I'm doing the works for us and her mystery girlfriend."

"Ben! That's so sweet of you. But..." Lizzie sat up and reached for the zip at the back of her dress. "But I can't encroach on you and your daughter. She barely knows me, other than as 'that woman with the undies'. Christmas is family time and —"

"And?" Down to his boxers, he crossed to the bed and took hold of the zip for her. "The offer isn't going anywhere and there'll be plenty of food. At least think about it?"

"Why are you so bloody lovely, Ben?" She wriggled her shoulders as he drew down the zip. He laughed bashfully and kissed her shoulder, bringing the dress down. "Hang on. I have a little surprise for you."

Lizzie pushed herself up onto her knees, took the hem of her dress and lifted it over her head. She heard Ben's reaction before she saw it.

"Can we pretend I didn't say I was tired?"

Lizzie, in her sheer bra and French knickers, gave her lover a kiss.

"You *are* tired, and we'll have lots of other nights together when you're *not* tired and I'll wear them for you." She draped the dress over the headboard and wriggled down under the duvet. She unfastened her bra and hung it over the bedpost, but decided to keep her knickers on, just as Ben had kept his shorts on. As soon as she was settled, Ben slipped beneath the covers beside her. Without a pause, he snuggled Lizzie, his arm protective around her waist.

"Goodnight, my darling detective." Lizzie kissed him on the lips and, listening to the steady rise and fall of his breathing, drifted off to sleep.

But after floating through the dark night, through dreams of glass and chrome, lilies and ribbon, Lizzie awoke. She reached for Ben, but he wasn't there. A node of panic began to grow inside her. Then she noticed light through the curtain. Not daylight, but the glare of streetlights from outside.

She rolled over in the bed and saw Ben stood by the window, the curtain pulled slightly aside. He was looking down into the alleyway, his face as stern and still as if it was hewn from granite.

Lizzie whispered his name. Her voice sounded unnaturally loud in the otherwise silent room.

"Throw me my clothes," Ben whispered urgently, not glancing round. "I think there's someone out there."

Lizzie shivered. She put one arm across her naked breasts and crept out of the bed. She pulled on her dressing gown and tied the belt. Some of Ben's clothes were on the armchair by the window, but there were the others he had discarded as he had gone into the kitchen. Without saying a word, Lizzie hurried in bare feet over the cold floor to fetch them.

By the time she came back, Ben was dressed again in his trousers and shirt. She laid the remainder of his clothes on the bed.

"For God's sake, Ben, be careful! You can't go out there by yourself."

"I'm not going to, hopefully. I'm going to phone —" He picked up his socks when, from somewhere in the street, a police siren sounded, blue lights flashing as the car flew past the building on its way to who knew where. From the alleyway came the sound of someone moving, and Ben stepped his bare feet into his shoes and told Lizzie even as he headed for the door, "He's taking off, call 999!"

"Ben, you can't —" But she sensed that there was no arguing with him. She picked up her mobile from the dressing table, where she'd left it on, set as an alarm clock, and rang the emergency number.

Ben had already left the bedroom by the time the operator answered, the sound of his running footsteps and the slamming apartment door signalling his departure in pursuit of the unknown prowler.

After leaving a hurried, whispered report, Lizzie waited in the darkness, alone and afraid.

A few minutes went by and Lizzie heard the approach of a car. Blue lights shone behind her windows, and she heard car doors slam and urgent whispers. Ben was down there.

Is he all right?

She desperately wanted to peer around the curtains, but only that afternoon in the interview room, Ben had warned her not to.

And how on earth was Ben going to explain himself? She had told the operator that her friend was staying over, without giving his name or his profession, but wouldn't someone want to know exactly who her friend was, in case it was material to the investigation?

More time passed and the car doors closed again, an engine humming for a moment before the unseen vehicle drove away. Then the intercom rang.

Lizzie went into the hallway. The decor seemed even more ridiculous now. Perhaps she should take down the sword and the shield and actually use them against whoever had been prowling around out there?

She essayed a deep voice, and said, "Hello?"

"Ms Aspinall, it's Arthur from the front desk. I've DCI Finneran here." His voice was professional, not betraying any of the interest he must surely have in all this coming and going. "He left in a hurry without his key. Should I send him up?"

"Yes, Arthur. Thanks. Night-night."

"G'night." There was a click and she knew that Ben would be at the door in two minutes or less.

Lizzie hovered by the door to let Ben in, her eye to the spyhole set in a *trompe l'oeil* arrow-slit. When he appeared within the spyhole's range, she noticed him dragging his feet, as if he was exhausted. But, wondering who else could be out there, she waited until he was right in front of the door before she slipped back its locks and let him in.

"Disappeared!" Ben exclaimed the word as soon as the door opened. "I don't understand how he was so damned fast."

"Had they gone by the time you got downstairs?" Lizzie closed the door behind him and checked twice that she'd secured it properly. "Do you want a cup of tea to warm you up? You look freezing."

"I had him in sight for a minute or more, he went over a wall and when I followed, not a bloody sign. Didn't hear a car..." He pressed his back to the door, his head hanging down until his chin touched his chest.

"If that battenburg hadn't gone past, he wouldn't have taken off and we'd have got him!"

"Oh, what? I just don't understand how someone could stalk me. Damn it. I should never have agreed to those 'at home' magazine features. Maybe someone thinks a celebrity actually lives here! Could that be it? And they think they can get to them through me, and that's why they sent me that creepy card?"

"I need to get these shoes off…"

"You get back to bed, I'll bring through some tea." Lizzie brushed his hair back from where it had tumbled into his face, and kissed his forehead.

She put lights on as she went into the kitchen, then wondered at the wisdom of it. But should a prowler force her to stumble about in the dark? Lizzie spooned some loose tea leaves into a pot and filled it with water from the boiling tap, then loaded up a tray and took it to the bedroom.

Ben was back beneath the covers, his jaw set, and she could see the faint movement where his teeth were worrying at his lip. He greeted her with a smile though, one hand raking back through his hair when he said, "He's getting careless."

"How?"

Lizzie drew a plush velvet stool to the side of the bed and set the tea tray on it, pouring two mugs of tea. Then she climbed back into the bed, still wrapped in her satin dressing gown, and put a plate of chocolate digestives on the duvet between them.

"Because this so-called *prowler* isn't very good at it." He caught his lip with teeth again, brow furrowed in thought. "He sent that card. He tells you he's in the shadows, but he makes so much noise that he can't *stay* in the shadows."

"He wants attention?"

"Not after ten ye—" He clenched his jaw, too late to catch the words.

"Ten years? Ben, what are you saying? What's going on?" Lizzie looked down at the surface of her tea. Something stirred. Where had she heard that before, only recently? Ten years ago. *Similar cases ten years ago in London.* "The stalker and the poisoner. They're one and the same. Aren't they?"

"I can't discuss these cases with you, I'm already—" He blinked, watching her through eyes that flashed with years of remembered hurt. "I need to talk to the task force on your brother-in-law's stalking case."

"Ben, I need to know what's going on. There's been a prowler outside my bedroom window, and then I got that horrible card. Do you have any idea how terrified I was when I received that?"

"I know," Ben whispered, dropping his gaze to the surface of his tea.

Lizzie closed her hand over Ben's.

"Darling, what happened?"

"It was years ago…" He looked at her again. "I got a card from him, and then he stopped. I let myself think that he was done, dead, locked up, *something*…"

"And he's not finished. He's back?"

"There's something different, I just can't see it yet." With great care, he set the mug down on the table beside the bed. Then Ben turned back to look at Lizzie, his hand stealing up to her face. "Are we more than room 423?"

"We're not nameless anymore, we're not James and Louisa, are we?" Lizzie leant her face into his hand. "You're my dear old Ben, and I—wouldn't be without you."

"He sent a card to me when Holly died." There was nothing remarkable about the confession, but in its simplicity hid the intricate cruelty of this figure in the shadows. "I shouldn't tell you any of this, should I?"

"I would rather know the truth, Ben."

"The picture on the card was lilies wrapped in black ribbon, something you'd get from Sainsburys, and in it he wrote that message. *I'm in every shadow*." He pinched the bridge of his nose. "This time around, he's started sending *actual* lilies, Liz. A day after a victim dies, he sends lilies to the bar where he spiked them, wrapped in the ribbon I brought to you. That's new, he never did that in London, but it's him. Before I was called up here, he sent a bunch to the station in London addressed to me. It's a game to him."

"That's—that's utterly macabre. Lilies? I can't imagine what must go through someone's head to make them— And to send a card like that, when your wife passed away? Oh, Ben, what an awful thing to have happened to you."

Ben fell silent and settled his head on Lizzie's shoulder. He picked up one of the biscuits and held it out to her.

"I'm not sure I'm hungry." But Lizzie took the biscuit from him anyway, because a chocolate digestive was a reminder of the normal world where almost everyone else lived. "How did he know your wife had died? Was he stalking *you*?"

"It was in the press…"

"A funeral announcement in the paper? I'm sorry. That sounds so blunt. I don't mean it to."

"Holly was killed on duty." He laughed, the sound bitter and mirthless. "No, she wasn't. She was killed days later— I'm making no sense, am I?"

"Not...not really." Lizzie pressed his hand. "Was she in the police too?"

He nodded. "We went to school together, went into the force together, did *everything* together. She pulled a drunk driver over, totally routine thing, and...and he panicked. Floored the gas..."

Ben fell silent, his breath suddenly far quicker, sadness crumpling his face despite his best efforts to control it. "They said she was brain dead, Liz, but I wasn't letting her go that easily."

Lizzie swallowed. "I don't blame you. I wouldn't have either. Not if I loved them."

"So for weeks me and Sam told each other that Hol was going to wake up, but she wasn't, was she? And he was dosing people with antifreeze and I was trying to hold it all together for my little girl." Ben wiped his hand over his eyes. "Holly got pneumonia. You saw the press conference, you heard that bastard ask about Susan Burns?"

"Yes. The one who was..." Lizzie couldn't say it. *Pregnant.* "Yes, I remember his question."

"Holly couldn't fight the pneumonia and we lost her, me and my little girl. About a week after she died the card arrived and that same day" — he took a deep breath — "I got a tip-off from a bar, someone acting suspiciously and I didn't — We were *always* getting tip-offs and every single one was a waste of time. And I didn't go that night, I told myself tomorrow would do and —"

Ben closed his eyes, clearly fighting the swelling tide of emotion. "That was the night he killed Susan Burns. She was the pregnant girl and she was drinking soft drinks and because of *me*, because I looked at the tip-off and thought, *another bloody glory seeker*, a woman and her unborn child died. And I'm so bloody ashamed, Lizzie."

Lizzie moved her mug and the plate of biscuits onto the tray. Then she held Ben tightly, running her fingers tenderly through his hair.

"No, you're not allowed to feel ashamed, not for that. There's only one person to blame for that woman's death, and that's the shit who's poisoning people. Not you! And what did you do that night, instead of go to that bar? I bet you tucked Sam up in bed and read her a story, didn't you? You weren't the copper, you were Dad. And you should be proud of yourself for that. Not ashamed, Ben. I won't let you feel ashamed for that, any of it."

"I couldn't have left Sam that night, not after the card…" He clung to her tightly, admitting, "I always wondered, though. Was *he* behind that tip off?"

"Maybe. And maybe, if was him, and if you *had* gone, it might've been too late anyway. He only did it to goad you, and stand about in an alleyway and watch you all rush about. I'm sure he was there today. Watching. Waiting. That's why I stayed inside. He was *there*."

"And every single day of these ten years, I've thought about those people he killed." He lifted his head to look at her, dark eyes wet with tears. "And *something's* different. Ribbons and flowers, that's not how his mind worked, it's too fussy. Something's changed, and it's going to be what trips him up."

Lizzie dabbed away his tears with her satin sleeve.

"Then you'll find him, won't you? It won't be long now. And no one else will be hurt by him ever again."

"I need to talk to the guys who're dealing with your brother-in-law." He blinked at the touch of her sleeve.

"But I'm so bloody sorry if I brought him to you, Lizzie."

"Because of the ribbon? But I've seen it somewhere before. I have a horrible feeling…" Lizzie lay back on the pillows. She felt so tired. "I have a horrible feeling that you haven't brought him to me. That he's been here all along."

Ben sighed, his head still resting on her shoulder. "Before that night— I've never been with anyone but Holly, Liz."

"You spent ten years without anyone loving you?"

"I was too busy being a mum *and* dad." She felt a smile twitch at his mouth. "I had to learn pretty bloody quickly—it's still the hardest job I've ever done."

"I'd say you did a pretty good job. But maybe now, it's time for Ben Finneran to be spoilt. Don't you think? And I'm so glad we saw each other across the street. I'm so glad I came to you."

"I didn't even think about it. When I saw you, I *knew*."

Lizzie smiled at him tenderly. She whispered close to his ear, "I love you."

"I waited ten years for you and I didn't even know it," Ben told her, bringing his hand up to caress her face. "I love you, Ms Lizzie Aspinall."

They kissed, slow and tired, until they finally fell asleep in each other's arms.

Chapter Fourteen

When Ben opened his eyes, the room was still dark, and for a moment, he wondered where he was and how he could be so cosy and content. Only then did he sense the warmth of Lizzie's body curled around him, her head resting on his shoulder and her hair teasing a gentle tickle to the end of his nose. Of course, he knew where he was now. He was in heaven.

He remained very still, the silence outside the window telling him that the world hadn't yet started to wake. It was his favourite time of day, a land out of time, when all the rotten blights that blotted out the sun had yet to show themselves.

Somewhere out there a poisoner was sleeping, or perhaps he too was awake. Perhaps he was snuggled with his lover, wondering at what his day might hold.

Ben forced that thought down and held her closer than ever. She had forgiven him for Susan Burns, for ignoring the tip-off that had let a woman die. Perhaps now he would forgive himself too, just as Susan's family had told him that he must.

Lizzie murmured in her sleep, a smile at the corners of her mouth. It would be the height of bad manners for a guest to wake up their host, wouldn't it, just to find out what they were dreaming?

She exhaled, her breath warm against Ben's skin. Was it wishful thinking, or did she sigh his name?

In his head, he ticked off the business of the morning. He could afford a little time, Ben decided, before he plunged headlong into a premier league footballer's stalking case and a man named Neil Mellor. Woe betide Lizzie's ex if he had taken to skulking in alleyways beneath his ex-lover's window though, because the last thing the poisoning case needed was a disgruntled former boyfriend muddying the water.

Yet somehow, Ben knew that the person beneath Lizzie's window had sent that card, had sent eight people to their deaths and a dozen others to intensive care. *Any good copper probably would knock my ex out of their enquiries first though*, Lizzie reasoned, *then gets onto the serious business of solving crime.*

It all seemed forever away, the thought of a world that contained not only Lizzie Aspinall but a stranger who would kill at random, poison people who were just enjoying a night out. How could such light and dark exist together? How could he hope to keep that shadow from her sunlight, to keep his work out of her world?

I will, was his silent promise. *I swear to you, Liz, I will.*

As if she had heard him, Lizzie started to wake up. She blinked several times and finally opened her eyes. The sparkling blue of her irises was as alluring as the Mediterranean Sea on a hot summer's day.

"Hello again," Lizzie said.

"Good morning, I think." He kissed her hair. "Back off to kip, my Parisian saucepot. It's really early."

"Is it? It's so hard to tell this time of year, though… It could be four in the morning or seven. But I don't feel tired. I'd rather cuddle for a while."

She snuggled her warm, soft body against him, planting a kiss on his shoulder.

"I love you, Ben…"

"Love you, mademoiselle." He felt her skin warm beneath his palm, felt the small band where it wasn't and for a few seconds clenched his hand. In one night Lizzie had taught him so much about forgiveness, Ben realised as he unclenched his fingers. She didn't mind that he wore a wedding ring, and Holly wouldn't mind that he had fallen in love again after ten empty years. He was luckier than he would ever have expected to be.

"*Ça va, monsieur*?" Lizzie kissed him again, taking his hand and weaving her fingers with his. "That's pretty much the limit of what I can remember from my French lessons! *Voulez-vous une baguette, Monsieur le detective*?"

"*Je suis* very, very happy." He rested his forehead to hers. "*Ma belle* Lizzie."

Lizzie caressed him, running her hand down the side of his body, over his waist, over his hip, to his thigh and back again. "When do you have to leave?"

"I can afford to lounge about for a *little* bit longer." He kissed her hair. "What about you?"

"I'm the boss. I go in when I choose. I mean, I might ring the office and crack the whip remotely, but…I'm yours for as long as you need me."

"Whip-cracking Lizzie? I like the sound of her," he teased. "I've got a pair of handcuffs if that helps?" He blinked, glad for the silly turn of the morning. "And a truncheon somewhere. And then there's the uniform, but I don't suppose you'd be too bothered about that."

In a voice that surprised him with its depth and its decidedly saucy tone, Lizzie said, "Oh, *Ben!* Grrrr... My naughty policeman! Have you discovered that I've been running a house of ill-repute in Montmartre, and you've come to close it down, but I'm trying to convince you otherwise by a cunning seduction?"

That actually shocked him into delighted silence for a few seconds. He blinked, opened his mouth to speak, then blinked again.

"Do you think this *gendarme* could be convinced by such an immoral sort of girl?"

"I most definitely think he could, especially as he's brought his truncheon into bed."

She brushed her hand over Ben's shorts, waiting for him to allow her permission to touch him, to go from conversation to cavorting.

"You're full of surprises," Ben grinned. "*Ma cherie.*"

"Would the *gendarme* like the bordello-keeper to make him happy?" Her hand swept by again, lingering a little longer.

"He wouldn't say *non*," Ben assured her.

"*Bonjour...*" Lizzie tugged down his shorts and closed her hand around his erection. She pressed her mouth to his, rolling him onto his back as she kissed him.

"*Et vous, mademoiselle.*" He slid his tongue against hers, sighing.

"You have a *très bon baguette, monsieur.*" Lizzie giggled.

"*Voulez vous* give *mon baguette votre attention*?" Ben gave her his best *slightly* suspicious copper look.

"I might just give it a little nibble…"

And Lizzie vanished from sight under the duvet, kissing her way down Ben's chest. He brushed his fingers through her hair, feeling his heartbeat quicken, and that delicious sense of anticipation that he had pushed aside for ten long years. Her kisses fell across his stomach, her tongue sliding just inside his navel and passing lower, through the dark hair that clustered there.

She made a delightful racket without even knowing she did so. Little moans in the back of her throat, sighs that sounded almost surprised, ill-suppressed snatches of giggle, and her tongue, slicking wetly over his skin. If he stopped to think about it, the very idea that this woman, younger, successful, independent and from a different world to him, would love Ben Finneran, might seem like a joke. Yet she did—she loved him enough to trail her tongue down the length of his cock, tasting and teasing, until he arched from the bed, his hips straining towards her.

Still she teased and still Ben's hand clutched at the bedsheet, the steady, harsh rhythm of his excited breaths assuring that he could draw this out for them both. He felt again the cold champagne glass she had rested on his stomach, the erotic fizz when she'd taken him in her mouth, and his erection twitched involuntarily. Lizzie met this with a surprised sigh that left Ben reeling, every sense knocked sideways by his lover's playful game.

With a groan of effort, Lizzie shoved back the heavy bedlinen. There she was, pink-cheeked and grinning.

"Would my naughty *gendarme* like to *arriv-ay*? Or…"

Lizzie wriggled out from their embrace and reached for the bedside table. She pulled open the drawer and her hand alighted on a box.

Well, this is the better sort of bordello. What else should a man expect?

She took the cellophane tab between her teeth and began to open the box of condoms.

"*Madame.*" Ben's eyelids were heavy with desire when he blinked. He smiled and murmured, "I'm looking forward to sampling the delights of *la maison.*"

He reached one arm above his head and took a loose hold of the bedframe.

"My naughty *gendarme* gets exclusive treatment at this establishment. Only special guests can romp with the *madame* in Edward VII's bed."

She tore the foil pack open with her teeth and threw it carelessly aside with a Gallic shrug. Straddling his legs, she rolled the condom onto him.

"Would you like me to keep this on?" She indicated her satin dressing gown, which had fallen open to reveal to that she had nothing on beneath but her loose, sheer French knickers.

"I would," he breathed.

"Are you ready for your *plaisir*?"

Ben tightened his hold on the bedframe with one hand, knowing how much she enjoyed his little efforts at peacockery. He tensed his muscles and settled his other palm on her thigh, savouring her rose scent. Ben caressed Lizzie's skin, locked his gaze on hers and warned, "The future of your establishment depends on its *madame.*"

She took his hand to her underwear, to nudge aside the fabric, then lowered herself just enough for the tip of his erection to tease her. She gazed down on him with a look that was at once mischievous and loving.

"Once you have had *plaisir avec madame*, you will not go to any other bordello, I promise you that."

His hips strained upwards towards her and he forced himself to keep them down, to hold himself back. He replied, "This *gendarme* has skills of his own, madame. You may find you want no other clients after enjoying our *plaisir*."

Lizzie winked at him.

"Is that so, *monsieur*?"

With deliberate slowness, Lizzie lowered herself, millimetre by millimetre, gasping silently as she did, her head tossed back, until she had taken him entirely inside her.

"Mmm…*monsieur*, you please me much already…"

Ben felt the muscles tense in her thigh and he bit his lip, knowing what was about to happen. Lizzie crossed her arms behind her neck, her loose hair tumbling into her face. Then, holding him tight inside her, she began to rise and fall upon him.

When his fingers tightened on the bedframe this time, it was entirely involuntary. He forced his eyes not to close, too enraptured by the sight of his lover's body riding against him. His hand slid from her thigh to the delicate curve of her waist and there it rested as his own hips began to move in time with her, driving her onwards.

Lizzie panted with the effort, her endearingly bad French still puffing from her mouth.

"*Monsieur*, you are *très bon*… *Mon dieu!* Your truncheon is so big, my naughty *gendarme*… Oh! Ooh!"

She brought her arms down from behind her head and trailed a hand across Ben's stomach. Then, her eyes meeting his with a grin, she stroked herself inside her knickers. Her bad French vanished, subsiding under her moans.

His own gasps of pleasure mingled with hers, and he danced his hand over her until his fingers were moving alongside Lizzie's, pleasuring her. She was as soft as the velvet beneath which they had slept, as warm as the air that had blanketed them and as outrageously beautiful as this jumbled palace of an apartment. Yet he didn't feel like a drab, middle-aged copper with her, because some of that joy, that carefully contained flamboyance, was infectious, and he was utterly enchanted.

Ben urged her fingers to move more firmly, drawing sinuous shapes over her core, his thumb teasing. In reply to her enthusiastic movements he met her with long, deep thrusts, gasping her name in a voice that was deepened with desire.

"Oh, Ben, oh, *monsieur*, oh, naughty *gendarme*...!"

He felt her orgasm, her trembles and shudders, the tightening of her core. She tried to keep upright but, sighing, she drooped down over him, her hair draped over his skin as she fell.

"Mademoiselle," he managed to gasp, "I have never known a girl like you."

Her breasts were heavy and soft where they pressed against his chest, her nipples pert and hard. He released the bedframe and brought his fingers to her hair, guiding her lips to his. He caressed his other hand around her waist once more and let it rest on her bottom, feeling the deep tremors running through her body. He would draw this out for as long as he could, but the feeling of her body on and around him, the scent of her skin, the heat of her tongue in their kiss, were combining to press him on towards his own orgasm no matter how much he tried to push it away.

Lizzie whispered, her mouth hot against Ben's ear, "Take your pleasure of me, *monsieur…*"

And that desirous whisper was too much to resist. It seemed as if every muscle in his body tensed and his fingers tightened on Lizzie's buttock. Ben's last conscious thought before pleasure claimed him was that he was making a lot of noise, then he thought of nothing but her as his body arched off the bed and flung him into the dizzying maelstrom of his ecstasy.

It seemed to go on and on, his hips moving wildly, kissing everywhere he could reach, but finally, like an ebbing tide, it was over. Ben lay beneath Lizzie, the orgasm playing itself out in gentle moans, a light sheen of perspiration beading over them.

Lizzie kissed him on his mouth.

"Did I please my naughty *gendarme*?"

"Your bordello is safe, *mademoiselle*," Ben gasped. "And I *will* be back for a second visit."

He drew in a deep breath and closed his eyes, utterly content here, safe in her arms. Perhaps, he finally accepted, they could really have a future, if she could forgive her *gendarme* the occasional late night and early call.

"My brave, dashing *gendarme*… Would you like some breakfast?"

"I would *love* some!" He blinked, a thought occurring. "Why don't you snuggle here and let me do the honours?"

Chapter Fifteen

Lizzie brought her sketchbook and folder with her to the bar. That way, it counted as work. She was meeting her sister, but she was now her client as well. Despite her initial reservations, Lizzie was looking forward to creating Versailles in Greater Manchester. She enjoyed a challenge.

She heard Donna before she saw her. Her sister was on the phone, as she so often was, chatting noisily about her next appearance on one of the innumerable chat shows that beat a path to her glittered door. The conversation seemed to be about a car that had turned up five minutes late. If that happened again, Donna furiously warned, there'd be hell to pay.

Was Donna being vacuous again, or was the stress of Matt's stalker getting to her? Lizzie didn't want to think about that, but what Ben had told her was weighing on her mind. A poisoner who stalked people, who had been repeatedly lurking outside her own window and was threatening her brother-in-law and her sister. And Donna was losing it over a car.

"Hi!" Lizzie waved as best she could with her arms full. She dropped down in the chair opposite her sister at the table. "How's things?"

"Horrible." Donna threw her phone into her bag and closed her eyes. "I've had the police at the house this morning checking up on Neil, of all people. Where was he last night, where was he the night before? Luckily he was at ours, but…*Neil*? He's like Matt's brother!"

Lizzie toyed with the cloth ties on her folder.

"They can't… They have to speak to everyone." A bottle of Pinot Grigio was already on the table. Lizzie poured herself a glass and took a mouthful before she went on. "Look, Donna, there's been a prowler outside my flat. I was worried that it might be connected to your stalker. I mean, it might be. And that's probably why they've had to talk to Neil. Exes come high up the list. Not that it would explain why he'd stalk Matt!"

Lizzie laughed nervously. Despite Ben's assurances that she had nothing to fear because he would protect her, she had walked all the way from her office to the bar with her heart in her throat. She went to take another mouthful of wine, but looked at it dubiously. She glanced around the bar at the other people who were there. Just innocuous businessmen and ladies-who-lunch. Everything normal, everything bland. She looked at her sister's glass, with a splash of wine in the bottom. She sipped.

"Oh God, he's bothering you now?" The colour drained from Donna's face despite her tan, her voice betraying her fear. "He sent us a creepy card, I passed it to the policeman this morning, but — It's horrible,

Lizzie, we've had to get this big bloke who follows us round all the time!"

She nodded towards the corner where a hulk of a man sat, unobtrusively turning the pages of a newspaper. "It's just in case anyone tries anything."

"You've got a bodyguard?" But what use was a bodyguard against poison? Lizzie leant over the table towards her sister, her voice dropping to a whisper. "What sort of card?"

"One you'd send for a funeral, and then..." She reached out for Lizzie's hand. "This copper this morning, he says, well, you know those poisonings? It looks like it's the same person. I'm scared all the time, Lizzie."

"Oh, Donna, I was sent the same thing! A *with sympathy* card. Why is this happening to us? I won't tell a lie, Donna. I'm frightened."

"The guy this morning," Donna opened her purse and peered at a card, "Finneran. He says this person has already killed people before. Why does he hate us? We play football and model clothes!"

Lizzie felt a glow inside her at the mention of Ben's name, the man she loved and who loved her. She wouldn't allow herself to give over to fear. She had Ben.

"And do interior design," Lizzie reminded her.

"He's not after you though, is he? He's fucking with you to get to me and Matt." She pulled a bewildered face. "He'd hardly pick on a curtain maker when he's got a prem player in his sights!"

"For the millionth time, I don't even make the curtains. I contract that out!" Lizzie tried to smile. But as she lifted her glass again, a memory stirred.

That first night, when she had gone to room 423. She and her sister had been at the Mezz bar. It had been crowded, and Donna had returned to their table with two identical cocktails. And Lizzie's had tasted bitter, too unpleasant to drink.

"Are you sure, Donna, that this person isn't interested in me? Lurking around outside my flat, sending me a card. And that cocktail, don't you remember? I couldn't drink it! It tasted foul." She slowly turned her glass. "Unless they thought *you'd* drink it? Or perhaps both of them were spiked and you didn't notice, and we were both okay because they hadn't put enough in, or…or… Oh, God, I don't know!"

Lizzie took her phone out of her pocket. She opened the stream of texts she had from Ben, where they told each other once every five minutes that they loved each other. She *had* to let him know about that cocktail.

"Let's talk about something happier." Donna laid a menu in front of Lizzie. "Did you ever see your mystery heartbreaker again?"

She smiled up at her sister.

"Funny old world, isn't it? Yes, I did see him again. And — oh, I have to tell you, or I'll burst! We're in love!"

"So…you're in love with a married man whose name you didn't know and who had you in tears?" She tapped the corner of Ben's card on the table. "Did you find out his name yet?"

Lizzie gestured to the card. "You already know it."

Donna's gaze dropped to read Ben's name and she asked, "*Him*?"

"Yes! And he's not married, either. What a misunderstanding *that* was! He's just, bless him, his wife died years ago, and he's too sentimental to take off the ring. He's loving, and sweet, and kind, and…noble. And I love him with all my heart."

Lizzie caught sight of her reflection in one of the mirrors that decorated the walls. She was very red, and very dimpled. And she didn't care one bit.

"And asking questions about your ex-boyfriend?" Donna raised her immaculately threaded eyebrows. "And investigating the cards *we've* received, so he's either the stalker, or he's got a massive bloody nerve! Can he *do* that? Isn't it like a doctor operating on his family?"

"It's all a bit awkward. Don't say anything. He's so professional, despite —" The interview room swam back into Lizzie's mind and she fanned herself with her drinks mat. "Did you see him on that press conference the other day, about the poisonings? He worked on the original case years back in London. He's so determined. He's not going to give the case up. If anyone can find out who's doing this to us, to the city, it's Ben."

"He let you down badly — are you sure he's telling the truth about his wife? I'm only thinking of you, Lizzie — it just seems a bit off that he's harassing your ex. He's not one of those controlling sorts, is he?"

Lizzie flung down her drinks mat and laughed. "Oh, for heaven's sake, Donna! He's not harassing anyone, he's a police detective who is investigating a serial killer. Besides, he told me about what happened to his wife, and…well, there's still news stories online about what happened. It's tragic and sad and awful. He's not lying to me, Donna. Besides, I had all that time with Neil to know what dating a right git looks like. And he's so different."

"I bet he isn't supposed to shag a witness though." It sounded so crass, put like that, so mechanical and cheap. "Shouldn't he be, I don't know, independent?"

"Shouldn't you show a bit of loyalty to your sister, and not hang about with my ex?" Lizzie poured them both some more wine. "Our relationship began before he knew I was in any way connected to all this. We can't just— I almost wonder if you don't want me to be happy."

As Lizzie said this, the piece of ribbon came into her mind. She had avoided thinking about it. Her failure to help Ben with his case, and the knowledge that she'd seen it somewhere before nagged at her. But there it was, unspooling in her thoughts, silver on black silk. Lizzie pressed her eyes tightly together to clear the image away.

"I can't just ask Matty not to see his best friend anymore, Lizzie, can I?" She tucked the card back into her purse. "Look, we sisters need to stick together. I know you're all loved up with your silver fox. How old *is* he? He's older than you by a fair bit!"

Lizzie did know his age. She'd seen it in the online reports, even though he hadn't told her himself.

"He's not quite ten years older than me. That hardly makes him a cradle-snatcher. Besides, there's a lot to be said for older men."

"So long as he treats you right and it doesn't get all tangled up with me and Matt's case," Donna shrugged and looked down at the menu. "I was going to ask if you'd come over tonight because Matt's off out with the lads after the game, but I guess you'll be cosied up with your copper."

Yes, I bloody well will.

"I don't really want to be on my own." Donna pouted. "And you don't have to see him *every* night, do you? You've only just met!"

"Okay...I'll come over." Lizzie couldn't really turn down her sister, after all, though she'd lie alone in the spare room, missing her *gendarme*. She didn't like the thought of Donna being by herself in that big house, even if she did have a contender for Mr. Universe patrolling the premises. Sisters together, they'd be, just like when they had been children in the fort they'd built under the dining table, using wooden spoons and spatulas to fight off their cousins. "In fact, I need to show you these ideas for your house. It might be easier if I visit."

"It won't hurt PC Plod to spend a night on his own. You're going way too fast as it is."

"Me, go too fast?" Lizzie laughed good-naturedly. "Exactly how long had you known Matt for before you were off to the Maldives for your wedding?"

"Matt's in the Prem," Donna reminded her. "Everyone in Manchester feels like they know him already!"

Lizzie folded her hands. She realised, too late, that she had adopted the same pose that Ben had used at the press conference.

"And *that's* why he's got a stalker."

"Sorry?" Her sister's face grew hard as granite. "Are you blaming *Matt* for the fact he's being stalked? Where the hell do you get that from?"

"I've told you before that you're not the first celebrity couple to get a stalker, and you definitely won't be the last. The more you pose about, showing off your lifestyle to anyone who'll print a photo of you, then the more you encourage it. That's just how it is. And no, it's not right that there's people out there who think it's okay to behave like that and terrify people, but this is what happens, sadly."

"So those people who got poisoned, they were asking for it? They encouraged it by having a drink, did they?" Donna shook her head, her eyes flashing with annoyance. "And maybe now you're *asking for it* by shagging a copper, sis. Have you thought of that?"

"Christ, you sound like Neil sometimes!" To avoid looking at her sister, Lizzie ran her eyes over the menu. For some reason, she fancied something French. "I'm not arguing with you, Donna. I'm just trying to — Look... We're both on edge with this stalking business, and us ragging at each other won't help, will it? We need to keep an eye out for each other."

"You're right." She nodded, a long sigh escaping her glossed lips. "And if you'd rather see your policeman, I'll be fine on my own. I've got my bouncer to trail round after me, at least."

"It's not a bother, really." Lizzie couldn't help the saucy grin that perked up her face. "The poor man could do with a night on his own to recuperate!"

"Well, there we are then. Grandad Plod can have a night with CSI and we can drink pinot and sing along to Little Mix!"

"Little who? But yes, let's spend the night in. Face packs and Cosmo, the lot! And cobblers to horrible stalkers who want us to be frightened."

Lizzie raised her glass.

"I'll whizz a car over to you at sevenish? And your stalker can spend the night wishing he was having *half* as much fun as we are!"

Chapter Sixteen

Neil Mellor was not the sort of man Ben would have pictured Lizzie with at all. In fact, he wasn't the sort of man he would've pictured if someone had said *physio* either. He wasn't so much glowing with health as *burnished* with it, his hair and skin shades of blond and brown that couldn't possibly be native to Manchester in December. In fact, Neil Mellor looked more like the professional footballers he administered to, muscular and chiselled in his T-shirt and tracksuit bottoms, an intricate tattoo inked in a sleeve down his left arm.

The trip to the Etihad had been fruitful, at least, with the players and their wives gathered to hand out wrapped gifts to local schoolchildren and here, at last, Ben could meet the *other* Aspinall girl. Donna de Luca was nothing like Lizzie, though she was every inch a WAG, and she and her husband were happy to confirm that Neil had been at their mansion in Alderley Edge all night.

'*Yeah, we was playing FIFA,*' Matt had said gravely as Donna patted his hand encouragingly. Ben had duly noted the information down before the footballer added, '*It's like football but it's a computer, yeah?*'

Thanks for the confirmation.

And now there were two crimes to consider and a whole other task force to work with. Yet he had a feeling more now than ever that the truth was right there, just out of sight, but moving on the horizon all the time. Ten years ago, the poisoner had kept his distance, had enjoyed the anonymity. Now, out of nowhere, he was showing up in person, leaving flowers, sending cards to premiership footballers.

What would have changed him, though?

What had brought him out of hiding?

The thought was still on his mind when he locked the car and headed into the station, aiming straight for the cafeteria. Crisps would help… Crisps *always* helped when a man had to think.

And just *why* was his daughter sitting in the cafeteria of a police station?

"Sam!" Ben called her name as he approached the table. "What's up?"

"Oh, Dad? Hi!" Sam raised her hand. Her eyes darted from Ben's across the room to Anj, who was approaching with a cup in each hand. "I was just—" She smiled, all teeth. "All right, how's it going?"

"I've been hanging out with footballers all morning. I'm thinking of getting a badly-spelled Japanese word tattooed on my arm." He stooped to kiss her cheek. "We hadn't arranged to meet, had we?"

"No, but…" Sam looked again towards Anj, who was hovering at Ben's elbow.

"DCI Finneran, good afternoon."

"PC Choudary, I take it one of those drinks isn't for me?"

"Dad, meet Anj. Anj, meet Dad."

Sam pushed back her chair and stood. She took a cup from Anj, put it on the table and reached for Anj's hand.

"Meet my secret girlfriend!" Sam grinned.

"It was a badly kept secret," Ben admitted with a smile. "But I was waiting for you to tell me."

"Awww, Dad, I can't keep anything from you! Bloody interfering old bill."

Anj extended her hand to Ben's. Something almost cheeky danced in her eyes. "If doesn't contravene protocol, sir?"

"You look after this girl." Ben shook Anj's hand. "You won't find a better one."

Anj's gaze fell on Sam, the cheekiness chased away. "I know."

"Anj is awesome, Dad. Although she hasn't hidden her pants in my coat pocket yet!"

"You're only young. That's a more advanced move." He took a step backwards and told them, "I'll get my crisps and leave you ladies alone. Before I *do*, though...how'd you feel about one more for Christmas?"

"Dad, who is it? That woman?"

"She does have a name, Sam."

"*Lizzie!*" Sam winked at Anj. "Of course she can come for Christmas!"

And Anj turned to Ben, the most subtle of quirks to her eyebrow. "I look forward to meeting her, sir."

"You already have," was Ben's mysterious answer before he turned and went in search of his crisps. At the counter he paused and took out his phone, tapping a message to Lizzie that said, *Sam's cool for Christmas if you fancy it. Love you xxx.* Then, crisps in hand, he headed back to the ever-more-chaotic incident room.

Before Ben could find his way to his desk, a blustery man in an old brown suit stormed up to him.

"Finneran! My office! And you can leave your bloody crisps!"

Ben knew better than to obey the second half of that command. Crisps left unattended wouldn't last five minutes, so he pushed them into his pocket and followed the DCS into his airless office.

"Close the sodding door behind you. Were you born in a barn?"

DCS Charlie Worthington paced back and forth behind his desk. He picked up a pen, threw it down, then hauled a handful of papers into his large, reddened hands.

"What the bloody hell do you think you're up to, you silly southern prat?"

"Just getting some crisps, sir."

"I'm not talking about your blasted crisps, DCI! You explain to me, *now*, why the hell you turn up in a witness statement, accompanying a lady home, eh? Got a smart answer for that, have you?"

"The same reason I was with her last night when a prowler was under her window." He gestured to the pile of papers, long since used to dealing with ulcerated members of the old guard. "That's probably in your paperwork too. She's an expert witness. We were discussing the case."

"Yes, I've got that. The 999 call." Worthington leafed through the pile with fingers like Cumberland sausages. "It came in just after one in the bloody morning, Finneran. Is that the usual time you southern jessies investigate your expert witnesses, is it? And strangely, the good lady's words were" — Worthington adopted a high-pitched whine—"*My friend's staying over, my friend has gone outside, please come quickly, I wouldn't want the prowler to hurt my friend.* Friend? That doesn't sound very impartial to me. And I'm the one who'll have the bastard CPS crawling up my arse, 'cos it's happened on my watch! If I find out you've bloody well compromised an expert witness — more like *sexpert* witness, you bloody prat—I'll grab your overactive balls and twist 'em off!"

"Is that it?"

Worthington hurled the stack of papers onto his desk.

"*Is that it?* I've got poisoners, I've got stalkers and I've still got all the other bloody snides and scallywags who populate this cocking city, then I've got Mr. Ponced-Up Southern Detective who's come up from that London, and he's rodgering my bloody witnesses! I'll give you, '*Is that bloody it*'!"

"Sorry. I'm not clear on what you want me to do?" Ben took a deep breath, well aware that he shouldn't be doing *anything* with Lizzie, let alone voyaging to make-believe Parisian bordellos. "I'll tell you one thing though. Our poisoner is Matt de Luca's stalker, and I know you're going to tell me that's bollocks, but the two cases are linked."

Worthington blinked. When he cleared his throat, it sounded like a cutlery drawer being shoved closed.

"What are you chuffing well on about, Finneran?" Worthington sat down in his chair and tipped a handful of antacid tablets into his mouth. His puce-coloured face was beginning to pale. "Sit down, Finneran, and stop buggering about. I may very well tell you it's bollocks, but I'm six months from retirement and I'm not leaving this bloody spaceship of a building with a carriage clock and an unsolved case. So go on. Explain."

Ben took a seat on the vinyl chair that had seen better days, puzzled by how, in a brand-new building, Worthington's office and all it contained seemed to have come from another era.

"So we've got this footballer who's being stalked. Death threats, all the usual sort of stuff. Now, he's had stalkers before, but this one —" He knitted his hands atop the desk. "He sent a sympathy card. Tie into that the fact that Ms. Aspinall's sister is de Luca's wife, and she's had someone prowling about outside her place. I really think we need to consider these two cases as one, sir."

Worthington turned his chair. He was in thought, his upper lip twitching as he stared out of the window.

"It's the cards that links them." Worthington was thinking aloud. "And the science boffins, what can they tell us about the cards? Just ordinary cards, sent by a bloody madman."

Ben was silent, that sense of missing *something* just there on the edge of his mind. Something was obvious, so obvious that it just didn't stand out.

Worthington spun his chair back to face Ben. He pulled a piece of paper off the pile towards him. "What's all that guff about the ribbon? Your expert... What did she say? She recognises it. Only bloody person to recognise it, but she can't remember where from. Not much of an expert, eh? But she's linked now, with de Luca's stalker." Worthington tapped his fingers on his desk. "Case I worked on, back when I was a young DC, before I had a divorce and an ulcer and flat feet. A load of burglaries. Random ones, but it always seemed like something linked them. And do you know, in the end, there was a burglary at this one house, and it turned out that was where the answer was. In that house. Just a family we'd otherwise overlook, but they had this old statue thing that turned out to be priceless, and there'd been a feud, years before, and someone hated someone else enough to burgle all those other people to put us off the scent. You know, like Agatha Christie, and *The ABC Murders*. We called 'em *The ABC Burglaries*! So that's where I'd start. Ignore all the random people in the pubs and the bars and all that. It's that family you want looking at. Those two girls. And by looking, I don't mean—have you seen those photos of that Donna girl in the Lycra? She's got an arse better than Kylie's! Find out, Finneran. Who'd hate those two girls enough to do all this."

"I'm already on it, boss," Ben told him with an enthusiastic nod. "One ex down, a list as long as your arm for Donna de Luca to go at. Every other player in the premiership and the championship. I'll speak to Ms. Aspinall again too, see if there's anyone in her past worth looking at. The thing that's throwing me on all this though… We *think* it's our man from ten years back because he's got the cards right, so how does that tie to these girls, and—The lilies don't fit, do they?" Ben tapped one finger thoughtfully on the desk. "Why would he start leaving flowers? We've got nothing, supermarket flowers tied with a bit of ribbon left somewhere in the vicinity of the bars. Nothing on CCTV worth anything. I'm wondering if our man got banged up and *told* someone? So they've taken on the job for him, but added the flowers to make it their own?"

"Flowers are a bit poncy." Worthington tapped a biro against his teeth. He swung his chair idly from side to side, then looked up at Ben. "Maybe they're an undertaker. There!"

"Drumming up trade, sir?"

Worthington sprang out of his chair, a vestige of that young DC awake in him once more.

"That's it! That's bloody well it! I've only gone and cracked the case! You look through those girls' backgrounds, and if you find an undertaker in there somewhere, then you've got your man!"

"I'll be sure to follow every lead," Ben replied diplomatically. "Lycra, undertakers, the lot."

"You bloody well do that, Finneran! Oh, bloody hell, I need a drink. Now sod off, you southern git, and eat your crisps. You've earned them."

Chapter Seventeen

Lizzie went to the intercom as soon as it buzzed. She stared at it in surprise when she realised that it wasn't the voice of a chauffeur that she heard, but that of her own sister.

"Hellooooo! Matt's got the whole squad up at ours getting lashed to celebrate their win this afternoon, so I've come to you instead!"

"Okay, I'll buzz you in."

Lizzie couldn't blame Donna for avoiding that. She wondered if she should suggest they go out for dinner, but the thought of that figure in the shadows made her nauseous. A couple of minutes later there was a knock at her door, heralding the arrival of Donna and, Lizzie realised as she opened the door, her minder from earlier.

"Lizzie, meet Dutch. He's going to sit in the corner and make sure we don't get murdered!"

What exactly do you say to a bodyguard?

"Hello, Dutch. Fancy a brew?"

"Yeah, can do, four sugars, no milk?" He gave her a thumbs up. "Cheers!"

"Dutch just needs your Wi-Fi password and he can entertain himself," Donna assured her as she sashayed through into the sitting room.

"It's *valance*. All lowercase." Just to be on the safe side, Lizzie spelled it aloud as she went into the kitchen. *Tea for the bodyguard, wine for us girls.*

"Matt insisted that I bring him, since he's got the City first eleven and half the backroom boys to keep him safe," Donna announced, following Lizzie into the kitchen. "No copper tonight?"

"Ben's at his hotel tonight, if he gets the chance to get home. He said he's got some leads to follow up and might be at the station till the wee hours. He sounded almost excited. Do you think they're closing in on...on whoever it is?"

"He wasn't bad-looking for an old timer!" Her sister's elbow nudged Lizzie in the back. "Do you have to give him a few hours notice if you're in a naughty mood? Pop a pill, constable, and get your bus pass. You've pulled!"

"Donna!" Lizzie laughed. "He definitely does not need any help in that department." She lowered her voice as she passed Donna a glass of wine. "In fact—don't tell anyone this—he's amazing in bed."

"Go on. Tell your little sis!"

"Oh, Donna... No!" Lizzie rummaged in a cupboard for some crisps and poured them into a bowl. She wondered if, several streets away, Ben was devouring a crisp sandwich. "Talking of bed, you do know what Matt plans to put on your bedroom ceiling?"

"Noooo," she drew out the word, long and low. "On the *ceiling*? Oh no, not a mirror?"

"That would be preferable. He wants his tattoo!" Lizzie hugged herself, laughing. "When he told me, all I could think of was you lying there with him above you, and that thing just...*there* overhead!"

"That's not happening. He's getting his velvet and his cherubs. He's not getting that."

"I did tell him it doesn't really go with the Versailles theme!"

"Our painting's done, you should *see* it. We look like proper royals!" Donna beamed. "I'm wearing my red Versace, Matt's in pure white!"

"Which royals would that be?" Lizzie tried very hard to keep her sarcasm at bay, but she wasn't sure she had succeeded.

"There's no need to be catty." Donna pouted. "Mrs. Plod!"

"He's not a *plod*, Donna. He's—he's so driven and determined." Lizzie wandered through into the lounge and dropped onto the sofa where only the evening before she and Ben had sat together. In the corner Dutch was, as Donna had promised, entertaining himself with an iPad and a pair of very serious-looking headphones.

"He watches sport *all night*," Donna confided. "Can you believe he's gay? I couldn't. He's super butch. Butch Dutch!"

Lizzie raised her eyebrows. "You're surprised he's gay?"

"I'm in football, Liz. You don't meet many gay lads."

Lizzie grinned to herself, recalling Jordan's favourite anecdote about a certain premiership footballer he had met in a sauna just off Canal Street. But she decided not to repeat it.

"You never know, that's all I'm saying. Do you want to watch anything on telly? I found loads of amazing old *Poirot* episodes. Shall we watch them?" Lizzie knew what the answer would be before she'd even asked and prepared herself to watch a rom-com.

Donna made a face and shrugged. "If you want. Ooh, you know what I watched at Nikki's? *Bridesmaids*. Have you seen it?"

"No, I haven't. What's that about, other than... weddings?"

"It's *hilare*! We'll watch it, yeah?"

"Well, if you like. But my memory of your wedding reception involves me crying in the loos. Is there anyone who does *that* in this film?"

"It's *not about you*! God, Liz, there are other people in the world, you know!" She set her jaw and shook her head. "I'm being stalked, Lizzie, I just want to laugh!"

"All right, we'll watch it then."

Lizzie turned on the slim, sleek television and navigated her way to *Bridesmaids*. As the opening credits began, she slipped back to the kitchen to fetch another bottle of wine. Donna was already hooting with laughter, but all Lizzie could think of was her sister's wedding reception, where she had decided, then and there, to leave Neil.

Chapter Eighteen

"You're in the Edwardian bedroom, Donna. I suppose Dutch could kip on the throne in the hallway. What does he actually do at night? Does he ever sleep?"

"Oh. Dutch is evening security. He just did lunchtime so I wasn't on my own today." Donna, who had been welded to her phone all night, glanced at the screen and scowled. "Oh God, Matt's hammered. Listen to this! *Don Don, proper sick, feel like shit.* Not even a kiss!"

"Sure you'd want to be kissed by someone who feels sick? Even virtually?" Lizzie stretched her arms and yawned. She would have an epic headache tomorrow, she knew. Too much wine, too much Donna. "That's lads-out-on-the-lash, though. I got so fed up of Neil rolling in at three o'clock, drunk as a skunk."

"Matt likes a drink. It'll be *horrible* at ours just now. A dozen millionaires and their hangers-on puking into the pool!" She knocked her empty glass against Lizzie's shoulder. "Now, bed... I want us to grab an early start tomorrow. The quicker you get it measured, the quicker I get to choose my fabrics!"

"Absolutely. And no naff tattoo on the bedroom ceiling, either!"

"Dead right!" She rose to her feet and waved, calling, "Night-night, Dutchboy!"

"Goodnight." Lizzie still wasn't quite sure about the etiquette of dealing with bodyguards. She nodded to the giant man as she went out into the hallway. Donna dotted a kiss to Lizzie's cheek and disappeared into the bathroom, her finger tapping at her phone again as she went.

Lizzie returned to the Parisian bordello and closed the door behind her. She changed into her pyjamas, and after brushing her teeth and scrubbing off her makeup, she went to the wardrobe and pulled out a plastic bag.

Inside it was Daisy, her rag doll. Lizzie released the doll in her homemade dress from her plastic prison and brought her into bed, curling up against the pillows that still smelt of Ben. Her phone buzzed, and when she reached for it on the bedside table, the screen turned itself on and she saw that the text was from him.

How's it going, mademoiselle? Love you xxx

Donna came over. There's some horrible lads-night-in going on at Casa de Luca. So she's staying over and there's a bodyguard in my lounge. And I've had too much to drink. Sorry. How's things at the cop-shop? L xxx

Been back about 40 mins. Swim, crisps, bed, beer. You phoneable? Xxx

Yes! PS: I had crisps too and thought of you xxx

She had barely time to press send before her phone rang with a video call, Ben's name flashing up on the screen. As soon as Lizzie answered it, she apologised.

"Sorry… I'm wearing pyjamas."

He was sat up against the headboard, his hair dark on the white pillows, an eyebrow raised. What she could see of his chest was bare.

"I'm not!" He reached across out of the camera's sight. When his hand was in shot again, it was holding a bottle of beer. "Cheers, Ms. Aspinall. You look lovely, by the way. I might shin up your drainpipe and knock on your window."

Lizzie unfastened the top button and grinned at him.

"Just for you, Ben."

"Tell me about this bodyguard," he asked. "Is he looking after you?"

"He's just sort of…*there*. We were watching crappy films, and he was in the corner, headphones on, staring at a screen. How the heck he'd hear bullets flying like that, I dunno!"

"I've asked for a few extra patrols to go past your place tonight, so you can sleep easy." Ben took a swig from the bottle and ruffled his free hand through his wet hair. "I had to swim off all my spare energy since I'm banned from the bordello tonight."

Lizzie ran her fingertips across Ben's videoed face.

"I really wanted to be with you." Lizzie sighed. "But she's my sister. I couldn't really say no, especially given what's going on. She's terrified, Ben."

"I'm guessing Mr. de Luca's got a bodyguard of his own out in the middle of nowhere if she's at your place?"

"Not sure, actually. I think she said something about — this was a few glasses of wine ago — something about Matt insisting she have the bodyguard tonight. He's got all those footballers with him, so what can go wrong, other than someone crashing a high-performance sports car into a gatepost?"

Ben chuckled then peered a little closer to the screen. He reached out once more, his hand returning to put his glasses on the end of his nose. "Who's your friend?"

Lizzie waggled the doll at the screen. "Daisy! My rag doll. Do you like her?"

"She's fantastic! Give me a second." The image on the screen went dark then settled on the ceiling of the hotel room, whilst in the background she could hear Ben rustling about. A few seconds later the camera was moving and it rested once again on her lover, cosy in his bed. "Ready for it?"

"Is this suitable for Daisy to see, or must I cover her eyes first?"

"Family friendly, *mademoiselle*." He moved one arm and very slowly, from the corner of the screen, a very old, very traditional teddy bear appeared. A blue ribbon was neatly tied around his neck, his button eyes glittering. "Daisy, Lizzie, say hello to Kendal Mint Cake!"

Lizzie held Daisy's hand and made her wave at the screen.

"Hello, Kendal Mint Cake!" Lizzie laughed. "Dare I ask why you call him that?"

"Because it's his name!" He brought the bear to his ear as though it were whispering, Ben's eyes widening as he listened. "Kendal Mint Cake says he's never seen two such pretty girls, the old sauce!"

"Daisy, what was that? Oh really! My rag doll tells me that she thinks Kendal Mint Cake is just her type. Rugged, mature, with a manly layer of body hair."

"Takes after his dad!"

"He definitely does. Although you're not wearing a ribbon round your neck!"

Ben laughed. "I don't think it'd suit me as well it does him."

"He's very dapper. Do you like Daisy's dress? I made it myself. I was only about seven though, so it's hardly *haute couture*."

"She's a stunner, just like her mum." His smile grew gentle. "You look really cosy."

"I am! But I'd be cosier if— Ben, tomorrow night, do you want to stay over again?"

"Yes please! Should I cook again?"

"If you'd like! Look..." Lizzie took a deep breath. Maybe it was too soon, but it felt right. "I've got a spare set of keys at the office. I'm out tomorrow morning, I've got to go to Casa de Luca again to do some more measuring, but if you're around in the afternoon, swing by and collect them. If you want to."

She saw the change in Ben's expression from happy to downright disbelieving just a second before he asked, "Really?"

"Yes. Why not? Life's for living, isn't it?"

"I love you, Lizzie Aspinall."

"I love you, Ben Finneran." Lizzie brought the phone to her lips and kissed the air a millimetre above the screen.

"Do I need to let you go to sleep?" Ben asked gently.

"No...I don't have to go to sleep yet." Lizzie snuggled down on her side and laid the phone on its edge so that Ben was still facing her. She unfastened another button on her pyjama top. "I'm going to pretend that you're lying here beside me."

"Do I need to hide Kendal Mint Cake's face?"

"Maybe." Lizzie's hand hovered over the next button. "These pyjamas are suddenly very warm."

"Kendal says night-night." He sat the bear off to one side, out of sight. "Ben says hello."

"Hello, Ben. Would you like me to undo my button?"

"Slowly," he instructed.

Lizzie's voice was a breath. "Like this?" She looked directly into the camera lens as she unfastened the button as slowly as she could, revealing the edge of her bosom.

"Don't stop." Ben pillowed his hands behind his head, blinking as he watched.

Lizzie had only two more buttons to unfasten, and once they were both undone, she pulled the top off and lay back on her side, her arm cradling her breasts. From the screen Ben watched her, his arms tensed *just* enough to show them off at their best.

"My handsome *gendarme*... Tell me what you'd like me to do."

Ben blinked again, clearly a little taken aback by the invitation. He shifted slightly in the bed and asked her, "I'd like you to stroke your breasts like I do. Slowly, caress them."

Lizzie released her shielding arm and her breasts were revealed to Ben's view. She let him look for a moment, then did as he had asked. Watching him on the screen, she stroked, telling herself that it was his fingers trailing over her skin. She moaned, long and low.

"God, Lizzie, I wish you were here," he told her in a husky voice. "Or that I was there."

"We'll be together tomorrow night," Lizzie said.

"Tomorrow night," Ben whispered, "Let's share that bath of yours?"

"I'd like that. And I'll get you some beers in."

"I was thinking of your plait that night during my swim ," he admitted. "And you in the shower, and how you taste and feel and how much I bloody love you."

"Oh, Ben, I spent all evening wishing I was with you and not stuck here with — without you." She pressed head back into the pillow as she slipped her hand under her waistband. "And now I'll spend all night wishing I was sleeping beside you, too."

"Tomorrow night we lock the door, take a cold beer into a hot bath and forget the world exists?" He pushed his glasses up into his hair. "Just me and you."

"That would be so lovely. That would be — oh!" Lizzie moved her hand inside her pyjamas. She wasn't sure that Ben could see, but it must've been obvious to him what she was doing, what she had begun without really meaning to. But now, she couldn't stop. "Ben — oh, touch yourself, Ben. Pretend it's me."

"I hoped you might say that," he admitted, a flush creeping over his throat. "I was too shy to ask."

"Says the man...who stripped...by a window!"

"Oh yeah, that was me!" He shifted one hand from beneath his head. "Do you want to see?"

"You are such a naughty *gendarme*, Ben." Lizzie smiled her sauciest smile. "Yes, I would. And do you?"

"I think it's only right, *mademoiselle*." Ben set the phone on the table and laid on his side so Lizzie was able to see the full length of his body. The pristine white duvet covered him to the waist and he pushed it aside, letting her see his erection. "I want you, *madame*."

"You have such a beautiful cock." Lizzie knocked her phone off the side of the bed in her haste to take off the last part of her pyjamas. "Sorry about that!" She picked it back up and laid it on the bedside table. "Can you still see me?"

"I can see you and you're as beautiful as ever." There was mirth in his voice though. "And just as Lizzie as ever too."

"So much for being the bordello mistress! *Bonne nuit, gendarme!*"

"*Bonne nuit, madame.* How's business in Montmartre?"

"Quiet tonight. But that's fine. I have time for my *gendarme* now. My handsome, lovely *gendarme*."

"Your *gendarme* has had a hell of a day." He pouted, lazily stroking down the length of his erection. "Dreaming of you."

Lizzie said his name in a rather terrible French accent and slid her hand between her legs. She heard his breathing grow quicker, saw him shift slightly on the bed to draw just a little closer to the screen.

"Tell me how wet you are," Ben whispered, his fingers tightening around his cock.

"Very wet… Wet enough for you to fuck me. Hard."

"I can still you feel you," he told her, "my *madame*, riding me."

"My bed still smells of you. It's as if you're still here with me." Lizzie's hips rose off the bed and she cried out his name, again and again. In response, his hand moved harder and faster, tightening with each jerk of his wrist.

"Oh, Ben, I want to see you come. I want to see your seed on your hand."

"Lizzie!" It was something between a gasp and a moan, his eyes closing as he grasped the bedsheet. She saw his muscles grow tense, his head flung back against the pillow as he came hard.

"You beautiful, beautiful man, I love you more than you can know."

As she watched him tremble through the embers of his orgasm, Lizzie's own peak came into view. Gazing at the image on the screen of the satiated, naked man, sheened lightly in perspiration from the effort of his orgasm, Lizzie was flung into her bliss.

"Lizzie," she heard Ben gasp, his voice exhausted but content, "I love you."

"I love you too." Lizzie passed the back of her hand across her face. She had tears in her eyes.

"Happy?" He asked the question softly, his voice tender.

Lizzie nodded. "And are you, darling Ben?"

"Ridiculously so."

"Ben, can I ask you something?" Lizzie settled herself against the pillows and pulled up the duvet. "If we'd never seen each other — you in your hotel and me in that bar — if the first time you'd ever seen me was when you came to my office with the ribbon… Would you still have fallen in love with me?"

"Yes," he replied without a moment's hesitation, snuggling beneath the duvet again. "And I would never have dared to tell you, and we'd have missed each other without even realising it. And you'd never have known, because I'd have just been that copper who showed up to disrupt your day."

"No, you would have been the handsome detective with the glittering dark eyes. And I would never forget you as long as I lived, because I wouldn't have let you go."

"I believe that too." Ben smiled and leant across to put his glasses down beside the screen. "Can I ask *you* something?"

"Yes, go on!"

"What was going through your mind when you were on your way up to the room that first night?"

"I felt reckless and so attracted to you, but there was something more. You and I were complete strangers to each other, yet something linked us. And I had to know. I had to find out what it was."

Ben was already nodding as she spoke. "I was just looking out of the window and, well, there you were. It was like the breath went out of me."

Lizzie twisted a length of her hair around her finger. She pulled at it awkwardly. "No one's ever said that to me, ever. I wondered who on earth you saw when you looked at me. Not boring Lizzie, but some version of me who I had never dared meet before."

"There's nothing boring about you, Liz. I don't think there ever could be."

"You're too sweet. And the way you looked at me, across the width of a street! I wanted you so much. Still do."

"You'll always take my breath."

Lizzie grinned at him and blew a kiss towards the phone.

"If I could, I'd leave this on all night, so that if I wake up in the early hours, I could look over and see you there asleep. And hear you breathing."

"Tomorrow night, I'll be there with you," he promised. "I'd be there now if I could."

"I love you with all my heart, Ben—" Lizzie was poleaxed by an enormous yawn.

"Off to kip, Aspinall." Ben yawned too. "And I'll love you even more tomorrow."

"Night-night."

Lizzie reached toward her phone and saw Ben's arm reach towards his. In the second that passed as they turned off their phones, it was as if their hands had touched through the ether.

Chapter Nineteen

In the back seat of Donna's BMW, Lizzie watched the city go by as they drove out to Alderley Edge. The radio was on full blast, Donna singing along to a pop song. Her sister's rendition was peppered with interjections. She'd met that singer in a club. She'd met the other at the nail bar in Selfridge's. Lizzie was about to say that she'd had commissions from two of them and their producer, but she wasn't in the mood to be a Billy Braggart this morning.

What would happen after this case was over? Ben still carried the badge of the Metropolitan Police. He'd have to go back down south. Or would he try to stay? He would. She was certain of it.

Lizzie was wearing a loop of thread on the ring finger of her right hand, the thread that Ben had used to fasten her plait. She had carried it in her purse, but she'd wanted to see it, to feel it on her skin. And if anyone asked, *It's to remind me of something.* Surely no one would find it odd for an interior designer to go about with cotton thread on their finger.

Donna was on her phone again, Dutch and the driver silent in the front seat as the world sped past, and in Lizzie's bag, her mobile buzzed a message from Ben.

Can't wait for tonight and that bath of yours. Love you xxx

Tell me what your favourite beer is and I'll get it in the fridge, ready for you. Kiss kiss, mon gendarme *xxx*

My favourite is anything I can tempt my madame to drink with me ;) xxxx, he replied.

Just you wait and see! I love you xxx

The BMW was in country lanes now, the hedges bare of their leaves, grey clouds streaking the cold, eggshell-blue sky. A light frost had fallen overnight, fixing a faint glitter where the watery beams of the sun caught against the thin crust of ice. It reminded her of the words to a carol that she'd sung at school.

Then the gates of the de Lucas' mansion appeared up ahead, and the air was ripped apart by Donna's scream.

There on the gate, where those wrought-iron initials tangled with each other, was a bunch of what looked like dozens of white lilies. A jet-black ribbon secured them in place and even from here, even from this distance and through the murky winter morning, Lizzie knew that ribbon would be broken by the embroidered fleur-de-lys.

Donna's hand flew out, locking around the driver's shoulder, and she shrieked, "Stop the car! Stop the car!"

The driver hit the brakes. It took the BMW longer to stop than it should have as there was ice on the road.

Lizzie was jolted forward with such violence that her phone fell out of her hand. She reached into the footwell for it whilst grabbing for her sister with her other hand.

"Donna, stay in the car!"

It was Dutch who moved first and, surprisingly, fastest. He was out of the car almost before it had stopped, his trainered feet moving nimbly over the icy road and his mobile already in his hand.

"Everyone stay put!" he called, though he must have known Lizzie wasn't going to listen.

Lizzie had found her phone at last and rang Ben. She was out of the car in seconds. She had to see the ribbon.

"Hello, gorgeous!" Ben sounded happy to hear from her, and behind his voice she could hear normality. The sound of chatter, cutlery on plates, of people going about their business.

The cold air was raw in Lizzie's throat as she gasped, "There's lilies on the gate!" She had drawn nearer, her heart leaping in her chest. Despite the frost, she could clearly see the design on the ribbon. "It's the ribbon, Ben! It's the same one!"

"Which gate? Where are you?" She heard a new urgency in his voice, a door slam and his feet hurrying down a flight of steps. "Who's with you, Liz?"

"It's Matt and Donna's house. We've just pulled up to the gates. Dutch is on the phone, Donna's in the car with the driver. She's hysterical! Matt's in the house...I suppose. What should I do, Ben? He said he was ill last night. I just thought he'd drunk too much!"

"I want you all to stay in the car until we get there." The phone was muffled and she heard him shout, "Anj! Lizzie, are you still there?"

Donna's door was suddenly flung wide and she hurled herself out of the vehicle, her feet struggling on the icy road like a new-born foal's. Usually so elegant and assured, Donna de Luca fell heavily to her tarmac before scrambling back up onto her feet, her heels abandoned as she ran towards the gate. Blood seeped from new grazes on her knees but she seemed not to notice, intent only on fumbling in her handbag for something. When her hand emerged, it clutched a small device the size of a matchbox and, with a gesture from her thumb, the gates began to slowly open.

Tied between the two halves, the ribbon split apart and the lilies fell, scattering over the ground. The black binding fluttered in the breeze but Donna could go no farther, screaming in despair when Dutch caught his tree trunk arm around her narrow waist. She beat uselessly against him and he told her, "Wait for the coppers, Mrs. de Luca. It might not be safe."

"Ben, it's Donna!" Lizzie knew he must be able to hear her sister's frantic screams in the background. "I've never seen her like this before. I don't know what to do."

But sensing menace around her, Lizzie stepped back towards the car, beckoning to her sister. "Donna, don't go up to the house. Come and sit with me in the car, where it's warm. Come on."

The thought of Matt, alone in that now-sinister house, filled Lizzie with horror. Were the flowers a joke and was Matt hungover, blissfully unaware? Or was he already cold, a— *What if Matt is dead?*

"Stay in the car. Wait for us to arrive," Ben told her firmly. "Can you put me onto the minder?"

"Yes, hang on."

Dutch was already on his way to the car, Donna shrieking and flailing in his grip. Lizzie held out her phone to him.

"It's DCI Finneran. He'd like a word."

Somehow Dutch managed to bundle Donna into the car, then he took the phone with a murmur of thanks and asked Lizzie, "Can you try and settle her?"

As Dutch retired a few feet away, Donna fell silent and pressed her hands to the car window, staring out at the open gates and the palace beyond. Those pale blue cars were still there, the lilies blowing across the driveway like petals before a funeral procession.

Lizzie climbed into the car. "Come on, Donna, love. Hold my hand."

She was a child again. There had been a storm in the night. The two sisters had hidden in the wardrobe, and in the morning their mother had found them asleep inside it, curled around each other, Lizzie's rag doll between them.

Donna turned to Lizzie, her face wet with tears, her eyes filled with terror and confusion. She looked down at her grazed knees then, with a sob, collapsed into her sister's arms.

"Shh...shhhh..." Lizzie couldn't tell her it would be all right. They would have to wait for the sirens.

It seemed like a lifetime before three police cars came screeching through the lanes, lights blazing, sirens wailing, and all the time they were waiting, Donna was sobbing in Lizzie's embrace. The first vehicle was the black BMW that had collected Lizzie from her office and behind it were two patrol cars, bringing with them the confirmation that this was *not* a hoax, nor something to be taken lightly.

Ben was first to leave the convoy, and he threw a single glance at the open gate before he approached the car containing the unhappy party. Dutch pushed open his door and climbed out, clearly intending to take charge of the situation.

Seeing Ben arrive, Lizzie dared to hope that the sense of dread that had descended when she'd seen the macabre floral offering would now dissipate. But one look at Ben's face told her otherwise, and she held Donna all the tighter. She saw Dutch gesture to the gates, apparently explaining that Donna had opened them, and watched the uniformed officers congregate behind Ben, waiting for his word. The world seemed to have slowed to a crawl and she peered from the window at her lover, who appeared to be throwing orders this way and that. From his pocket, Dutch produced a bunch of keys and Ben took them, then approached their car, gesturing Lizzie to lower the window.

The window whirred down, and the cold air pushed its way inside the warm car. Donna's frightened wails echoed about the frozen lane.

"DCI Finneran?" *Ben, my darling Ben.* She darted out her hand to seek his. He caught her fingers and held them, his gaze full of love and concern.

"I'm going to go up to the house. PC Choudary's going to stay here with your car. There's nothing to be afraid of. We just need to establish contact with Mr. de Luca."

Lizzie nodded to them. "Hello again." It was the PC who had driven her before.

PC Choudary gave her a reassuring smile.

"Donna" — Lizzie ran her hand over her sister's hair — "they're going up to the house. Have you heard from Matt this morning?"

As Ben withdrew his hand, Donna shook her head, still sobbing. "No, nothing since last night. He's dead, isn't he?"

She raised her head just long enough to give a glimpse of her tear-stained face, then collapsed again, clinging to Lizzie.

"No, Donna, don't say that. He might just be hungover." Lizzie tried to smile. "He might be sat in your kitchen right now with his coconut milk, nursing the world's worst headache."

Donna lifted her head and looked through the windscreen to where Dutch and the driver were deep in discussion. She drew in a long breath and blinked, drawing her hand shakily over her eyes. For a few moments Lizzie thought she was going to speak, but instead she threw open the car door and jumped out, running towards the driveway where Ben and the officers were now approaching the house.

"Donna!" Lizzie was after her like a bullet from a gun. Her flat shoes allowed her to catch up with her sister, and she grasped her in her arms. "You have to let the police go in first. It might not be — "

Safe?

Lizzie glanced round at the police. PC Choudary had already clutched hold of Donna's arm.

"Let's wait in the car, Mrs. de Luca." Her voice was kind but had a stern edge.

Donna allowed herself to be returned to the car, quietly sobbing in Lizzie's arms as the minutes ticked by. Outside, she watched Dutch and the driver pacing, their faces darkened with concern. Then, as the sky grew even more grey overhead, she saw Ben walking briskly along the driveway. His grave expression gave nothing away as he gestured to PC Choudary and she left the car to speak to him. More minutes passed before Ben approached the car and opened the door. He climbed into the passenger seat and turned to speak to the women.

"He's dead, isn't he?" Donna reached out and clutched at his shoulder. "Tell me!"

"Mrs. de Luca." Ben's voice was calm, steady. "Mr. de Luca's unwell but he *is* alive. "An ambulance is on its way. We have to secure your home as crime scene. I'm sorry."

Donna's mouth gaped wide, as though she couldn't understand what she was being told, as though this was barely even English to her.

"Oh, thank God! Dear old sis. That's good news, isn't it!" Lizzie held Donna's hand. "I'll come to the hospital with you. We'll ring Matt's mum. He'll be all right."

Her last words were almost a question, and she turned to look at Ben.

"When the ambulance arrives, we'll be staying here at the house." Ben kept his gaze on Lizzie as Donna collapsed again. "I'll ask PC Choudary to go with you to the hospital."

Lizzie nodded. "Let's hope he'll be all right, Donna."

When the ambulance arrived, it barely braked as it cruised past the cars that were waiting in the lane and sped up the driveway to the house. Lizzie knew she was about to cry, but she pressed back her tears to be strong for her sister. For all that Matt was hasty with his fists, he wasn't a bad person. He didn't deserve to be—had he been?—poisoned and rushed to hospital. Lizzie could only hope that he wasn't suffering.

"He's going to die." Donna sobbed as they waited. "He is, isn't he?"

"Donna, come on now. We don't even know what's happened to him. And he wouldn't want to hear you say that." Lizzie adopted her best gung-ho tone. "He'd want you there on the side of the pitch, cheering him on!"

Not that Donna attended football matches, but the sentiment was well-meant.

"Ben, don't you think? We can't give up on the poor fella." Lizzie brushed Donna's hair away from her face. "We need to cross our fingers and our toes. And our eyes!" She did just that, clowning desperately to chivvy her sister along.

"I'll go and see the paramedics." Ben attempted a supportive smile. "I'll see you girls at the hospital?"

Chapter Twenty

Matt de Luca, premiership footballer in the prime of life, was wired up to machines, his eyes open, his lips parted, unable to speak.

His private room was full of hospital staff. Donna was sat by the bed, clasping Matt's pale hand, her face stained with her tear-damaged makeup. Matt's parents had arrived in matching blue football tops, announcing that they had fought through a scrum of reporters to get into the hospital. They vied for position with Donna beside the bed.

Lizzie could only wait outside with PC Choudary — or Anj, as she was now allowed to call her — and drink tea supplied by the Royal Voluntary Service lady in a tabard who came round with a trolley. She didn't want to make small talk with Anj, didn't want to distract her from her job. Instead, every so often, Anj patted Lizzie's hand and ask her how she was. And Lizzie, who didn't want to cause a fuss, would always answer, "Okay."

A man in a brown suit that had seen better days strode up the corridor and peered in officiously through the window of Matt's room.

"Ride me sideways, what a bloody palaver!"

Anj rose from her seat. "DCS Worthington, sir?"

"Look at this mess! Bloody hell! I've got a season ticket and all! We've dropped the ball, Anj. Dropped the bloody ball." He turned to look at Anj then, apparently realising for the first time that another person was sat there, eyeballed Lizzie. "And you are?"

"Lizzie Aspinall."

He put his hands in his pockets and rocked back on his heels. "That explains a lot." Then he strode off again, shouting something to a police officer who was just emerging from the lifts.

The officer was followed by two official-looking men who, she heard him tell Worthington, were from *the club*.

Honour the badge.

Into the room they went, and yet Lizzie was still here, still alone, still forgotten.

Minutes passed, footsteps came and went, interested hospital staff wandered too innocently along the corridor then, finally, the lift doors opened and Ben emerged. He looked tired but determined, his hands raking through his hair as he crossed to where Lizzie and Anj waited.

"How're you holding up?" Ben asked Lizzie softly.

"I'm okay." Her voice was high-pitched and unconvincing.

"You're doing really well, Lizzie." PC Choudary turned to Ben. "She's bearing up for her sister, sir."

"Well, I have to, don't I? That's what sisters do. We look out for each other. Poor old Don…"

Lizzie rose from her chair and looked through the window. Donna was prostrate across her husband, sobbing again. As a nurse pushed the door open to leave the room, the grieving wife's cries echoed along the corridor. It was the most pitiful sound Lizzie had ever heard, and yet she hadn't been allowed in to comfort her.

"Ms. Aspinall," Ben asked. "Can you spare me five minutes in private?"

"Yes, yes, of course." Lizzie twisted her hands together. Did he have some news? But surely it could only be bad.

He stepped back and gestured her along the hallway. They passed the lifts and Ben opened a door into an empty room. The bed was neatly made, the blinds shutting out the night.

"What is it, Ben? If it's bad news —"

"I just wanted to know you were all right." He closed the door.

Lizzie didn't reply at once. She looked up at those dark brown eyes and saw Ben's concern there. She rested her head on his shoulder and sighed. "I'm numb."

"I'm so sorry, Liz." He put his arms around her. "I had no idea —"

"It's my fault. He sent Donna a text and said he felt ill. I could've done something then, if I'd only thought!"

"No," he told her fiercely. "Don't ever say that!"

"I just— What do we do? Sit around and wait for him to die? Because he's not going to survive this, is he? I can see it in their faces, all those medical people swarming around him. My sister's going to lose her husband, and there's nothing we can do."

Finally, all the tears that Lizzie had held back in her determined effort to be strong for her sister came spilling out. She heaved with the torrent and held Ben tightly, as if he were the only thing left in the world for her to clutch on to, the only life raft left in the sea. He clung to her in turn, shushing her, kissing her, holding her.

"We're doing everything we can," he whispered.

"Will Donna be safe?"

"She's safe."

"Thank goodness!" Lizzie lifted her face to Ben's and ran her fingertips along his jaw. They paused on his lips. "I love you, Ben."

"I love you." He gently kissed her fingers. "And I'm sorry."

"I wonder if he stayed at home because he thought he'd be safe there? Because that's what I thought myself last night when Donna turned up. I thought, *we could go out, go for a drink in a bar, but we'll be safe at home.* And then look what happens to poor Matt."

"Do you want to go in and sit with them?" Ben stroked her hair tenderly. "You look tired out."

"I offered to, but they said no and Matt's parents are there now. And Donna. I'm not sure I'm much use. I'll just get under the doctors' feet. One of the other wives from the club is on her way, apparently. She's one of Donna's friends. I offered my spare room, but Donna's going to stay with her friend instead. Perhaps I should go home?"

"It's getting on for midnight. I'm going to send Anj home and get off back to Manchester. Can we give you a lift?"

"Yes, please. If it's not a hassle. I'd get a taxi, only I haven't got any change."

"You're my girl, and you're not getting a bloody taxi!" He kissed her as carefully as if she might break. "Come on, let's get some fresh air."

They left the room, deliberately walking apart, Lizzie dabbing a tissue to her eyes.

"I'll see if I can say goodnight to Donna first."

Lizzie's hand was on the door to Matt's room when it opened. There, in the doorway, in front of a tableau of officials and family and footballers whose transfer fees alone were more than she would make in her lifetime, stood Neil. His eyes were ringed red from crying, his tanned skin bleached pale by sorrow and, without a word, he reached to enfold her in a tight hug, whispering her name.

Lizzie stood as still as she could. She had loved this man once. Did that count for nothing, now that he was in despair? Putting aside the fact that they had once shared a semi-detached in Chorlton, Lizzie was the sister-in-law of his best friend, a man who was dying right in front of their eyes. A man who she was sure was being murdered by the poison in his system.

But Lizzie wouldn't hug Neil. She couldn't. She'd forgive him overstepping the mark just this once, while emotions thrummed, but feeling Neil's loveless arms around her so soon after being in Ben's tender embrace only made her realise how right she had been to walk away from him.

"Neil, it's awful, I know, but *please* — "

She pushed her way out of his arms and stepped back from him. And she knew what they'd think, all of them, all those football people. *The hard bitch.* Well, so be it.

"Where's your heart, Lizzie?" He looked at her as though she were the person who had put Matt in hospital, had run wires and tubes into him and left him for dead in that sterile room. "Isn't he your family? Shouldn't you at least *pretend* you're upset?"

Lizzie ignored him. She tried to reach Donna, but the room was too full of people.

"I'm...I'm just saying goodnight, Donna. Will you be okay?"

Franki, the other WAG, was stood behind Donna, false nails like talons gripping Donna's shoulders. At Lizzie's words Donna erupted into tears again, raising her fist with Matt's limp hand in her grip.

"What sort of a thing is that to say?" Franki blinked at Lizzie in disgust. Her false eyelashes were so thick with mascara that they resembled bats' wings.

"I only... Good night, everyone." With fondness in her voice, as if at the bedside of a poorly child, Lizzie addressed the figure in the bed. "Night-night, Matt. Sleep well."

"You!" Donna looked at her through bloodshot eyes. "You're not normal! What sort of thing is that to say? *Sleep well? Sleep well!* "

She threw down Matt's hand and launched across the room as a banshee in full flight, her acrylic nails extended like claws as behind her Lizzie heard horrified murmurings not about Donna, but about *her*. Donna was close enough for Lizzie to smell her perfume when Ben pushed between them, those talons catching his neck in the second before he caught Donna's hand. She crumpled like a paper doll, clinging to him, her face buried against his chest. Franki and Matt's mother were at her back then, helping the sobbing Donna to the bed.

"I think you'd better go, don't you?" Franki gave Lizzie a look of pure disgust as she spoke. "We'll look after Don."

Lizzie edged from the room, her voice stiff as she reined in any shred of emotion that could be misinterpreted. "Thank you for looking after my sister. It's nice to know that so many people care."

She looked once more at Matt, thinking of him lying on the floor of his mansion, alone and dying, all through the night.

Funny how people only care when it's too late.

Once in the corridor, Lizzie ran. She didn't know where to, but she only wanted to be as far away as she could from them. She stopped, realising that Ben was running after her. With tears in her eyes, she laughed.

"I said *rococo*, and Matt thought it had something to do with coconuts!"

He said nothing but put his arms around her and drew her into his embrace, holding her to him. She felt him stroke her hair, heard him hush her, smelled the cologne on his skin and tried not to think of the crowded room with its firmly closed door.

"Will you take me home, please, Ben?"

"Let's get Anj and get out of here." He took out his phone and tapped the screen. Lizzie vaguely heard the sound of another phone ringing somewhere along the corridor before Ben said, "See you at the lifts, Anj? Home time."

Footsteps sounded along the lino floor and Anj arrived. She nodded to Ben.

"The second shift have just come on. I've filled them in." She gave Lizzie an encouraging smile. "Families, eh?"

The three of them walked into the lift.

"Do us a favour, Anj?" Ben pressed the lift button. "Can you stop at the first drive-through we come to? My treat."

"Right you are, sir. There's a Maccy D's about five minutes away."

"I'll even tell you what Sam likes," he replied mischievously. "The milkshake machine had better not be turned off. I need chocolate. Anj, I should probably — "

He pressed the button again and the door closed, leaving the three of them alone.

"Anj, I should probably tell you that Lizzie's a bit more than a witness. She and I are a couple." He put his arm around Lizzie's shoulders. "Liz, Anj is Sam's other half. We're all one big, happy conflict of interest."

Lizzie and Anj laughed, then Lizzie put her arms around the young police constable and hugged her. They were in an awkward three-way cuddle.

"Sam has excellent taste, I must say, if you look after her as well as you looked after me today. Thank you so much, Anj. I would've fallen to pieces without you."

"Not a problem, Lizzie." Anj grinned.

"You two need to know that there's a massive amount of press outside. Anj, you go out first and bring the car round, they won't bother with a lone copper. Liz, you stick close to me and pretend they're not there."

"Will they know who I am?"

The lift doors opened. Lizzie grimaced as a hospital porter squeaked by with an empty gurney.

"I'll text you when I'm in position." Anj strode purposefully away.

"They'll probably know and they won't be after blood or any of that. Matt's a local hero, and you're family. They're not going to give you a hard time." He put his hands on her shoulders and met her gaze. "Just take a deep breath, ride it out and think of your milkshake."

"Will do!" Lizzie would've felt a lot happier if she could' hold hands with Ben as they ran the gauntlet past the press, but she knew without any doubt that it was impossible.

They waited in silence until Ben's phone chimed.

"Here we go." He kissed her forehead then, close enough for their arms to brush as they walked, Ben and Lizzie made their way along the corridor to the foyer of the hospital. Outside, a sea of faces and cameras waited, the press clustered together awaiting news of Manchester's current favourite son. They perked up at the sight of movement in the fluorescent-lit lobby, phones and recorders already being proffered as Ben opened the door.

Lizzie kept her eyes ahead. Camera flashes went off in her face, making her blink in their constant lightning glare. She almost lost her footing in the disorienting brightness, but she regained her balance. Some of the reporters knew who she was, her name shouted by voices she didn't know.

"Lizzie! What's the latest news on your sister's husband? Is he going to pull through? Lizzie!"

In silence, she walked steadily onwards, her eyes fixed on the vanishing point. Ben's fingers were gentle on her elbow, steadying her, keeping her close. His free hand was raised to shield her from the cameras that came too close, but the gentlemen of the press were pushy, tired and cold and needing *something* to file for the morning edition. They crowded in closer until Ben snapped, "Get out of her damn face. Have some respect!"

Then the car was there in front of them and he pulled open the door and followed Lizzie into the back seat.

"I'll give you a tenner for every one of those vultures you take down." Ben patted his hand on the headrest of Anj's seat. "Get the lights on. Let's get out of here."

Some of the press had followed them to the car, and Anj smiled as she revved the engine and put on the lights and the siren. As she sped out of the hospital car park, she laughed. "I'll ring ahead, wind down the window and see if their aim is good enough to lob our burgers through as we drive past!"

"I'd love to see that!" Lizzie smiled and rested her head on Ben's shoulder.

"It's one of the benefits of going out with a copper." He kissed her hair. "Free junk food."

Ben would have been as good as his word but found his offers to pay politely declined by the young man at the drive-through window. Instead, with the car well-stocked with enough food for the three of them plus Sam and more besides, Anj had them outside Lizzie's building in record time. Ben gathered up his share of the bags and milkshakes and opened the door, climbing out and waiting for Lizzie to join him. He handed Anj a twenty-pound note and told her, "Get yourself a cab from the station to Sam's, tell her I said goodnight?"

"Thanks, DCI Finneran! Night!"

Lizzie delved for her keys in her pocket and she and Ben entered the apartment building. The concierge greeted them with a nod as they passed, as politely discreet as ever. Ben returned the nod, following Lizzie across the lobby.

As they went up in the lift, Lizzie observed, "This all feels so delightfully normal. I can only apologise that I *still* don't have any beer in for you. Things got a bit..." She winced at the accumulated memories of the day and, with a deep breath, shoved them aside as best she could.

"Let's make it normal," Ben urged. "Let's eat our chips and drink our milkshakes and just...*be*? Last night, seeing you — I never thought anything like that would happen to me, Liz. Let's think of that instead of today?"

"It's not something I'd ever done before, I must admit! But it was fun, wasn't it?" Before Lizzie's eyes was the sight of Ben, naked, pleasuring himself. A shiver of anticipation shot through her at the memory.

"You've gone red." He pressed the cold milkshake cup to her cheek. "Do you want a live replay later?"

"And if I said yes?" She grinned at him, but a thought got in the way. "Just so you know, when Neil hugged me at the hospital... You do realise, don't you, that I don't feel anything for him anymore? It was like being hugged by a lump of wood. I don't know why he did that. He's taken the break-up well, then *that* happened. I just want to eat chips and take my *gendarme* to Paris."

"If you said *yes*, I'd be happy to comply, *mademoiselle*," he told her with a pantomime gravity. "And your ex is feeling a bit fragile, it's not surprising. You don't need to worry, Liz, I didn't think you were about to fling yourself into his arms."

The lift doors opened on Lizzie's floor and they walked arm in arm along the corridor to the front door of her flat. In minutes they were curled up on her sofa, devouring their drive-through dinner, Ben's favourite film playing quietly on the television in the background as they ate.

"I wish she hadn't opened that gate," Ben murmured thoughtfully, pausing with a chip halfway to his mouth.

"Why's that?" Lizzie slurped her milkshake, then pressed her fingertips to her forehead. "Ooof, brain-freeze! But why? Because the bouquet fell apart?"

"The other bouquets were little things, supermarket stuff, but that was a pretty big bunch of flowers. I'd have liked to have seen how many there were, how the knot was tied on the gate, just the full picture really." He finally ate the chip, his eyes narrowing with thought. "There's something with the CCTV that's making me feel off. I can't put my finger on it, but it's not right."

"I did try to keep Donna in the car, but she really lost it. She saw those flowers and screamed. I've never heard anything like it. It terrified me."

"He has CCTV," he mused. "We know he has it, he's a celebrity, he has a minder, a stalker, all that. Yet on the night he dies, a fortunate gust of wind throws the camera off centre. Then our killer just *happens* to come from left to right to reach the gate and avoid getting caught on film. If he'd come right to left, we'd have got him on camera. That feels *too* lucky to me."

Lizzie shuddered. "That is *horrible*. Are you sure it was the wind that knocked the camera?"

"It was stormy, but… We can't make any conclusions yet. We need to get that looked at, see how the time matches up versus the worst of the wind, all that scientific stuff." He screwed up his empty burger wrapper and threw it into the paper bag. "And we don't even know how the poisoner got to Matt yet. That's going to be a big one."

In thought, Lizzie rattled the straw in her milkshake cup. "Same ribbon?"

"Same ribbon." He nodded. "But a stack of differences *again*. London, ten years ago…targeted working-class pubs, no flowers, no messages, no taunting the police, nothing but one card. Manchester, targets upscale bars, sends lilies tied with ribbon, stalks, turns up at a victim's *home*, flaunts it as though he wants to be caught. What happened in ten years to turn him from someone in the shadows to someone in the spotlight?"

"Upscale bars are easy. That night when we first… Well, Donna bought these cocktails and they had this bizarre taste. I couldn't drink it. It was that bitter, like medicine. But was that the poisoner or more likely some stupid trendy drink that tastes disgusting? I didn't mention it before. I didn't want to waste your time with it. But now? Well, all this business with Matt, it's made me wonder."

"What?" He turned to look at her. "That night we met?"

"Yes. You saw me try to drink it! It was there on the table."

"Was that your *first* drink in the Mezz that night?" He had taken on a new urgency, she realised. "How long had you been there?"

Lizzie put the milkshake down on the side table and knitted her fingers. "Let me think… Half an hour? We went in. I got the first round. White Russians, a classic. And they were fine. We went to that table by the window, because it wasn't as crowded there. And we chatted, so we took a while with the first drinks. Then

Donna said she'd get the next round in. And while she was off at the bar, I happened to look across the street. And that's when I noticed you. When she came back, she was all annoyed because she said she couldn't get hold of Matt. Then he texted her and it turned out he'd been tanning. So when I decided to go, she said Matt would finish my cocktail as I'd only sipped it. And they were going off for sushi afterwards. Thrilling lives of celebrities. A leftover cocktail and a nagging wife."

"This is the first time we can possibly pinpoint the *exact* time he spiked," Ben told her. "The others had all been out for a while and had a few drinks. The bars were crowded, their CCTV showed nothing we could use, but we *know* the time you were there, we *know* Donna was at the bar. It might just have been a really nasty drink, but if someone slipped something in there and they have cameras, we could see them!"

"You're kidding? I should've said something earlier, but I thought..." Then Lizzie realised something. "Does this mean that you remember the exact time that we first saw each other?"

"It was quarter to seven, give or take. I know it was quarter to seven because Sam was going down to London for the night and her train got in at twenty-five to, and she rang me to say she'd arrived safe."

Lizzie squeezed Ben's knee and gazed into his dark eyes. "DCI Ben Finneran, you have 'copper' written through you like a stick of rock."

"And this copper's wondering about that thread on your finger?"

She had forgotten about it, with all the horror of the day. Now there it was, on Ben's knee. She hoped he wouldn't think it was an *aide memoire* for a client's colour scheme, even if everyone else would.

"Do you recognise it?"

"Come to bed," was all he said in reply.

Lizzie took his strong jaw in her fingertips and brought his lips to her own. "Yes, *gendarme*."

"*Madame*," he scooped her up as he rose to his feet, "let's make each other happy."

Chapter Twenty-One

As they shed each item of clothing, they came closer to shedding the day and the world outside the bedroom. Together they tumbled into the bed, their lips together for ever-deeper kisses, their hands sliding over soft, warm skin. For tonight Lizzie could leave the hospital behind.

In Ben's arms, Lizzie was wanted, cherished and adored in a way she had never been before. She tried to show him, in response to his every touch, how she returned his feelings, with her own caresses, her own deep kisses.

The world outside disappeared as, illuminated by the moonlight, they made love beneath the velvet covers. Ben held Lizzie's hand as they scaled the heights of pleasure, his gold wedding band pressed to the cotton that was looped around her finger, bound to each other.

Once their bodies had stilled, they embraced on the edge of sleep.

"Have I made you happy?" Lizzie whispered. "As happy as you've made me?"

"Happier than I thought I'd ever be," Ben murmured, his lips brushing her ear. "Happy enough to finally make a decision."

"A decision?" Lizzie looked into his eyes, so dark in his moon-silvered face.

"Since Holly died, life's been just me and my girl. She's growing up now and I was just rattling about in a house that was too big for me." He brushed his fingertips over Lizzie's face, smoothing her hair from her cheek. "We put the house on the market, and just before I came up here, it sold. I was going to buy a smaller place down there but now— How would you feel if I moved up here? Not *in* here, don't worry, but I don't want to be at the other end of the country."

"What—! Do you—? You'd live up here?" Lizzie's heart raced. "Ben! Oh, that would be so wonderful! I've been dreading the idea of you going back to London. I even wondered if I could move down south. I'd do anything to be with you, Ben. I love you."

"I was going to jack the job in and go off and see the world, but— Oh, Liz, I wouldn't want to be away from you, so this is as far as I want to travel now."

"Why *don't* we travel the world together, bit by bit?" Lizzie glanced around her Montmartre bordello. "We should start with Paris."

"Could you do that? With your business?" She saw the hope in his face though, heard it in his voice. "We'd have the house money—"

"I'm allowed a holiday sometimes! And if I was feeling particularly naughty, I could even say it was work. You know… I have this idea. After that book I did, the publisher wanted me to write something else, and I told them that what I long to do is a book on historical interiors. In Britain and everywhere else! And the more I thought, the more I realised it wasn't going to be just one book. It'd be a whole series, country by country. But I'd need the time to do it, and — well, it's only really been in the past few months that I've been able to consider that I *could* do it, and not —" Lizzie linked her fingers with Ben's and brought them to her mouth to kiss them. "Let's just say there was something in the way before, and leave it at that."

"When this case is done — and it *will* be — shall we do it? You and me and the open road?"

"Oh, yes, please, we have to! It'd be so wonderful!"

"Sam'll be a happy girl that her dad's finally getting a life!" He pulled her into a tight embrace, whispering, "I love you."

That same recklessness that had led Lizzie to follow the thread to the man in room 423 emerged from behind the fear and the sadness of the past few days. She was giddy with happiness in her lover's arms.

"We could go anywhere, Ben. We could do *anything!*"

"And whenever a hotel has a 423, we book it for James and Louisa!" He kissed her again, clearly fired by the very thought of it. "And they fall in love all over again!"

"Oh, we *have* to!" Lizzie kissed him and rolled him onto his back. "We're going to have such fun together, Ben. I know it!"

"Louisa was a hell of a girl, but she's more James' type." He caught his hands in her hair, bringing her down for a kiss. "I think Ben prefers his gorgeous Lizzie...but then there's the *gendarme*, and he's crazy for his *mademoiselle*. This flat's getting crowded!"

Lizzie yawned. "You need to sleep, *gendarme*. You have a villain to catch."

"I promise that I will, Lizzie." He met her gaze, determination showing in his eyes. "Whatever happens, I'm going to get them off the street. That starts tomorrow, with the CCTV."

Lizzie snuggled against him. She felt so safe in his arms. How could they ever come to harm? As his lips pressed to her shoulder, she could almost *hear* him going through the case in his mind, the flowers and the poison and the sheer bloody mess of it. How must it be to have such a responsibility though, to have the weight of lives and families and funerals resting on him?

No wonder he wanted to leave it all behind.

Chapter Twenty-Two

"Finneran?" It was more of a question than a command from the puffy-eyed DCS who was standing by Ben's desk. Either Worthington hadn't slept or his liver was about to pack up for good.

Ben looked up from his computer screen, his own eyes tired from being here since before dawn broke. The antifreeze had been found in the worst place possible. The bottle Matt de Luca had taken to his match the previous day. The bottle everyone in the dressing room and dugout had enjoyed unrestricted access to at some point during the afternoon. It was another needle in another haystack, and that was *before* he went back to the Mezz, let alone returned to the hospital where the footballer remained unresponsive.

"Boss?" Ben pushed his glasses up into his hair. "What's up?"

DCS Worthington rapped his knuckles on Ben's desk, his other hand in his trouser pocket, fidgeting with some change. He had none of the bluster of yesterday.

"A word, if you would. Come on over to my office."

Worthington began to walk across the incident room, treading carefully, as if the soles of his shoes were too thin. Halfway across the room, he stopped and looked back over his shoulder. He attempted a grin with his saggy mouth.

"Haven't got all day, lad!"

This was time Ben could ill-afford to use, but he rose from the desk and followed Worthington, every eye on him as he went. Once he was in the office, he closed the door and waited for whatever today's explosion would be.

"Take a seat, DCI Finneran." Worthington pulled back his own chair and sat down, adjusting his tie, fiddling with his cuffs. Once Ben was seated, Worthington folded his hands together and pursed his lips as if he was about to whistle. "I saw you last night, leaving the hospital, with a witness."

Ben felt the words like a punch in the gut. He felt his mouth drop open, heard his voice say, "And Officer Choudhary, sir. We were seeing her safely home."

"I met her yesterday, briefly. I can see why, Finneran. She's a lovely-looking girl, your damsel in distress. But you've got to be careful. I've already said to you, you can't compromise the case."

"I know." Ben pinched the bridge of his nose. Of course he knew, every officer did. "I want to catch this bastard more than anyone. We've had ten years to think about each other."

"By rights, Finneran, by rights, I could throw you off the case. You realise that? You're too bloody close. But I know that if I told you to sod off home and cool down, you'd go maverick on me and investigate it anyway. So I'm going to keep you where I can see you. You've been too close for ten years anyway. Nothing's going to stop you now, you tenacious bugger. And I don't want to retire with this unsolved. You're the only bloke who'll get it done. But just be careful. Make sure no one upstairs gets wind of you and her."

"I met her before she was anything to do with that case," he told Worthington carefully, but then he thought of the house that he no longer owned, the wife he no longer had, the daughter who was growing up and the woman he loved. "And I know that we... I appreciate the chance, sir, really."

"*I'll* pretend I didn't see you bundling her into the car. And *you* bloody well catch this killer!"

"We ate chips and then she gave me the best lead we've had in weeks. She was in the Mezz last week with Donna de Luca. Night was quiet, we can pinpoint the time and there's a *chance* someone messed with their drinks." He leant forward. "If that's on CCTV...we might finally see our man."

Worthington went rigid, his eyes wide like a bloodhound that had caught a fresh scent.

"Should get you to seduce witnesses more often. Bloody hell!"

"They were very good chips. I can't take the credit."

Worthington's shoulders rose and fell as he laughed. "I like you, Finneran. I do! Reminds me of them ABC Burglaries, actually, because I —"

There was an urgent knock at the door and Ben glanced over his shoulder as, to his surprise, the brave officer outside turned the handle without being admitted. Worthington looked ready to erupt, but before he could force the words out, the young man exclaimed, "Matt de Luca's dead!"

"Jesus bloody wept!" Worthington stared at the silent telephone on his desk. "Where's this come from?"

"It's all over the web. Club hasn't confirmed it yet but Twitter reckons Pep's doing a press call at ten!"

Worthington already had the receiver crooked against his shoulder, sausage-like fingers stabbing at the phone. "Oh no, he's bloody not! We're not having anyone talk to the press except through us!"

Ben was out of the office before Worthington had finished dialling the number. He arrived at the hospital to find that the crowds at the hospital had grown, swelling with the news of the footballer's death. Now it was an ocean of sky-blue shirts and scarves as seemingly every season ticket holder made their pilgrimage. The press jostled for position, and when Ben tried to get into the building, it was like tackling a rugby scrum. The television in the foyer told him that in the city and at the stadium where Matt had reigned as emperor, an ocean of flowers and cuddly toys was piling up, the screen flashing images of people on their knees, weeping for their lost prince.

DDL – Live 4 Eva, someone had sprayed across a flag that now flew at the centre of that ever-expanding tide of tributes. Matt's face smiled out of posters and T-shirts and the ship sailed on, bobbing across ten thousand badges on teddies and hoodies, socks and scarves.

People wanted answers now, Ben knew as he arrived at the stainless-steel doors to the morgue, and that was going to be on him.

It's going to be a hell of a Christmas.

Chapter Twenty-Three

As soon as Lizzie saw the ticker roll across the bottom of the television screen, she rang Donna's number. It was engaged. She rang their parents, and their number was engaged.

Lizzie hurried into her clothes, having planned to work from home today in her pyjamas. A brief slick of makeup, in case the photographers had her in their sights again, then she was gone.

Arthur on the door looked up as she ran through reception.

"So sorry, love!"

Lizzie nodded to him and was out in the street. She flagged down a taxi and the driver had already heard. He had no idea who she was, didn't twig when she told him to take her to the hospital where Manchester's recent monarch had breathed his last.

"Such a big fan, such a shame. Poor bloke, hope they find whoever did this and the death penalty's brought back just for them!"

Lizzie saw again the tattoo on Matt's back. His totem. *'It's spiritual to me.'* A devil's head, for the king who wanted Versailles.

The taxi couldn't get to the usual drop-off point for the hospital, as the police were trying to divert pilgrims. Lizzie wound down the window.

"I'm family. I'm Donna de Luca's sister."

She could see their disbelief all too clearly.

"You'll have to get out here and walk, love."

Lizzie paid the driver, who was finally rendered silent, and she hurried through the crowd. She kept ringing Donna's number, hoping to get a clear line. If only she was persistent enough. She reached the doors to the private wing that Matt had been in, and it was blocked by police.

"Please let me through. I need to speak to my sister."

"Is she a patient, madam?"

"No, she's Donna de Luca."

An eyebrow shot up. "Journalist are you, trying to sneak in?"

"No, I'm not!"

Lizzie moved away to an angle of the building. She gave up ringing Donna and instead rang Ben.

"Lizzie!" Behind him she could hear a lot of noise, voices shouting and feet hurrying. "I wanted to give you a chance to sleep in before I called. You've heard the news? I'm so sorry."

"I can't get hold of Donna or our parents. I don't know what to do. And I can't get into the hospital either because no one believes that I'm Donna's sister!"

"You at the hospital now? Go to the nearest uniform and give me his shoulder number, I'll take it from there."

Lizzie took a few steps so that the police who had shunned her earlier were in her line of vision again.

They nudged each other and grinned as they saw Lizzie appear. With great satisfaction, Lizzie texted the shoulder numbers of both officers and waited.

Seconds later the radio of one of the officers crackled into life and he sighed theatrically before answering.

"This is DCI Finneran," Lizzie heard Ben say. "There's a young lady with you right now. She's Mrs de Luca's sister. Can you take her up to join her family, please?"

Lizzie glided towards him. "Hello again. I really *am* Donna's sister."

A crowd of footballers, agents and backroom staff in shiny suits had congregated around the family room. Lizzie was piloted in by the policeman.

"Watch your backs. That's it. Family member coming through."

Lizzie only wanted to comfort her sister, even if that meant sitting in the corner with a cup of tea for three hours, unable to approach Donna because the people crowding around her drowned out Lizzie's quiet consolation with their cries of woe.

"Can you give us some space, Lizzie?" Donna wailed. "I can't breathe!"

"I'll just…" No one noticed Lizzie as she squeezed her way out of the room. She rooted in her pocket for her phone. She'd ring Ben. He'd know what to do, what would happen next. Matt's body had already been taken away for the post-mortem. How was it possible that someone who was so young, so alive, could now be lying on cold stainless steel in a pathologist's lab?

Like every other phone that day, Ben's was engaged. Lizzie decided to send him a text.

If you have a moment, would you give me a ring? Not urgent! Worry not — L xxx

"Hey." A hand landed on her shoulder. "We must stop meeting like this."

Lizzie put her phone in her pocket but didn't let it go.

"Neil."

She took half a step away from him. His aftershave was layered on so thickly that she twitched her nostrils, about to sneeze.

"Why'd you act like you're scared of me, Liz?" He lifted his hand. "What the hell did I ever do to make you go off like this?"

"Just stop touching me!" She raised her hand. "You can't keep doing that. We're not a couple anymore. You can't just walk up to me and touch me!"

"I'm putting my hand on your arm, not up your skirt!" His voice was an angry bark, but he bit his lip to silence it. "My best mate just died, yeah? My brother?"

Lizzie flinched another half step from him. She kept her tone measured and calm, hiding her desire to raise her voice. "My sister — my *actual* sister — is in that room, mourning her dead husband. I'm not willing to have a pity contest with you, Neil. We're both…on edge. And don't — don't raise your voice at me, either, I had enough of that when we were living together."

"I sat up all night with Don. Where were *you*?"

"I went home. What was I supposed to do, Neil? I was shoved out in the corridor. I tried to help, but *what could I do*?"

"You should've been there," he told her angrily. "You should've been there for your Don and you never have been. She's sacrificed everything to be with Matt. No privacy, can't even go for a run without the paps getting in her face, can't go down the Spar for a pint of milk without a full face of makeup. It's not easy being her, you know. You're fucking selfish, Liz. You always were!"

Lizzie breathed deeply. She remembered the afternoon she had slipped back to Chorlton to collect the last of her things. She'd thought he would be at training, but his car had been in the driveway. She'd decided to go into the house anyway. She'd been civil, so had he. Until she struggled with the chest of drawers and had had to pull it hard to open it. Neil had thundered up the stairs, yelling at her not to smash the place up, and he had yanked the drawer so hard that one of the handles had come off. He'd swung the drawer away from her, almost catching Lizzie's face with its corner, and its contents had spilled out in a wide arc across the room.

With a sneer etched into his face, he had proceeded to smash up the drawer. Lizzie had backed away against a wall, watching his relentless attack on the humble piece of flat-pack furniture. His rage, his hurt pride at her leaving him, had come pouring out. And as he'd kicked at the drawer, and wrenched its sides off with his powerful arms, he'd shouted *'You're selfish. You're fucking selfish. This is all your fault, you and your fucking curtains. All these years I've wasted with you, and you weren't even fucking here because your business is more important than me!'*

She pushed the sound of the breaking wood out of her mind.

"I *have* been there for Donna."

"You're jealous because she got a prem *megastar* and you. Make. Curtains."

"I never wanted the life that Donna has. She wanted it, and she went after it. When you and I got together, all she said to me, constantly, was 'Can Neil introduce me to this player and that player and some other

265

player?' She made as much use of you as she could. Perhaps you can be matchmaker for her again, Neil, just as soon as she's cast off her widow's weeds."

"You're a cold bitch, Liz." He took a step away, as though she were poison. "Her heart's broken, and you're running about with a fancy man and no time for her. You're a class act."

"How — how the —? *Fancy man?*"

"Lizzie first, Don second." He shook his head in pity. "Cold fucking bitch."

"I'm not — I'm not a bitch. I'm *not!*" Lizzie pressed her lips together, failing to hold back her tears.

Neil shrugged and turned his back. Then, as he walked away, he punched the air and began to chant, "Matt D-L! Matt D-L!"

His voice echoed around the corridor, and acolytes and hangers-on appeared from who knew where to join in the chant for their dead hero. The chant grew louder. It rang in Lizzie's ears until it was all she could hear. She wandered away along the corridor and pushed her way into the ladies' toilets. Once the door was shut behind her, she heard her phone ring in her pocket.

It was Ben.

"How're things going?" There was still noise behind him, crowds now.

"Neil knows about you, about us. I don't know how, but he does."

"Does he know who I am, or is it just that you're seeing someone?" Ben's voice was soothing.

"He said — He said I'm *'running about with a fancy man'*. I have no idea if he realises you're a copper."

"Don't worry about that. Are you with Donna?"

"I've been sitting in the family room. It's why I rang you, really. I'm just sort of there, if you see what I mean. I haven't been able to talk to her. She doesn't stop crying, and all these WAGs keep turning up and they're all crying too. It's— My nerves are shot. I just wanted to talk to you, and when I left the room, Neil appeared."

"You sound worried sick. Has he done something?"

"He wasn't very nice to me." As if he had said he hadn't liked her shoes.

"I'm sorry." She heard movement, the voices growing a little quieter. "Get home, get a cuppa and try to relax. I'm going to be really late tonight, but I can come over if you won't be in bed?"

Despite her tears, Lizzie grinned. "Even if I *am* in bed, you should come over. I'll tell Arthur to buzz you up."

"Have what's left of the day to yourself and, while you're at it," she heard a smile in his voice, "get your Christmas tree up. You're running out of days!"

"All right then. It'll be up when you come over this evening, I promise, but you'll have to help me decorate it."

"Deal. Now home, bath, food, relax. And think of your old copper, pounding the pavement looking for answers."

"I think of you all the time anyway. And I'll get you beer! Goodbye, Ben. Take care, won't you?"

"I always do. Love you, gorgeous!"

Lizzie blew a kiss at the phone. She put her fingertips to her warm cheek. She was blushing.

Chapter Twenty-Four

Lizzie had brought the Christmas tree home in the taxi. It wasn't as big as she would've liked, but it was as large as she could carry by herself. She found a plastic bucket in a cupboard and, after a heroic struggle, righted the tree in it. Her fabric stash sufficed to dress the bucket in red cotton with a big white satin bow.

Tomorrow, she'd buy glass ornaments from the German market, and she'd get lights. Bundles of them, and not just for the tree. She'd drape the flat with ropes of them. Because lights shone against the darkness, lights guided you home.

Lizzie cracked open a bottle of Bailey's. It was nearly Christmas, after all. She raised a toast to the late, great Matt de Luca, and polished off the glass in one go.

The smell of the Norwegian spruce made her feel that Christmas wasn't going to be a solitary day. She'd be with the man she loved, and they would be happy. Even if she mourned Matt, his death and thought of

Ben's bereavement, it made her feel, intensely, that they should live in the time that they had.

She spent the evening binging on comedy Christmas specials, and as it grew time to go to bed, she realised that what was missing, other than Ben, was the smell of mincemeat and spices, stuffing and a turkey, and the sulphur from crackers. She'd buy a saucepan, a huge one, and they'd have mulled wine. They'd ladle it up and become tiddly without realising, and fall asleep on the sofa together.

No calls or texts came from Ben. But Lizzie didn't expect any. He was busy, after all. Once she had washed, got into her pyjamas and snuggled into the ridiculous big bed with her rag doll, Lizzie sent Ben a text.

Off to bed now with Daisy. Arthur will let you up. Ring and I'll open the door. Christmas will be lovely with you. Your L xxx

Lizzie sank into dreams about Christmas and about her Ben. But at some point in the night, for no reason that she could fathom, she woke up. She checked her phone and it was four in the morning. *Where's Ben?* Lizzie got out of bed and rang down to the concierge. No one had called for her.

Just as Lizzie ended the call, her phone rang again, but with an unknown number.

She couldn't answer it. What if it was the stalker? But it was four in the morning. What if it was Ben?

"Hello?"

"Is that Lizzie?" It was a young woman's voice, thick with cold or sorrow. "It's Sam, Ben's girl?"

"Oh, hello, Sam!" *How nice of her to ring. Although why at this time? Unless something's —* "Sam, are you okay? Is your dad okay? It's the middle of the night."

"Dad's in hospital, can you come? He's all right — he isn't, but he will be —" She sniffed back a sob. "We're at the infirmary."

No, no, this isn't right. This isn't meant to happen. Ben's invincible. Ben protects everyone. This can't be true.

But it is.

"I'll come at once. Tell him Lizzie's on her way?"

Without waiting for a reply, Lizzie ended the call and changed as fast as she could into the clothes she had discarded earlier on the bathroom floor. She was crumpled and her eyes were sore in the bright bathroom light, but she didn't care. She threw some things into a bag and ran off downstairs.

Trying to get a taxi at this time of the morning seemed impossible, until Lizzie stood, in desperation, in the middle of the road, and managed to flag down a cab.

"Couldn't leave you just stood there, lass, not if it's an emergency!"

The journey was swift in the near-empty streets, and Lizzie soon arrived at the hospital. The front entrance was garlanded with tributes to her late brother-in-law. Her pace slowed. There were so many flowers, football shirts, homemade print-off photos, teddy bears and guttering candles.

Hero to so many. And now he's dead.

What a dreadful waste of a life.

Lizzie met Sam at A and E. The young woman looked utterly exhausted, her legs clad in what appeared to be pyjamas patterned with pugs, her body buried in a heavy green parka and trainers on her feet.

Her eyes were bloodshot but she wasn't crying now, though she clearly had been.

"Hey." She managed a smile. "I'm sorry for ringing so late."

Lizzie stroked her arm.

"Honestly, it's all right, Sam. I'm glad you did. I'd woken up for some reason anyway. What on Earth has happened to him, Sam? And are *you* okay? Have you had something warm to drink?"

"Someone—" She took a deep breath, obviously willing herself not to cry again. "Someone beat him up. A bunch of lads interrupted. It sounds like it was really bad and—" A few tears escaped, her voice cracking. "He's all bruised and—this is really creepy, it's stressing me out—whoever it was dumped a massive bunch of lilies there when he ran off, like funeral flowers. I reckon it's to do with that footballer? People really love him. What if they're trying to get revenge or something?"

Lilies. Lizzie again saw the bunch tied onto the gate, how the bouquet had burst apart and the petals had been scattered by the wind.

Whoever had attacked Ben had not intended him to survive.

"Can I see him, Sam?"

The younger woman took her hand and together they walked down an empty corridor, their footsteps echoing. After a minute or so, Sam pushed open a door and stood back to let Lizzie enter the dimly lit room, where she could already see Ben beneath the bedsheets. At the sound of movement, he lifted his head just a little to show a face that was blooming with purple bruises, his right eye blackened and his upper lip split. Dressings were dotted here and there on his bare arms and the top of his chest, where the neatly folded blankets didn't cover him.

His hands rested atop the covers. The left was bandaged, but he raised his right in a tired gesture of welcome.

Lizzie wanted to hold him but didn't know how she could without hurting him. So she took his hand and pressed her lips to the top of his head, to his thick, near-black hair that still had the metallic scent of the night-time.

"Ben, my love, who did this to you?"

"Probably City fans," he told her. He was trying for cheeky but the words sounded painful and he closed his eyes. Sam hovered in the doorway and he told her, "Get in this room, Samantha Finneran. I want my two best girls with me."

Sam's trainers squeaked across the highly polished lino. Lizzie stretched out her hand to Ben's daughter, and once she reached the bedside, Lizzie wrapped her arm around Sam's shoulders. She wouldn't think about the lilies, wouldn't contemplate how close she had come to losing Ben.

"The Christmas tree's up in my flat. Need to get some decorations for it, but the place smells of Christmas now, save for all the food."

"That's Dad's job," Sam told her. "Christmas stockings, mulled wine, turkey and all the trimmings. You're coming for dinner, aren't you? My house is a bit crappy but it's allowed to be. It's student digs."

"You're welcome to come to mine. I've got a spare room. It's got a four-poster bed!"

"We can't all descend on you," Ben murmured. "There's Anj too. It wouldn't be fair."

"I'm in Anj's debt anyway. And you, Ben Finneran, shouldn't be worrying about that. You can't go back to the hotel in this state. You could come back to mine. You need looking after."

Lizzie paused and turned to look at Sam. She was aware that she was overstepping the mark. His daughter might be young, but Lizzie didn't want Sam to feel shoved aside if she was already planning to help him recover.

"That is, if — ? Sam, were you going to take your dad home? I don't mean to encroach."

"He's bad enough with a cold," Sam teased. "He's all yours!"

"How long are they keeping you in for, Ben?"

"It's a few bruises," he told her. "I bet I'll be out for dinner."

"Tomorrow — or at least, this evening, then? Is there anything you need that I can pick up?"

"I'll sort all that," Sam assured her. "You concentrate on warming his chicken soup."

"Let's pull up a couple of chairs, Sam, and keep the old plod company."

Lizzie and Sam sat together by Ben's bed, Sam's head on Lizzie's shoulder. She stayed awake as long as she could, listening to the collective slumbering breaths of the Finnerans, listening for the footsteps of the stalker, the poisoner, whoever it was out there who dealt only in destruction. But after a while, Lizzie began to sleep, her head resting on the edge of Ben's pillow. When she woke up a few hours later, Sam was lying asleep across Lizzie's lap. Lizzie stroked the sleeping girl's hair.

Ben's eyes flickered open. Very slowly, as though every movement hurt, he brushed his hand to Lizzie's face.

"Good morning," Lizzie whispered.

"Hello." He managed a smile but it became a wince, thanks to the split in his lip. "You should see the other guy."

"He better hope I don't or I'll—" Lizzie stopped herself. Violence upon violence wouldn't solve a thing. "Do you remember anything about what happened?"

"I was walking to the car," he told her. "Next thing, I'm dragged off the street and being used as a punchbag. I can usually handle myself, but, well, you can see how that went."

She didn't want to see, but the proof was there before her, her lover's body brutalised into a painful mass of bruises. And if this was what they could do to Ben, a tall man, usually fit and healthy, then what— A prickle of terror shot up Lizzie's spine.

But she wouldn't allow herself to be frightened. She had to be brave for the people she loved.

"Someone must've seen who it was, surely. Did you, or was it too quick?" Lizzie almost sounded like Ben when she declared, "They won't get away with this. I won't let them."

"I didn't get a look at him. It was like being hit by a bloody train." Ben closed his eyes, drawing in a long and deep breath. "I hardly managed to get a punch in."

Lizzie sighed her lover's name. "Do you want me to find a nurse? Do you want more pain relief? Just tell me what you need, and I'll look after you."

"I needed my girls with me, and they're here." He smiled a lopsided smile. "I love you."

Lizzie bent towards him and, as lightly as she could, on a tiny patch of unbruised skin, kissed his cheek. He shifted just a little, but it was enough to press closer to her kiss, and his sigh this time was one of contentment.

Chapter Twenty-Five

The day passed in a blur of doctors and police, a curious mix of concern and camaraderie that lifted Ben out of his self-reflection. With Lizzie and Sam departed for the hotel under strict instructions to secure Kendal Mint Cake above all else, he did his best to convince the doctor *not* to sign him off sick, eventually managing to barter the medic down from three weeks to a fortnight.

It wasn't ideal, but he could still think, could still get onto the system, even if he couldn't pound the streets. He could still feel that bearpaw grip on his throat, see the ground rushing up to meet him, suffer through every kick that landed in his ribs and kidneys, and in the air, the scent of lilies.

This changed everything about the case, the poisoner turning to beating.

Something had made it personal.

Night had fallen when Ben was discharged, and he left the hospital with Lizzie as his support, travelling to her flat in a car personally supplied by Worthington.

Yet all the time he was turning over the previous night in his mind, not as a victim, or a man in pain, but as a detective whose quarry had changed, had gone over the edge somewhere.

Tonight though, he couldn't think of that, because he was too full of painkillers and the knowledge that he had survived purely by luck, that a bunch of drunks looking for a place to relieve themselves had seen off a killer. Tonight he was safe in Lizzie's arms, just being Ben.

When the front door of the flat opened, the homely smell of the Christmas tree met Ben's nose.

"Fancy a brew and a biscuit? Do you want to sit in the lounge, go to bed or get cleaned up? Kendal Mint Cake is on the pillow with Daisy. Hopefully they've been behaving themselves!"

"I need to get cleaned up and have a drink of something." He paused, narrowing his one good eye. "I smell Christmas?"

"You'll see the tree in good time. Let's get you in the bathroom. I know — hot chocolate! Can you drink that with a splash of brandy, or will it make you go funny on all those pills?"

"I'm sure I can force it down."

"Good. I'll get the bath running and you just sit tight. Lots of bubbles?"

Lizzie helped him every wincing step into the bedroom and perched him on the edge of a plush armchair. Singing a Christmas song to herself, she went into the en suite. He settled back gingerly, smiling at the tree, at the sound of her voice, at the knowledge that Sam was safe with Anj, that they were all — for tonight at least — where they should be.

This morning he'd felt old, half dead, used up and wrung out, but now he felt a little bit more like Ben, though a bruised, sore version of himself. He looked down at his bandaged left hand, remembered the force of a trainer stamping down on it and the way he had clenched his fist to protect his gold wedding band from that hellish foot. The band was in his pocket now, and where it would go next, he wasn't sure. Holly would have loved Liz, that much he knew, and she deserved better than to be dating a man who wore a wedding ring when she didn't. The time had come to put that gold band safely away until Sam met someone worthy of it. It might need resizing, of course, but it deserved to continue on its journey.

He reached into his pocket and felt the wedding ring there. It was Sam's now, and in the back of his mind, he heard Holly's voice, rich with mirth, telling him, '*About bloody time, Fin.*'

Lizzie appeared with a tray. Two mugs steamed on it.

"Your bath is ready when you are." She tenderly kissed the top of Ben's head. "I'll put this tray down and get you undressed."

"I'm going to give my wedding ring to Sam." He lifted his head to look at her. "I want us to be us, and I know Hol would understand that."

Lizzie lowered her eyes, apparently fascinated by the mugs on her tray.

"I think Sam would like that." Lizzie raised her glance to Ben's. "She was asking me about us, when she and I went to the hotel. I told her I felt a bit embarrassed being in that room with her, and she said she was glad, because she'd wanted you to find someone."

"I know we've only known each other a few weeks, but it feels like a lifetime to me. I love you so much, Liz." He rested his hand over hers. "I want us to be together."

"I do too, more than I've ever wanted anything." Her cornflower blue eyes were brimming over with love for him. But then came the pert grin and the dimples that he loved so well. "Let's get you into the bath, DCI Finneran. You look altogether too roguish in that leather jacket of yours!"

She went off with the tray and returned without it, ready to heave Ben up from the armchair. His closed his good hand around hers in a firm grip and rose on rather shaky legs to stand, telling her, "I've had this jacket longer than Sam's been around!"

"It looks like you stole it from Steve McQueen."

"It's older than I am," he admitted as they made their careful way through to the bathroom, where a deep, inviting bubble bath waited. The rich fragrance was in stark and welcome contrast to that of the hospital, which still clung to his hair, and he paused to breathe it in, to return to sanity.

Lizzie carefully peeled him out of his jacket. It took time, pausing for breath after freeing one arm, preparing himself for more soreness. Once the jacket was off, Lizzie draped it around her shoulders.

"Does it suit me?"

He had a sudden image of Lizzie in that Parisian lingerie of hers with that same vintage jacket, lying back on the luxurious Montmartre bed. He tried to blink it away, but it wouldn't shift. Of course, he wouldn't tell her, because she might just laugh.

"I was just thinking of how good it'd look with even less clothes." So much for that plan then. At least he could blame the painkillers. "And how gorgeous you are."

"Nice to know you're still as saucy as ever! Now off with that T-shirt." She hung the jacket on the back of the bathroom door then came back to Ben and put her hands on the hem of his top. "I hope this won't hurt too much." She began to inch it up.

"Before you go any further..." He took a deep breath, but he had to tell her before she saw the purple bruise that marked the treads of his attacker's training shoe. "My stomach took a bit of a kicking, and it's not pleasant. I just don't want you to get upset."

"Don't worry about me. You're here now, *almost* in one piece, and that's what matters."

He saw her swallow as she raised the T-shirt, her eyes darting between his glance and the bruises that he knew were now visible. If there had been anything he could do to take away the hurt he could see in her eyes now, he would have, but there was nothing for it but to brave it out and make it into something to be laughed at, not some madman who had made this personal.

"It's harder than it looks, being a *gendarme*."

Lizzie's mouth twitched at the corners, a flash of desire shining behind the gentle concern in her eyes. Her voice was soft and loving. "Arms up, and let's get this T-shirt off."

Ben obeyed as meekly a child, gritting his teeth simply because he wasn't about to show her how much it hurt, which was only going to add to her worry. She would see the bruises, the cuts and grazes, but she didn't need to know that it was agony.

Lizzie's fingertips hovered over Ben's bruises, as if she wanted to touch but couldn't. She was trying to smile.

"Nearly there. Jeans next."

"You might have to help with that," Ben teased. "My hand's all bandaged, after all."

"Don't worry. I have experience in these matters." Her cheeky tone slipped away. "Are your legs bad too? Just so I— Tell me if it hurts, won't you?"

"Just a bit bruised here and there," he assured her. "He gave me a bloody hard kick in the balls too, so I might not be the most acrobatic *gendarme* for a few days."

"What the hell is wrong with people?" Lizzie avoided his eyes, carefully unfastening his button fly. "A poisoner, kicking you there? What for?"

She knows.

His efforts to keep it from Lizzie were all for nothing, Ben realised. She had known all along, and he would hardly blame her if she sent him back to the hotel where they had first met. Who knew what kind of madman might be targeting him, after all, and here he was in her flat, bringing that madman to her door.

"I mean, if it is the poisoner? Sam said they found lilies in the alleyway. She assumed it was a City fan, that it's to do with Matt—and it *is* to do with Matt, isn't it, but only because..." Lizzie looked up at him from where she knelt on the floor. "You'll be safe here. I won't let anyone hurt you again. They've got to come through me first!"

"I don't even know if I should be here, Liz," Ben admitted quietly. "I hadn't even thought— I don't want him following me to you. Maybe I should be on my own. That way, nobody I love's at risk."

"You should be here because we want to be here together. Sod them, whoever they are. I'm not going to be scared. And right now, there's absolutely no way I'm letting you go. You need looking after. You can't possibly be alone."

And he couldn't argue, because it was true and he knew it. He had come through so much— Holly's accident, her death, raising their girl alone, looking after her and the memory of his wife, and a career, and a house, and— It had been a long ten years. Yet now, here in a new city chasing shadows, he finally needed someone to look after *him*, and he couldn't imagine that there was a luckier man on earth, bruises and all.

Lizzie gave him an awkward grin. "At the risk of sounding indelicate, shall I yank them down quickly?"

He made a point of squaring his shoulders, as though facing up to an angry bull, and nodded. "Do it."

"After three. One, two!"

Down they came, a count too early, the oldest trick in the book, like ripping off a plaster.

She guided him to sit on the side of the bath, and Ben was divested of his shoes and socks, which he could never have bent over to remove himself.

"All ready now, Ben. If the water's too hot or cold, just say and I'll sort it. Hold my hand and dip in a toe. And don't get that bandage wet."

The temperature of the water was perfect, but as he settled into it, Ben was reminded of the evening he had promised that they had never had, sharing this bath and drinking cold beers. Instead, here he was, bloodied and battered, more helpless than he had been in his entire life.

"I'm sorry, Lizzie," he murmured. "It's pretty embarrassing, getting a pasting like this."

"If it had been a fair fight, *my* money would've been on you. The bastard who goes about doing this is a nasty little wimp—spikes people's drinks and sneaks away, jumped you in the dark. And *you're* not a wimp. I saw you run out into the street after them. Fearless. At least it seemed like it."

She showed him his bottle of shampoo. A slice of normality.

"Shall I wash your hair? I won't if your head feels sore, though."

"Would you? It smells of hospital." He turned his head to watch her. "I went after that CCTV of yours. Owner's back from Bali a couple of days after Boxing Day. I've got to sit tight until then. Shall we include Bali on our research trip?"

"I think we shall. Close your eyes!"

Warm water cascaded over his head and Ben closed his eyes. The click of a bottle, then her fingers, massaging his scalp, foam running down his face. He listened to the sounds of Lizzie's movements, the sigh of her breath, and again he was struck by how close he'd come to never being here again, to never being *anywhere*. Yet the killer had claimed his premiership scalp just hours earlier, then abandoned the shadows that concealed his poisons and risked the chance of being face-to-face with the police officer who had been chasing him for years.

And it made no sense at all.

"What do you think changed, Liz?" He murmured the question. "He's won, but why did he go after Matt de Luca? Why turn poisoning into beating? There's something obvious and I'm missing it."

Lizzie paused, her fingertips circling Ben's scalp. "Here's something I was wondering today, while I was stuck in that family room with Donna. If that cocktail I had *was* spiked, and if Donna's was too, why wait and kill Matt? Was it a warning shot? But then, weren't all the other poisonings random? That's not random, is it? Me, Donna, Donna's husband, then you get beaten up."

"And ten years ago, when all this began, Matt was fourteen years old, so it's not some old vendetta being played out. We've had psychologists on this, the works. They tell us *'he plays God with strangers'* and now, out of nowhere, he doesn't." Ben opened his eyes, blinking the water from his eyelashes. "If those lilies tonight hadn't been tied with *the* ribbon, I'd have called it a copycat and been looking at your ex, but the ribbon changes all that. Don't suppose you or your sister have any crazy-eyed florists or undertakers lurking among your ex-boyfriends?"

Lizzie laughed. "No! I have very few exes, anyway. But Neil was so nasty to me. I'm a *'cold, selfish bitch'* with a *'fancy man'*, according to him. That kick in the balls makes me wonder if it really was him, after all. It would make sense. What bloke wouldn't want to kick his ex's new man in the nads? But then, how do you explain the lilies and the ribbon? Unless…"

"Don't stop at *unless*," Ben urged. "Keep going."

"He's got a temper. I witnessed him smash up a piece of furniture when I left him. You don't think — It's ridiculous me even saying this, but what if it really is Neil? He was living in London ten years ago, then moved up here."

"He has a watertight alibi for the night I chased the guy under your window," Ben reminded her, "and for at least *one* of the murders. He was sitting behind the dugout all evening, right there on Sky Sports."

Something about it bothered him though. Could this be a jealous boyfriend hiding behind something bigger? He would have known of the ribbon and lilies from the de Luca house. Perhaps he just stepped into something far bigger than he was.

"Can I be a pain and ask you to grab my phone, Liz?"

"You're *never* a pain." She kissed the air an inch or so above his soapy hair. "Is it in your jacket?"

"It is," he replied, pleased that, if nothing else, at least he'd got her Christmas gift before the axe had fallen. "I'm going to ask Worthington to bring your ex in for the beating. If it was him, he'll have the split knuckles to show for it."

Lizzie didn't say anything, but he heard her cross the large bathroom to where his jacket hung on the back of the door. She was almost beside him at the bath when Ben heard a stifled noise in Lizzie's throat.

"Here's your phone." Her voice was oddly robotic.

"I'm really sorry, Lizzie." He held out his hand not for the phone, but to lace his fingers through hers. Could he do this to her, to the man she used to love?

No, he wasn't sure he could.

"If you want me to pretend we never thought about Neil, I won't make that call." He kissed her hand with his split lip, feeling her soft skin. "We'll let it go past as a moment of madness."

"No, I want you to. I *need* you to. If it was him who attacked you, I'm not going to stand in the way. I just — a horrible little voice in my mind is telling me that if it *was* Neil who attacked you, then it was *my* fault. He'd want me to think that. But I'm mustering the strength to shout it down."

"One person's to blame, and we'll bring him in tonight. We'll see if we can link him to the attacks too, but those alibis…" Ben let the sentence hang. "Should I make the call?"

"Yes, Ben, you have to, before he hurts anyone else."

He took the phone and selected Worthington's number, then neither of them spoke as Ben listened to the tone and waited for his boss to answer. The information was swiftly relayed — suspicions about Neil Mellor, the power of jealousy — the strength of the man, and Worthington took it all in, seemingly rather fired-up at the thought of making a collar of his own after years behind a desk. With a parting shot to remind Ben that *he* was on sick leave until the new year, he rung off, leaving Ben to ask Lizzie, "When *did* the two of you get together? What month?"

Lizzie passed Ben his mug of hot chocolate and she took one for herself. She perched on the edge of the bath, swirling her free hand in the water without looking at Ben.

"Funnily enough, it was around Christmas, nine years ago. We had a mutual friend, someone I knew from uni. Neil had just got the job up here, and our friend insisted we all go out together for Christmas drinks, starting with a slap-up curry in Rusholme. I drank far too much and Neil acted the gentleman and escorted me home. I thought he was very charming. He took me to the door and didn't attempt anything. Then the next day our mutual friend said Neil wanted my number. And…that was it, really. My business was beginning to take off, and he got commissions with the players and was so helpful. Ingratiating, as I see it now. Controlling. Then we moved in together and… I couldn't see it at the time. He was manipulative. Chased away my friends. Made me feel guilty and belittled me, my business. Said everything I had, I owed to him. I told myself I was being silly, and so did my family, but… I'm sorry. You don't need to hear all that. It's pathetic."

"I want to hear it. I want us to know each other." He took a sip of hot chocolate. "But the London poisonings were ten years ago, so if we're talking about Neil, where was he in the interim? What happened between his leaving London and meeting you that stopped him in his tracks?"

"He went abroad. His family are up here, you see, so after moving from London, he was in America for a while, then the job came up at the club and he applied so he could come home. I've seen photos of him out there, when he wanted to rub it in about his ex, who was a six-foot-tall cheerleader."

"If you're about to tell me she met a sticky end," Ben warned playfully, trying to make this seem less terrible than it was. Could she *really* have been sharing her bed with a killer for nearly a decade? Had Lizzie been the factor that stopped him in his— "You were sick on the first night with him?"

"I was *very* drunk. And yes, I did throw up, when we got out of the taxi, and he held my hair back, which seemed a bit above-and-beyond. But I was so grateful to him, and— Oh, he didn't! He couldn't! I'd drunk a lot, and I'm not proud of myself, but—" Lizzie closed her eyes. "As for Bree, that cheerleader, I have no idea what happened to her. I sometimes wondered if he just made all that up and she was some woman he happened to have a couple of photos of."

Had he dosed her, made Lizzie sick to be her white knight?

Ben forced himself to rewind, to be the cool, analytical police officer he had been trained as. But could it *really* be Neil? No, he reminded himself. There were still those alibis and those televised matches. If Neil was involved, he wasn't working alone.

And it was Worthington's problem for tonight.

"Ms. Lizzie Aspinall," he blinked, his black eye stinging, "why *aren't* you in this bath with me?"

"I don't want to squash you and make you sore. But if you *insist*, DCI Finneran."

She pulled her jumper up over her head and, her eyes beginning to glow, hurled it across the room as if the striptease dancer had returned, which wasn't entirely out of place in the bathroom of a Montmartre bordello, even if her clothes were less *Parisian lady of the night* and more *sensible Manchester woman in winter*.

Ben watched her appreciatively, even if his bruised body didn't allow him to show it. He shifted a little painfully to let her join him among the bubbles, promising, "You're safe now, Liz. Neil'll be brought in tonight and once I see that CCTV... I just know our man's on there."

Lizzie danced her fingertips lightly over Ben's knee, where it stuck out above the surface of the bathwater.

"You realise, don't you, that what we have, it was never like that with him."

"What you had with Neil doesn't change anything about us," he assured her. "I don't expect you to have lived in a convent for thirty years waiting for a man to strip off in a hotel room window for you."

He sat back against the bath with a sigh, wondering what was happening with Neil Mellor at this moment. Did he have an alibi or were his knuckles split and bruised? Did he wear Nike trainers, the tread of which was currently on Ben's stomach, and if he did — and Ben was sure of it— where did he get that black ribbon with its distinctive fleur-de-lys? He knew beyond a

The Man in Room 423

shadow of a doubt that the poisoner was the man who had attacked him tonight, and if that was Neil Mellor —

"I think it's Neil," he whispered. "He had access to Matt's house on the night of his death, to his water bottle all that matchday, but I can't work out how he did it on those nights when he was in the dugout. Did he put it in the bottles somehow or — "

Ben shook his head.

"I'm getting ahead of the investigation. Let's see if it was him to start with."

"If it is him, then maybe that would explain how I recognise the ribbon. Maybe it was in our house somewhere? Maybe at his mum's, even. But..." Lizzie sighed and cupped a handful of water over herself, tipping it from her neck, down her chest and onto her breasts without the slightest coquettish intent. "I can't picture it. And yet I know I've seen it."

"Don't think about it," he told her. "I never get the answer when I'm thinking about it."

"Do you know that I've dreamt about the ribbon? I chase it, like the string of a balloon, and it always slips out of my grasp."

"We'll get there when I'm not so bruised," Ben murmured, his eyes still closed. "I'm just dreaming of all those exotic places that you and I will be seeing soon, all those beaches where we get to roll in the surf in between the odd bit of writing books for you and spending the house money for me."

He revelled in her company, in the touch of her skin on his beneath the bubbles, on the sheer sight of her there in the low light. Somewhere out there a possible killer was about to be apprehended or might have been already. The thought of Neil Mellor's thick wrists in handcuffs was one that filled him with a sense of satisfaction he could hardly countenance. Ten years of torment, families who couldn't enjoy peace, the dead who couldn't rest easy… It would all be over soon. The victims would finally have the justice they deserved.

And he'd be free of it too, no longer wondering where the killer was, what he was doing, if he was going to strike again.

They would all be at peace.

Peace was the last thing Ben was able to enjoy when his phone buzzed into life and, seeing Worthington's name on the screen, he snatched it up from the side of the bath and answered. What he heard was the last thing he would ever have guessed, and for a moment, Ben wondered if he was still in hospital or perhaps the pills were stronger than he'd thought. Yet the more Worthington talked, the more it became a stone-cold reality and he met Lizzie's gaze, realising that he was going to have to tell her.

"Lizzie," Ben said gently as he let the phone fall onto the thick bathmat, "that was the boss. He's been to Neil's house."

She brought her arms in a protective gesture to cross her chest. She was still, then met Ben's eyes with her own, so large and blue.

"Please just tell me. I can hear it in your voice, Ben. For God's sake, say it."

"I'm so sorry, Lizzie. It looks as though Neil —" How did you even begin to say it? "He killed himself, Liz."

She broke their glance. Her arms tightened across her, her chin fell to her chest, the end of a loose length of damp hair dropping into the water. She curled her legs under her and she cried.

And he watched her, because he didn't know what else to do, because he was a copper with no experience of women other than his wife, and how the hell could he comfort a woman whose lover of nine years had just been found dead?

Perhaps he would get it wrong, Ben reasoned, but he couldn't do nothing, so he reached out and took her hand, saying nothing as he held it in a careful grip.

Lizzie returned his clasp. She grasped the edge of the bath with her other hand, the defensive gesture gone.

"I don't even know why I'm crying. For myself…because I lived unhappily with that man for all that time? Or for the people whose loved ones he killed? Or for him, because he's dead, and I'm angry, and I cannot find it in myself to pity him or mourn him?"

She heaved a deep breath and gazed into Ben's eyes again.

"Or am I crying for you, because you spent ten years waiting to catch him, and he's slipped beyond the reach of earthly justice?"

"He won't be the first. The main thing now is that nobody else is going to die," Ben told her. Yet he wished for each of those parents, for the spouses and the children and the friends left behind, that Neil Mellor would have heard the final bang of a cell door behind him. "It was him, Liz. Worthington says the house stank like a funeral parlour, potted lilies out in the conservatory."

Lizzie grimaced. "And to think he moaned about the roses I put on the mantelpiece! Oh, he really was an utter git to live with, Ben. In the end, I used to do things on purpose just to annoy him." She laid her head back on the edge of the bath. "What the hell was I doing with him?"

Then, as if something had occurred to her, she lifted her head. "Have they found the ribbon?"

"They'll start looking at his house tomorrow, piecing it all together. He was the attacker, Liz. Apparently his knuckles were split wide open." Ben sighed, still wondering at something he couldn't quite place. "He must've been out of control, thought I'd got a look at him…"

"And thanks to him, I can't even give you a hug! But at least it's all over. I just wonder why he killed Matt when they were friends. Did he flip out and get jealous because Matt had that career, and the money and a wife? Next to Matt, Neil was a nobody."

"You can give me a hug." He smiled. "If he didn't manage to break me, a hug from a gorgeous girl certainly won't, even with a fine bosom like yours!"

Lizzie laughed, her face lighting up. She pulled herself onto her knees and, holding on to the edge of the bath, lowered herself down to Ben. She stopped with just a whisper of her skin lying against him.

"Is that too much?"

"It's never too much." He put his arms around her, drawing her closer still. "When he was beating me up, I couldn't think of anything but you and Sam. I thought I'd never see either of you again—"

Ben swallowed and closed his eyes tight for a few moments, wondering at the man who now lay dead on a hospital slab, a man who could turn on his best friend without motive, who could play God over perfect strangers who just wanted a drink with friends.

Lizzie whispered, "We both survived. And we mustn't waste a moment."

"I know," he told her gravely. "As soon as we've had our Christmas, I'm going to find somewhere up here, just until we're ready to travel."

Although her arms were loose about him, Ben noticed a slight tightening in them. Her breath caught. "Move in here?"

Did she mean it? Was this grief and worry and —

"I wouldn't want you to regret it. I can be bloody untidy, Liz." Yet he would love to.

"Do you think I would want to go to sleep each night alone in a pristine flat or get into bed with you every evening in an utter tip? There's no contest. Tidy or untidy, I love you."

"Sleeping every night in a bordello with the finest girl in France?" He cuddled her closer than ever, despite the bruises. "It's a *oui* from me!"

Lizzie hovered her mouth over his split lip, almost kissing him.

"*Mon naughty gendarme!*"

"Always!"

Chapter Twenty-Six

Ben, Lizzie and Sam had decorated the flat. It was gaudy, with 1970s paper globes, and had been festooned with so many fairy lights that it could be used as an alternative runway for Manchester airport. They were determined not to be miserable. Their first Christmas together was going to be a time for joy and vast amounts of mulled wine.

Atop the tree sat Daisy and Kendal Mint Cake, happily snuggled together among the branches whilst four Christmas stockings hung beside the fire, with even Anj not ignored since her promotion to Official Girlfriend.

By the time Christmas Day dawned, Ben Finneran would be an official — if still somewhat bruised — resident of the Parisian bordello. He was ready to venture out, he told Lizzie, and where better than to room 423 to pack bags, say goodbye to the bed where they had shared so much fun and finally pay off the hotel bill.

Lizzie knew she'd have to make space in the flat for Ben and his belongings.

"Seeing as we've got everything sorted for Christmas, I'm going to root through my stuff. I could just shove it all in storage, but somewhere I've got all the little frocks I made Daisy years ago. I have to show them to you. They're inept and adorable!"

"Doesn't matter," Ben told her happily as, with some effort, he managed to battle his bruises long enough to lace his boots. "Kendal Mint Cake wants to see his girl in all her finery."

Lizzie gave him her fondest grin. "Now off you go, because the sooner you leave, the sooner you'll be back, and the sooner it'll be Christmas."

"And you'll come as soon as Jordan's done?" He pulled on his leather jacket and stooped to kiss Lizzie. "We need to say a proper farewell to that bed, don't forget. And I need your help with the cases, but I wouldn't be so ungentlemanly as to admit it."

"I wouldn't miss a farewell to that bed for anything. And you must say *that thing you said* when you let me in and kiss me by the door."

They hadn't been able to make love since Ben's attack, but there were signs that Ben's robust constitution had rallied. In fact, in the two days since his return from hospital, he had been positively *perky*, in all senses of the word.

"Your key, *madam*!" Ben pressed the key card into Lizzie's hand as her mobile began to ring. "I'll see you later in 423, Louisa."

"I look forward to it, James." Lizzie checked the screen of her phone. "Oh, it's Donna...I better take this. See you later, handsome boyfriend."

"And you, gorgeous girlfriend." He kissed her again, scooped up his wallet and was gone, the flat door closing a few seconds later.

"Donna, hi, how are you?" Lizzie opened the hall cupboard, cunningly hidden behind the sword and shield, and assessed the pile of boxes before her.

"My husband has died and the man who killed him did it for me. Do you know that?" Her voice was deepened with grief. "I had a text from Neil the night he…he…"

She stopped, sobbing, her voice catching. "He said *'now we can be together'* and I didn't understand but now I do. He did it for me, Lizzie!"

Despite her happiness with Ben, despite having walked out on Neil, a flare of anger burst inside Lizzie. She bit her lip but couldn't help almost murmuring under her breath, *How long had my ex been in love with my sister?* But she had to be supportive for Donna. They had both gone through unimaginable trauma, and it wouldn't do to be jealous about a dead man.

"I'm so sorry, Donna. That's a horrible thing to discover. Make sure the police know? Even if they can't put Neil on trial, they're tidying up the loose ends. They'll need to know you were sent that text."

Lizzie dragged several suitcases from the cupboard. At the back was an old cardboard box that had come from the loft of their parents' house. If the rag doll's wardrobe was anywhere, this was it.

"I've told them already." Donna sniffed. "I'm going away with Franki after lunch. She's asked me to spend Christmas at her place in Southern France so I can grieve for Matt properly. I haven't had a chance to think about the funeral yet, but we're having a concert for him, because his people want to mourn him too, the people who looked up to him. It's for our fans. They really viewed us as City's royal couple."

Lizzie rolled her eyes, but fortunately Donna was unable to see from the other end of the phone.

"A concert? Wow, that's really sweet! Have fun in France, won't you? The weather should be a lot better there than it will be in Manchester!"

But even if it was sub-zero outside, Lizzie and Ben would be as cosy as could be.

Lizzie wrinkled her nose, holding back a sneeze as she pushed the cardboard box across the hallway. Lizzie paused. Maybe this wasn't such a great idea after all, as the flat was relatively clean, and the dusty old box would make a mess. But she was sure the dresses were in the box, and it was only dust, after all.

"How's the plod? Feeling better?"

"Almost. He's just gone out, actually. First time since the attack. He's moving out of the hotel." Lizzie would wait until Donna had come back from France to tell her that Ben was moving in. She couldn't wave her own happiness in the face of someone who had just been widowed. "It's a shame you can't pop by for Chrimbo. We're having quite the party!"

"There'll be a few of the squad in France, so I expect they'll do their best to help me take my mind off my loss." Donna's voice took on a pious tone. "Will you tell plod that I don't hold him in any way responsible for what happened to Matt? I'm sure he did the best he could manage. It just wasn't quite good enough."

Lizzie gave the cardboard box an extra-hard shove.

"Like I said, Don, they haven't finished tying up the case yet. We, both of us, stupidly didn't go to the police about that dodgy cocktail in the Mezz. Do you remember? Ben thinks it might've been spiked. They'll be able to look at the CCTV from that night soon, though, once the bar owner's back from holiday. They might find Neil in the act on video. Makes me shudder just to think of it. He could've killed us, Donna! Maybe he was going to kill you because he thought he couldn't have you and me out of revenge for dumping him, and when it didn't come off, he decided instead to get Matt out of the way. Horrible, messed-up man."

"Neil wasn't there." Donna laughed. "I would've seen him, wouldn't I? Nobody messed with anyone's drink. Tell him not to waste his time, Lizzie. Unless he was in disguise as the barman, and I think I would've spotted his tattoos!"

"They have to check the tapes, Donna. They can't leave any stone unturned. It might have taken very little, the tiniest distraction and he'd have poured the poison in, without you even knowing he was in the bar."

Lizzie opened the lid of the box. The familiar smell of their childhood home rose from inside it. An undefinable smell of misty autumn mornings at the beginning of the school year, with the leather scent of new T-bar sandals and the distant promise of Christmas.

"Neil? You were always so bloody stupid, Lizzie, such a drama queen!" She laughed again, but Lizzie could hear the familiar childhood rage rising in her voice. "My husband's dead, and it's *still* all about you, isn't it? It's like I'm broken and I need my sister for *me*, but no, *you* had a spiked cocktail, Lizzie with her nasty ickle drinkie! I'm the one who's still stuck in the shadows waiting to bury my bloody husband!"

"I tried to be there for you, Don, but your friends shoved me aside. And Ben and I did invite you for

Christmas. You know you're welcome here, but you're the one who's — who's —" *Lizzie's hair in pigtails, Donna tugging so hard the elastic bobble snapped, because Lizzie wouldn't let Donna play with Daisy.* "You're buggering off to the French Riviera instead. Hope you have a great time, but don't ever say I wasn't there for you, because I *was*."

"You never have been. I hope you have a *wonderful* Christmas, Lizzie, and I didn't mean what I said! I *do* blame your stupid old plod for Matt's death, and Neil's too! Stick that in your fucking stocking!"

And the line went dead, but Lizzie was left with the satisfaction that, no matter how hard she tried, Donna de Luca couldn't slam down a mobile phone. That would annoy her no end.

Under some plastic beads and childhood scribbles that had once been on show stuck to kitchen cupboard doors, Lizzie found the red ballet-slipper case that she had been hunting for.

She grinned like a child and lifted it onto the dining table. The lock was rusty and she knocked it open easily with the teaspoon Ben hadn't put away after breakfast. Exposed to view for the first time in nearly thirty years, Daisy's dresses had the power to drag Lizzie all the way back to her childhood — a wardrobe sewn by hand, from scraps of fabric and ribbon, from Mum, and nans and aunties. Here was a frock made from old curtains, and here was a frock with —

Lizzie's phone leapt into life, *Jordan* written across the screen. She shoved back her chair and went to the front door.

"You can use the intercom, you know!" But her tone wasn't chiding. She was only playing the grumpy boss. "I'll buzz you up."

Jordan arrived like a beardless Father Christmas, snuggled in a seasonal jumper complete with illuminated fairy lights, his arms full of brightly wrapped gifts from clients, many of them shaped suspiciously like bottles of champagne. He was full of gossip for Lizzie, all of his cheer and silliness eating away at the last trace of the annoyance Donna's call had left. It was also eating into the time she could be spending in 423 with Ben — *James* — of course, but they had forever now, so they didn't need to steal afternoons.

"Thanks so much for holding the fort while I've been busy. I owe you one, Jords. I better get on though and tidy these away." She raised an eyebrow. "I was once a top designer of *haute couture*, as you can see!"

"Busy being in her own episode of *Poirot*!" Jordan exclaimed, peering at the dresses. "Though your copper's a bit nicer to look at. You've had a right few weeks of it, Vivienne Westwood!"

"If it hadn't been for Ben, I don't know how I would've— Jordan! Are we still on for New Year's Eve?"

Lizzie shut the case again, but it was so full that the lock wouldn't stick. It burst open and the dresses scattered across the table.

And there it was.

The ribbon.

Black silk with a silver design of fleur-de-lys. When she had been eight years old, Lizzie had used it to trim a dress for her rag doll. It was only now, seeing the ribbon against the red gingham frock, that she realised, at last, why she had recognised it.

She had only been allowed a scrap of it, just enough for the trim. Their nan had produced it from her old sewing box. There had been a huge length of it, still on its original reel.

Jordan was saying something but Lizzie didn't hear him. The voice of her sister in the grip of a tantrum echoed down the years.

'No, Lizzie can't have the ribbon. I need it!'

Was it possible that Donna, who had been given the whole reel of ribbon that day to suppress her tantrum, when Lizzie had only been given an end, had kept it for all this time and had used it for so macabre a scheme?

"You all right, boss?" Jordan lightly brushed her arm. "You've gone white as a sheet!"

"Jordan, I'm sorry, I must get hold of Ben." She grabbed for her phone and swiped Ben's name.

* * * *

Ben heard his phone buzz in his jacket, which was hanging from the polished wooden coat hook in the office of the Mezz's manager. *Funny how things turn out*, he mused, watching the young man with the badly fitting T-shirt click through various files and drives in search of the CCTV feed for the night Lizzie and Donna had come to the bar.

Ben had been walking up the hotel steps when his phone rang and there, four days ahead of schedule, had been his chance to see the CCTV that might put a full stop on this whole sorry affair. Bali hadn't happened, the owner explained, thanks to an angry wife, a passport and a cigarette lighter, so if Ben really wanted to spend Christmas Eve trawling through grainy video footage of an uneventful evening in one of Manchester's most popular bars, he was welcome to do so.

Of course Ben had tried to call Lizzie and of course Donna had tied up the line, but he would have a couple of hours at least, he knew, and that would be more than enough time to get this done. This would tie up the last strands of thread and explain how, if Neil *had* been in that bar, Donna didn't see her own husband's best friend standing close enough to spike her drink.

Of course, maybe nobody had spiked anything and it had just been a bad cocktail, but time would tell.

"Bear with me a few more minutes," the bar owner told him apologetically, "I'll get there one day!"

"Like Bali," Ben replied with a sense of mischief he didn't feel.

"Hmph!" His companion huffed his reply. "Not if my wife's got anything to do with it!"

So Ben listened to his phone buzz and kept his eyes fixed on the screen, even though it wasn't the night in question. People had died here in Manchester, just as Susan Burns and her unborn child had died in London, and if Lizzie had been a guinea pig ahead of the attack on her brother-in-law, he needed to know who had spiked her drink.

Because he had the strangest feeling that it hadn't been Neil Mellor.

Chapter Twenty-Seven

Lizzie ran up Princess Street, dodging around last-minute shoppers, the cold air raw in her lungs. She tried to ring Ben again and again, but he wasn't answering. He'd be in room 423. Lizzie was running to him with the rag doll's dress in her pocket.

She had left him an out-of-breath voicemail, with the noise of buses and a brass band playing carols in the background.

"Ben, it's me. I remembered! The ribbon belonged to my nan, and she gave the reel to Donna! Neil sent her a text. *'Now we can be together.'* Did they do all this together? The lilies, the ribbon and Matt. Did they? I'm nearly at the hotel, I'm just coming up the steps."

At the top, Lizzie stopped, panting, every breath burning her throat. The doorman touched the brim of his hat.

"Merry Christmas, young lady."

With an effort, she said, "Merry Christmas to you too."

She spun through the revolving door and hurried across the hotel lobby, past the armchairs and the decorations and the Christmas tree. It took a while to find a free lift, but finally a pair of brass doors opened and Lizzie was on her way to the fourth floor and to Ben.

She leant back against the mirrored wall, her face reflected back at her. People often said she and Donna didn't really look alike, and as Lizzie stared, she tried to find points of difference and similarity between herself and her sister.

I don't want to look like a murderer.

Donna, with her narrow blue eyes made to look bigger with eyelash implants. Donna, with her dark hair burned blonde with bleach, tricked out with extensions. Donna, with her lip-plump and her Botox. Donna, with her false nails and her skyscraper heels. Donna, who wasn't entirely real.

The lift stopped on the fourth floor, and Lizzie took out her phone to ring Ben again.

There was a missed call from Donna.

Lizzie strode along to 423, her heart hammering in her chest. Another set of lift doors opened behind her, and as Lizzie went into the room that had changed the direction of her life, a hand came down on her shoulder.

"Oh, Ben, there you—"

Lizzie was shoved forwards, the door slamming shut behind her.

She was looking into her sister's face.

"Oh, sis." Donna pouted, her hair hidden beneath a wide-brimmed hat, her eyes beneath oversized sunglasses and on her feet, oddly, trainers. "You know how to pick 'em."

She drew back her hand and slapped Lizzie with enough force to send her reeling onto the bed, still the angry little girl she used to be.

"I mean, a *murderer*? Only *you* could bag a murderer while I bag a footballer, don't you think?" Donna opened her handbag and rifled through it. "Do you want to know, before I kill you, the how and why and all that rubbish? Like when we used to watch *Batman*? You probably don't, but I'd really love to tell you, because you never, ever gave me credit for being smarter than you."

Lizzie, still reeling from the slap, struggled to move off the bed.

Where the hell is Ben? Why isn't he in his room?

"Kill me? Donna, no! Don't, for God's sake! Come with me, and we'll find Ben, it'll be all right, I promise!"

Lizzie clutched onto the bedsheets, just as she once had in a transport of desire. And now it was only out of paralysing fear.

"Find Ben? Look... Wherever darling old *Ben* is, he's not going to see that CCTV. He doesn't *need* to see it." She took a small glass bottle from her bag, the sort that once held a half of vodka and now held a bright green liquid. "Neil was like a puppy sniffing round after me, Liz, because *you* couldn't give him what he wanted. And there was no way I was going to fuck a pathetic little thing like him when I had Matt, was there?"

"But Matt was so bloody thick. I mean, you met him, you know he was an idiot, but bloody hell, he was insured up to his *fucking* eyeballs." She leant back against the table where Lizzie had sat whilst Ben had plaited her hair. "And I just said once to Neil — and I was only being a bit silly — *'I'd be better off if he was dead.'* That doesn't make me horrible, does it? And your boyfriend said, '*I can make that happen. I can make your dreams come true, Donna.*'"

"Of course it makes you horrible, you bitch! Matt loved you. I saw it on his face at your wedding. He glowed with love for you. He adored you. Trusted you. How could you?"

"Because Neil told me he'd done it before, Liz, in London! And he stopped because of *you*, and because you broke his heart, his silly, stupid heart, he started again. Those people who died up here, *you* did that to them." She unscrewed the top from the bottle with her gloved hand. "But we had to lay a trail, so it looked as though there was a nutter out for Matt, you know? And that's what we've been doing in the bars…laying a trail. And we were too good for your old copper, and when the police break into this room and find him stabbed and you poisoned, well, they'll say, *poor old plod, victim of a crazy girlfriend* because believe me, I'm *really* fucking good at laying trails now. I'm good at the show, because your idiot Neil would never've thought of flowers, and I'm good at flushing away the shit, because let's be brutal, but what self-respecting widow on her way to the Champions League is going to want a crappy physio hanging off her bra straps?"

Lizzie looked from her sister to the door. She might just be able to make it, if she could only command her terrified limbs to get her off the bed. But then this was Donna. She could placate Donna if she was nice, if she gave her what she wanted, if she caved in, if she pleaded. '*Sorry, Lizzie, you can't have the ribbon. Just let Donna have it and she'll calm down.*'

"The police know it was you. They already do, because I've told them. Because I saw the ribbon, I remembered! It belonged to our nan. Think of her, think of what this would do to her if she was still alive! She hated it when we fought. It's too late, Donna. Surely you must realise you can't run from this. Give yourself up, before you make this any worse!"

"This didn't have to happen. People won't do as they're told. Neil beats up plod, plod insists on looking at cameras when we're all happy to just blame Neil on his own, to say, *well done, Neil, you were a one-man band*! I didn't even *mind* giving away the credit for my share of poisonings!" She brought the bottle to the bed and climbed up to straddle Lizzie, pinning her arms to her sides. Then she reached out and pinched her sister's nose tight. "So open wide, and drink your medicine. It feels like being pissed, Liz. You might even enjoy it!"

Once Donna had Lizzie pinioned to the bed, glaring at her with nothing but ice in her eyes, Lizzie realised that there was no time to plead. It might be too late, unless she fought. Lizzie sharply twisted her head to the side, her lips pressed close together. With all her might, she jack-knifed her hips up off the bed. She was still wearing her gloves, so she couldn't scratch, but she balled her fists and struck the insides of Donna's thighs.

Donna was unsteadied, and Lizzie braved herself to open her mouth, to shout, "Think of Mum and Dad. You can't do this, Donna, you can't! You'll destroy them!"

Lizzie took a deep breath and pressed her lips together again, feeling the glass bottle against her skin, liquid spilling over her face. She kept up her struggle, kicking her legs and rolling her hips, hitting out with her fists, trying to displace Donna as her attacker pressed down more heavily on her. Another hard slap across Lizzie's face, then her nose was pinched again and the bottle was pressing to Lizzie's tightly closed lips.

Lizzie fought for every second of life that remained to her, just in case someone came, someone heard. Because she couldn't die now, she couldn't leave Ben alone in the world.

Where is he?

Lizzie fought back tears. She had never felt so forsaken as she did at this moment, but she turned her fear into anger, fuel for the fight for her very existence.

She wasn't going to die in the bed where she had been brought back to life.

Chapter Twenty-Eight

Finally they found it there, in grainy, time-lapsed footage. Ben smiled as he watched Lizzie enter The Mezz just minutes before they fell in love, remembering the world before he even knew she existed. He saw her climb the steps, open the door, cross to the window, all of it mapping the land of their relationship, the little choices that could have changed everything. They might have gone on to another venue, chosen a table elsewhere in the room, sat in opposite seats so she hadn't looked over into the hotel, or at least, not into 423.

Yet she had, and now they had each other.

Then he watched Donna, tall and confident in high heels, her blonde hair poker straight, her enormous handbag dangling from one bent elbow, stand at the bar. The barman serving them in his trilby hat, throwing bottles into the air and catching them, performing a dizzying display of bartending acrobatics for his glamorous client. There was nobody else at the bar though, just the girls, and Ben felt the familiar knot of disappointment as he realised that there had been no spiking of the drinks that night, just a cocktail that hadn't been to Lizzie's taste.

And Donna, Donna with her bag and her stalker and her millionaire husband and —

"Life insurance," Ben murmured, the jigsaw suddenly complete in his head. Neil always at the house, a drunken Matt and a sober Donna, always ready with an alibi for the physio, but Matt didn't know, couldn't know, because he was drunk or on the pitch or — It seemed different because it *had been* different. Neil had no longer been acting alone. He'd had Donna now, Donna with flowers and money and every reason to want her husband out of the way.

Her husband and her accomplice too... What plan could be better than letting her partner take the fall for something that was done together?

As the lightbulb flicked into brilliant life in Ben's brain, he watched Donna take a small bottle of something that even the poor CCTV image could see was green, unscrew the cap and pour it into one drink.

She'd used her own sister as a guinea pig.

Ben went to his jacket in two strides and took out his phone. He saw the missed calls and —

So many missed calls.

"You need to preserve this footage." Ben turned and hurried to the window. From here he could look out onto 423, he realised, and in there — not a man at a window nor the woman he loved, but two women engaged in a fight that looked like it was to the death.

"Call 999! Room 423, The Midland!" And then he was running faster than he could remember running in his life, already punching in Worthington's name as he went. His bruised ribs were burning, his brutalised muscles screaming for rest, but there was no way on earth he could stop now.

Chapter Twenty-Nine

Spit it out, spit it out... The liquid that had seeped by sheer force through Lizzie's closed lips tasted sweet. Her gullet instinctively rose to swallow it down, but with her last reserve of energy, Lizzie jerked up her head and projected a mouthful of spit and sweet poison at her sister.

Lizzie took another deep breath, as if about to dive, and pressed her lips tight again as another slap stung across her face, then Donna peeled Lizzie's lips back from her teeth with her sharp false nails. Lizzie screamed through her closed mouth just as the door of room 423 banged open.

"Get away from her!" Ben's voice was breathless, furious and punctuated by the door slamming shut behind him. At the sound of it, Donna lashed out instinctively, smashing the bottle against the bedside table and sending a shower of antifreeze into the air, its scent filling the air. As nimble as any girl should be who worked out whenever there was a camera pointed at her, she bounded down from the bed and flew to meet Ben before he could react to the scene.

The jagged glass teeth caught the light as they flew and Lizzie heard a horrible, wrenching breath escape Ben's lips as her sister plunged the broken bottle into his chest. He seemed to tense, his shoulders stiffening as she raised the bottle for a second strike. With a deep red stain spreading over the blue shirt he wore, he took a step back, his bruised face paling into the colour of fresh milk.

"No, not Ben, no! You mad bitch!"

Lizzie found a reserve of energy from somewhere deep in her marrow, and she dragged herself off the bed. As the jagged bottle began to fall again, Lizzie screamed like an Amazon going into battle and ran between her sister and her lover. She grabbed hold of Donna's hair and yanked it so hard that an extension tore out, jerking Donna's head to one side. With the whole weight of her body, Lizzie shoved herself at Donna, ramming her face-first into the wall.

Ben slumped forward, his hand catching Lizzie's and pulling her away from her sister with what seemed to be his last vestige of strength. Donna, though, neither moved nor fell for what seemed like minutes but must only have been seconds. Then she went down as though she had been poleaxed, the broken bottle she had been holding jammed deep into her breast. Her blood slicked the pale wall as she slid down it, mapping a bright red trail that led straight down to the body of Donna de Luca.

Lizzie was suddenly so cold that she was trembling. She guided Ben to the floor, cradling him in her lap.

"I've killed my sister…"

But Ben was still alive, even if his breaths were shorter and shallower by the moment. She had a hazy idea that she was supposed to stop the bleeding somehow, and she pressed her palm flat over his wound. She tried not to look down at the pooling blood, nor at the wide eyes of her dead sister, but only at Ben, her loving and beloved Ben.

"Don't die, Ben. You can't leave me when we've only just found each other."

There were sirens outside then, lights and noise, and in her arms, Ben whispered, "I love you, Lizzie."

He drew in a curiously contented, ragged breath and closed his dark brown eyes.

* * * *

Six months later

The row of cypresses on the distant hill swayed together in a breeze that Lizzie couldn't feel. She paused in the opened patio doors and, shielding her eyes from the bright sun with a tanned arm, looked out across the bright blue of the swimming pool. Her hair was still damp from her swim.

Lizzie's loose dress billowed about her as she went out onto the patio to fetch her straw hat from the sun lounger. Her attention was drawn to the gate in the white stucco wall, almost hidden from view by the bright purples and pinks of the huge bougainvillea that cascaded over it. Every moment, she hoped to see his face there. She turned away.

She'd bought a magazine in the airport and had left it out on the patio table. As the breeze arrived at the villa, the magazine's pages frantically turned, as if by an invisible hand. Lizzie grabbed it. They were still printing photographs from Matt's memorial concert, still showing the ranks of glamorous WAGs in black cocktail dresses and large sunglasses, surrounded by flower tributes.

But there had been no lilies.

Lizzie hadn't attended. Too many gentlemen of the press would've been there, even the ones who had camped outside her apartment building. Pressing the intercom at all hours, somehow getting her phone number.

'How does it feel to be the sister and ex-girlfriend of a pair of murderers?'

'No comment.'

And all the while, her own pain had been ignored.

So she had come here, just as she and Ben had planned before the ground had been ripped out from beneath them. A villa up in the hills, up in the sunshine, away from Manchester, away from her home.

Away from the memories.

She didn't cry so much now though, the sunlight and birdsong slowly but surely beginning to mend her sadness. She didn't think of the hotel room that often either, of Ben in her arms, bleeding from the wound in his chest, his eyes closed and his limbs still.

Why dwell on those unhappy memories, after all?

"Sam says hello!" Lizzie heard Ben's voice a second before the gate opened and he strolled into view. He slipped his phone into the pocket of his shorts and added, "Apparently it's raining in Manchester."

He looked up into the blue sky, shielding his eyes against the sun despite his sunglasses. "I told her it's nice enough here!"

"It's glorious! I see you got to the baker's in time, before they ran out of bread. You'll be pleased to know I've refilled your beer supply in the fridge."

Lizzie almost skipped across the path to Ben, past the pots of geraniums, her arms outstretched to embrace him.

"You've only been gone an hour, Ben, and I missed you!"

"You should, because I'm amazing." He caught his arm around her waist, drawing her in for a kiss. "Scarred and bruised and two lives down on my nine, but I'm still amazing."

"And modest as ever, of course!" Lizzie ran her fingers through his hair, enjoying the feel of him, his warmth and liveliness. His heart beat against her chest through his loose shirt and her thin sundress—the heart that had come so close to stopping. "Do you want to have lunch now or"—Lizzie feathered her lips to Ben's neck—"after our siesta?"

"Proposal first, then siesta, then lunch." He kissed her very gently. "Do you fancy marrying an ex-copper, Ms. Lizzie Aspinall?"

Lizzie pulled his sunglasses down to the end of his nose. His dark eyes were dancing with mischief and love.

"Oh, Ben! Yes, of course I would. And do you want to marry an interior designer, who's skived off for a month to write a book?"

"More than anything." He beamed, stroking his fingers over the loop of thread that she still wore around her finger. He reached his tanned hand into his pocket and withdrew a small box. "I was going to give you this for Christmas but, well, I got stabbed instead. So, I *will* get you a proper engagement ring, but until I spend long enough out of bed to go shopping, I thought this might keep our thread safe."

"We can have our Christmas now." Lizzie unhooked the lid of the old jewellery box and carefully opened it.

On a small pillow of dark blue velvet, the colour of the midnight sky, was a silver locket on a fine chain. It was shaped like a rose, its surface sparkling with tiny pieces of red glass.

"It's the most beautiful thing I've ever seen!" Her hands trembled as she lifted it from the box. Inside its lid, etched many years ago by other lovers than they, it said *Ma cherie, un souvenir de Montmartre*.

"I love you, my naughty ex-*gendarme*."

"I love you too," Ben whispered. "My wonderful *mademoiselle*."

Want to see more from these authors?
Here's a taster for you to enjoy!

The Colour of Mermaids
Catherine Curzon & Eleanor Harkstead

Excerpt

Of course Eva wasn't going to turn down her invitation to the private viewing at the Hawley Gallery. Daniel Scott, *enfant terrible* of the international art world, was exhibiting in Brighton of all places.

She arrived fifteen minutes early, but the gallery was almost full. It seemed as if everyone who was anyone on the Brighton art scene had turned up for vast amounts of free drink and air-kissing. Eva waved to people she knew, and finally spotted her friend Lyndsey on the other side of the room in front of one of Daniel Scott's canvases. Somehow, a glass of Prosecco had appeared in her hand by the time she had squeezed through the crowd to reach Lyndsey.

"Hello, gorgeous!" Lyndsey put her hand on Eva's arm and leaned in to dart her lips to her cheek. As she did, she dropped her voice and whispered, "Not many laughs on these walls tonight!"

"Hello, darling!" Eva kissed Lyndsey back, her friend's summery floral scent enveloping them both like a cloud. "No, his work's not a laugh a minute, is it? But it's so exciting that the exhibition's *here*. And thanks so much for sorting me out with an invite."

"I don't actually understand what it *is*. I don't think I like it." Lyndsey peered up at the canvas before her. From it, *something* vaguely human glowered down, a twisted, misshapen silhouette of a human face in a mist of fog. She cocked her head to one side then the other and shrugged. Then she smiled and murmured, "It needs a kitten or two, then we'll talk."

Eva laughed. "Like the ones on tea trays that grannies used to have? You do crack me up! I love his paintings... I'm always drawing *things* in my illustrations. It must be so freeing to paint emotion."

"I haven't met him yet, but Rupert says he's *super* intense." Lyndsey took a glass of Prosecco from the tray of a passing waiter. "He wouldn't let us so much as hang a single work until he'd been through the space a dozen times. We've had some tricky artistic types through, but *nothing* like this. Rupert'd let him paint the place neon green if he wanted, though, for the exposure we're getting."

"I can't say I'm surprised that he's intense. I mean, to produce art like this." Eva recalled the photos she'd seen of him in newspapers and magazines, dark eyes like coals that seemed to burn through the paper. "Then again, I bet he's been really spoiled over the years. Don't you think? Mr Rockstar Artist!"

"I just want another lovely sculptress to come and give us all biccies like that one from Cornwall." Lyndsey pouted. "She was so nice, like the perfect mum! I mean, nobody came to see her work but...that meant biccies for the office!"

"Sorry about that, Lynds... I was busy." Eva hadn't been, of course, but at the time she hadn't wanted to go out and her own studio had been her sanctuary. "She sounds lovely, though. No biscuits from Mr Scott, I take it?"

"No, nothing from Mr Scott other than shirty emails from his people about the quality of the light and the spacing between the works." She took a sip from her glass. "You know none of them are for sale, and we've had offers on every single one?" Lyndsey dropped her voice again and confided, "I can't tell you how much because Rupert won't tell me. He just says think of an insane number and then add at least one zero. Mr Man-in-Black apparently *might* let some go once the exhibition closes. Personally, I can't think who'd want one! Would you want these things above your bed?"

"Possibly not!" Eva looked up again at the canvas. She had trouble turning away from it. She'd seen his paintings reproduced in books and everywhere else, but actually seeing his artwork up close — close enough to see each individual brush mark — made the emotion it represented all the more intense. "But imagine it in the lounge, it'd be quite the conversation piece at parties!"

"The problem is, to buy this you'd have to sell your house, so you'd have no lounge to hang it in!"

"That's true!" Eva laughed. "Thing is, don't you think he should, I dunno, up his game a little? Develop his style a bit? It is exciting seeing all these works up close, but it's as if he's painting to a tried-and-tested formula. The Daniel Scott Method!"

"Are you accusing our *enfant terrible* of painting by numbers?" Lyndsey affected mock outrage. "Tell me more, Ms da Vinci!"

Eva gestured towards the painting while she sipped a mouthful of Prosecco. "Well, I do paint myself, as you know, and I try to...do different things. I mean, imagine if he broke from type and did a landscape. Although I suppose if you get to be as famous as him you're trapped in one style, because everyone expects to see a Daniel Scott, and this is what they want."

"Oh, don't stop there," a male voice said from behind the two women. "I'm enjoying learning from a master."

Eva didn't recognise the voice, although it seemed familiar. Some annoying hanger-on, no doubt, who thought they were an expert. But when she turned, her eyebrow already raised in scornful retort, she was facing Daniel Scott himself.

His coal-black eyes held Eva fixed to the spot. "I…erm… My God, Mr Scott. If I'd known you were stood right behind me, I really wouldn't have said all that. Sorry. Erm…" She swallowed, then held out her hand to him, an awkward grin on her lips. "Eva Catesby. I am actually an artist, before you ask! Not just an opinionated bystander."

"Eva Catesby." He took her hand very briefly and narrowed his eyes as though trying to recall her name. "Did I see you exhibited at the Met last season? Or was it the Tate Modern? You'll have to remind me, I seem to have forgotten."

Because, of course, he has to be an egomaniac.

Eva rolled her eyes. "How unfortunate that you can't remember. By the way, you also appear to have forgotten your sunglasses. We *are* indoors." She indicated his Ray-Bans, which were perched on his dark hair.

"Eva!" Lyndsey whispered urgently, no doubt seeing her job as PA to Rupert Hawley flashing before her eyes.

"That's why they're not on my face," he replied, deadpan. "As you correctly say, everybody wants to see Daniel Scott and they'd be disappointed if I didn't have my sunglasses. I've always been a people pleaser."

"Is that so?" Eva arched her eyebrow again. He was dressed entirely in black. His suit, his shirt. Was it an act, and at home he tooled about in flip-flops and Bermuda shorts? "Of course, some people are much harder to please than others. And I'm one of those people, I'm afraid. What can I say? I'm sure you're not all that fussed by the views of a provincial artist you've never heard of."

"Mr Scott." Rupert Hawley was suddenly beside them, as if conjured from nowhere. He was almost bowing, Eva realised, his hand extending to shake Daniel's. "I was hoping to announce you, you managed to evade me!"

"I was meeting the locals," Daniel told him. He subtly turned from Eva, angling his body away from her a little. "Tough crowd."

Rupert glanced to the two women for just a moment, but word of the artist's presence seemed to have spread and an interested crowd was gathering. Everyone was eager to meet the star in their midst and none of them, Eva knew, would tell him that he needed to try something just a *little* different next time he put brush to canvas.

"That's Brighton for you." Rupert managed to force a smile to accompany his words. He moved to put his hand on Daniel's back as though to steer him away, but it hovered there before falling. *He can't touch the icon, can he?* All he could do was wring his hands and say, "Let me introduce you to some people. Excuse us, ladies."

"Ms Catesby," Daniel addressed Eva, the hint of a smile chilling on his lips, "thank you for the notes. I'll keep them in mind."

"Oh my God," Lyndsey groaned as they departed in a crowd of excited chatter. "Oh my God, oh my God. Why did you do have to do that? You didn't have to do that!"

"Do what?" Eva sipped her drink as she watched Daniel walk away. *Cocky sod.* Although, she had to admit it, a very good-looking sod, which was probably part of the problem. A man who had lucked out thanks to the universe granting him both a handsome face and talent. "I was merely expressing an opinion. That's the point of a private viewing, isn't it? I mean, I know everyone *really* just comes out for the free booze and schmoozing, but there are paintings on the walls, and we're allowed to comment on them. It's not my fault he was eavesdropping. His work is great, but I just think… Bloody hell, if he pushed himself, it could be amazing."

"It's *Daniel Scott*," Lyndsey reminded her. "His last exhibition was at the Pompidou and when he came back to England he didn't go to the Tate or the National, he came to our humble little gallery. You were really rude to him, Eva, that wasn't on. It costs nothing to be nice, you know."

"I did apologise, but then he came out with all that egotistical bollocks, and I saw red." Eva adopted a snooty tone. "*I've exhibited at the Met, I've exhibited at the Tate Modern, I'm a great big poser with my sunglasses on my head, I dress in black because I want everyone to think I'm a badass, I still sleep with my teddy.*"

"It was rude," Lyndsey told her again. "And you were saying you loved his work, why didn't you tell him that?"

"Because that's all he ever hears!" Eva watched his progress through the room, handshaking with some of the most annoying people in Brighton. Everyone was smiling and fawning over the man. "Look, when I do outreach with those kids, I don't just say *well done* to everything they paint. I'll say, *well done*. And next time, what if you do *this* a bit differently. There's nothing wrong with pushing people. As long as it's a gentle shove."

"He's going to complain about you." As Lyndsey spoke, Daniel glanced over his shoulder at them for a moment. Eva flashed him a sarcastic grin and momentarily raised her glass. He raised his own in turn, the red wine catching the light before he turned away again. "And Rupert will blame me for inviting you and I'll lose my job. You know how moody Rupe can be. You'll have to go out for drinks with him again and save my job!"

"Oh God, Rupe and his lacklustre snog." Eva wrinkled her nose and giggled like a gossipy schoolgirl. "There's someone I won't be going on a date with again. Ewww!"

"Bless his socks, give him another chance." Lyndsey laughed. "You know, in three years of working with him, he's never had a girlfriend for more than a couple of months. You looked so cute together, and he still likes you!"

"He's a nice bloke, but really…" Eva shook her head. "He's not for me."

Whereas Daniel Scott…

What a thing to think. But he *had* been a bit flirty with her, although he was probably like that with everyone. Eva watched as Daniel lowered his head to speak to a woman who fashioned genitalia in colourful pottery. She was giggling at him. *Giggling.* Eva looked back up at the painting again. Something in it which she hadn't seen before, which she wouldn't have been able to describe even had she attempted it, made her come out in goosebumps.

"Do you want to see the rest of them?" Lyndsey touched her arm. "And maybe accidentally bump into Mr Scott and grovel at his feet? Tell him he's amazing and how sorry you are? *Pweese*?"

"I'd love to see the rest of them, but speaking to him depends on how likely he is to keep talking to that woman about her pottery pudenda." Eva snorted with laughter. "Am I mean? It's just…my foundation art course was bulging with them, and *she* somehow makes a living from crockery cocks!"

"She's probably not being rude to him." Lyndsey slipped her arm though Eva's. "Come on, talk me through these scenes of horror, it's not a world I often inhabit!"

"After that show last year of the comedy seagull photos, I'm not surprised you find them a bit" — Eva glanced at her friend's benign face, then up at a canvas of swollen, dark paint, which seemed to throb before her eyes — "unfathomable. You could see that one, for example, as…a bruise. An emotional bruise. We all have them. I suppose that's what frustrates me. He's putting all this emotion on canvas, and it could be dark and disturbing, but I feel almost as if he's cranking them out to order. Do you see?"

"I liked the seagulls," Lyndsey smiled nostalgically. Then she glanced over her shoulder, satisfied that Daniel was at a safe distance, still surrounded by acolytes. "But when I look at this… It's like there's something wrong with him. What's going on in his head?"

"Who knows? Does *he*?" Eva tipped her head to one side, to see the painting from another angle. "But don't you think that's the point of art, really? I look at this and it makes me think of…well…splitting up with Miles. An emotional bruise, which faded. And everyone else looking at it thinks of something painful that happened to them. And maybe — *maybe* — he does it on purpose, but in his production line way, stirring those feelings up, forcing people to *look* at that pain inside them. Or maybe horrible things *are* going on in that handsome head, and he spills it out in paint." Eva sighed. "Maybe it's a cross of the two."

"Oh God, he's looking at us," Lyndsey whispered, quickly turning her attention to the painting. Years in gallery administration had left her with the talent for looking both interested and appreciative even when she wasn't, a skill that Eva knew her friend was justifiably rather proud of. A skill that had saved her career on more than one occasion. "You've *really* upset him, Eva, so you'd better hope what's in his head *isn't* as horrible as his pictures."

Eva met his glance as she combed her fingers through her long hair with a careless swish. He was doing a very good job of not looking upset at all, despite what Lyndsey seemed to think.

"He's smiling, Lyndsey. He doesn't look upset to me."

"I'm not going to look at him. He might put me in a painting if I do!"

Sign up for our newsletter and find out about all our romance book releases, eBook sales and promotions, sneak peeks and FREE romance books!

About the Authors

Catherine Curzon

Catherine Curzon is a royal historian who writes on all matters of 18th century. Her work has been featured on many platforms and Catherine has also spoken at various venues including the Royal Pavilion, Brighton, and Dr Johnson's House.

Catherine holds a Master's degree in Film and when not dodging the furies of the guillotine, writes fiction set deep in the underbelly of Georgian London.

She lives in Yorkshire atop a ludicrously steep hill.

Eleanor Harkstead

Eleanor Harkstead often dashes about in nineteenth-century costume, in bonnet or cravat as the mood takes her. She can occasionally be found wandering old graveyards, and is especially fond of the ones in Edinburgh. Eleanor is very fond of chocolate, wine, tweed waistcoats and nice pens. She has a large collection of vintage hats, and once played guitar in a band. Originally from the south-east, Eleanor now lives somewhere in the Midlands with a large ginger cat who resembles a Viking.

Sign up to receive their newsletter at
https://curzonharkstead.co.uk/newsletter/

Catherine and Eleanor love to hear from readers. You can find their contact information, website and author biographies at https://www.totallybound.com.